BEST LESBIAN EROTICA 2001

BEST
LESBIAN
EROTICA
2001

Tristan Taormino,
Series Editor

**Selected and
Introduced by**

Pat Califia

CLEIS
PRESS

Published in the United States
Cleis Press Inc., P.O. Box 14684, San Francisco, California 94114.
Printed in the United States.
Cover design: Scott Idleman
Cover Photograph: Phyllis Christopher
Book design: Karen Quigg
Cleis Press logo art: Juana Alicia
First Edition.
10 9 8 7 6 5 4 3 2 1

"Monica and Me" © 2000 by Rachel Kramer Bussel will appear in *Starfucker: The Book* edited by Shar Rednour (Alyson, 2001); "Lipstick" © 2000 by Aimée Nichols was published in *Shades Beyond Gray* and *Biblio Eroticus #6;* "How to Fuck in High Heels" © 2000 by Shar Rednour is an excerpt of her book *The Femme's Guide to the Universe* (Alyson, 2000); "Dress Pinks" © 2000 by M. Christian was previously published in *Uniform Sex* edited by Linnea Due (Alyson, 2000); "Inquiring Dykes Want to Know" © 2000 by Shelley Marcus first appeared in *Strange Bedfellows* (XLibris, 2000); "Splitting the Infinitive" © 2000 by Jean Roberta previously appeared online in *Jane's Net Sex Guide Newsletter* (1999); "She Who Waits" © 2000 by Catherine Lundoff was published in *Taste of Midnight* (Circlet Press, 2000); "Blood and Silver" © 2000 by Pat Califia is from the book *No Mercy* by Pat Califia (Alyson, 2000); "Business Casual" © 2000 by Lauren Sanders first appeared online at Nerve.com.

TABLE OF CONTENTS

Foreword
Tristan Taormino

In the 1980s, when lesbian erotica was still in its infancy, women were most interested in getting their writing and images on the page and out into the world. Cutting-edge erotica was a direct response to the feminist sex wars; the mere act of writing and publishing it was radical. From high femme to leatherdaddy, dykes wanted to express, defend, and celebrate their sexual identities. Their very presence in lesbian communities and willingness to be out and proud was revolutionary. Putting themselves in print was downright dangerous. By the early '90s, the sex-positive movement was in full swing, and how we were putting out and what we were putting into words seemed less hotly debated. Some of what was so tumultuous in the '80s was being taken for granted by a new generation of post–sex war girls. As I began this series in 1996, the lesbian erotica market was nowhere near the size it is today; it was still difficult to get sex writing published. And with *Best Lesbian Erotica*, I was looking for the edge, the fringe, the not-so-normal.

This anthology series has always been about pushing at boundaries, but the trick is that those boundaries are always changing.

What is racy, relevant, and sexy among queer women is constantly transforming. In this first year of a new century, radical sex in and of itself is not *the* hot-button issue for lesbian feminism. The battleground has shifted from sex to gender.

The proliferation of gender identities beyond butch, femme, and androgynous is an exciting, confusing, stimulating moment in our history. Young women (and some not so young) are critiquing, playing, and performing gender at bars, in bedrooms, and on stages all over the place, crafting new identities like boydyke, girlfag, neofemme, boi, grrrl, transman, and drag king. As a smut editor and a sex educator, I have felt this change very deeply on many levels. Slowly but surely, the writing that appears in my post office box has been affected by all this work on gender. Joan Nestle was struck by this phenomenon and wisely said about the writing in *Best Lesbian Erotica 2000:* "The stories in this collection are freer, fiercer, more touched by both gender-specific erotics and gender play than any I have read before."

Our basic notions about gender, especially a two-gender system, are on fire right now, with different forms of female masculinity emerging from the sparks every day. Rising from all this smoldering, some of our sisters have crossed over and do not call themselves women anymore. Lesbians have a unique opportunity to confront their issues about men when some of their ex-lovers, best friends, or even girlfriends decide to identify as men. Still others refuse the male/female binary altogether, a terrifying but necessary choice.

This year, as always, I wanted to see if I could push the series a little bit further, with gender issues specifically in mind. So I teamed up with FtM writer and activist Patrick Califia-Rice. Some people have told me that it is inappropriate to have someone who does not identify as a lesbian selecting stories for a lesbian anthology. Patrick Califia-Rice is one of the finest erotic writers of our time—a difficult point to argue considering what he has contributed to sex writing. My choice of Patrick was also personal.

I dedicated the very first volume of *Best Lesbian Erotica* to Pat Califia because, more than any other writer, Pat Califia had an enormous impact on my own relationship to sex and porn. Working with Patrick on this particular project has been a great opportunity for me to challenge my own expectations, misconceptions, and phobias about transgendered people. When all is said and done, we're both still perverts, freaks, and rebels on the erotic frontier. To me, Patrick Califia-Rice has plenty to do with lesbian erotica—and plenty to say about it.

One of the challenges I face as series editor (and as editor of sex mag *On Our Backs*) is to represent lesbian sexuality in a finite number of pages. Lesbian sexuality is not one thing. It's not ten things or fifty things. There is such a wide variety of gender and sexual expression among queer women, it almost boggles the mind. I always feel like I'm precariously juggling the vanilla with the BDSM, the butch/femme with the andro-girls, the romantic with the anonymous, the fuck buddies with the married couples, the separatists with the trannies, the vulva-lovin' with the cock-suckin'. And then, of course, there are plenty of people and stories that fall between the lines, defying these already unstable categories—they're both; they're neither; they are something altogether different. I'm learning that this is what gender—and the gender revolution—is all about. And for that knowledge I thank you, Patrick, Kate, Riki, and so many others.

There are several pieces—among them "F" by Karin Pomerantz, "Sometimes She Lets Me" by Alison L. Smith, "Pawn of the Patriarchy" by Elaine Miller, "Dress Pinks" by M. Christian, and "The Rock Wall" by Peggy Munson—that have deliciously gender-specific sexual dynamics.

Rachel Kramer Bussel's "Monica and Me" and Shelley Marcus's "Inquiring Dykes Want to Know" prove that sex and politics are inevitably intertwined—and that the personalities who capture the media's attention might also catch ours in a different way. Unlikely pairings fuel the lust and surprise of "sex hall" by MR Daniel and "If You Can Make It Here, You Can Make It Anywhere" by A. J. Stone.

Romance rears her hard clit in interesting ways in "Lipstick" by Aimée Nichols and "Water Music" by Elspeth Potter. Lauren Sanders and Toni Amato dive headfirst into longing, obsession, lust, and pain in their moving stories "Business Casual" and "Grande Jeté."

Other authors track the delicate terrain of the many forms of sexual awakening: Gitana Garofalo's "How I Learned to Drive," Thea Hutcheson's "The Stars in Her Mouth," Sacchi Green's "Of Dark and Bright," and Susan St. Aubin's "Blood." The playful, witty story "Splitting the Infinitive" by Jean Roberta may just make you think about English composition in a whole new way. Shar Rednour's "How to Fuck in High Heels" will definitely make you look at pumps differently. Uninhibited imaginations coupled with futuristic technology, vampires on the hunt, and she-wolves roaming the woods create the unique fantasies of Skian McGuire's "Back in the Saddle," Catherine Lundoff's "She Who Waits," and Pat Califia's "Blood and Silver."

The stories in this year's collection are brave, funny, provocative, romantic, surprising, and full of passion. All of them dare to explore multilayered erotic feelings, sexual encounters, and carnal worlds.

Let them seduce you—enjoy the experience.

Tristan Taormino
New York City
September 2000

Introduction:
Speaking in Tongues
Pat Califia

There's a certain kind of interviewer who is out to get me. I don't know why, but this type of journalist usually comes from New York City. New Yorkers like the food in California, but there's too much happiness here, too many expressions of affection and invitations to brunch, too many fat people having lots of good sex, too many nonsmokers and vegetarians, too many massages and herbal antidepressants and brightly colored tattoos. So they get a little nervous, a little defensive. They go into attack mode so they don't lose their edge and die when they go home. I have to confess that I am guilty of being nice to New Yorkers on more than one occasion, just because it makes them so nervous. "Why are you doing this? What are you after?" they sometimes blurt out, searching in vain for an ashtray, a taxi, or a hotdog stand.

The not-very-hidden agenda is to show that I'm outdated and my work is obsolete, so everybody can ignore the politics of sex, stop collecting queer smut, and go back to reading the *Nation* or the *New York Review of Books*. One of the opening salvos in an interview like this is the question, "What new direction can your writing possibly take now that pro-pleasure feminists have won the sex wars?" Another tack they take is to ask, "Is there any point to writing about S/M now that it's become so mainstream?" Or they murmur, "There's already so much porn about lesbian sex, written by lesbians," implying that one more book of that sort would be passé, a burden upon the reader and reviewer.

What these soignée reporters don't know is that I've been asked these three questions for the last fifteen years. Liberals have wanted to pretend that the sex wars are over ever since they began. There are several motivating factors. One is intellectual laziness. It's so much more convenient to just lump all feminists together and pretend that there's one set of goals, one point of view about what causes the oppression of women and how to remedy that oppression, one leader to quote. Gloria Steinem is so photogenic, even after all these years, practically glamorous. Why ask her awkward questions about obscenity laws, international policy about prostitution, the forced psychiatric treatment or incarceration of lesbians and gay men, sex education for young people, or women and AIDS? Viewers will head for the kitchen and start looking for ice cream in the freezer.

Another cause for this benighted point of view is ignorance. The gay press is usually too busy putting fashion photo spreads together to pay attention to issues of censorship or freedom of expression. Designers, manufacturers, and distillers don't want to be associated with certain topics (like dangerous sex, upsetting art, street-level activism, or revolution). These days, both gay and straight magazines are simply glossy, tree-killing vehicles for sneaking advertising into your lovely home. The mainstream media certainly don't give a fuck, especially if material that depicts sexuality has been proscribed in a foreign country. They'd rather analyze how long Al Gore kissed his wife at the Democratic convention, and if there was any tongue, how is that going to play in the Bible Belt?

There's also political cowardice. There are three types of material that draw most of the governmental and other types of censorship—same-sex activity, S/M and "child" pornography (which features anyone under 18, or a computer-generated image of someone who appears to be under age 18). Cops or customs officials create dangerous precedents when they rationalize seizing books, magazines, or videos about these things. Even people who consider themselves to be staunch supporters of the First Amendment usually don't care. It's just too difficult to defend sodomy, cunnilingus, bondage, and flagellation. Who cares if pedophiles are being entrapped online or in their own homes by cops posing as sexually active minors? These are dangerous people (even if they never owned any child pornography until a cop sent them some via the Internet).

Unfortunately for the lining of my stomach, anti-porn feminism is still alive and kicking. Janine Fuller knows all about that, but I doubt you've ever seen an interview with her, not even in the so-called alternative press. For a decade, she has been pushing a censorship case that pits a tiny gay bookstore in Vancouver against Canadian customs. It has taken this long for the Supreme Court of that country to hear the case. In the meantime, Canadian customs officials routinely seize writing or images that feature anal penetration, S/M, or anything else they consider "degrading." Two men can legally fuck each other in Canada, but they can't look at porn that features anal sex, if it's imported from America, or read explicit safer-sex guidelines about it. Lesbian sex is not illegal, but descriptions of lesbian sex have been seized and destroyed. The law that justifies these seizures was put into place on the advice of American anti-porn feminists like Andrea Dworkin and Catherine MacKinnon.

These women and their colleagues also remain active in the international debate about regulating the sex industry. They have vigorously opposed any attempt to legalize or decriminalize sex work so that services can be provided to women who want to leave the industry, including women who were coerced into becoming prostitutes. Instead, they insist that prostitution is a crime against women, and must remain illegal so that no woman thinks it is a legitimate profession. There is no sense that these middle-class women might have common ground with poor women who sell sex in order to survive and feed their children. Prostitutes are attacked as if they were the supreme anti-feminists. Most recently these loonies succeeded in generating international condemnation of the Clinton administration because the president and his wife supported legislation that made a distinction between voluntary sex workers and forced prostitution, and suggested that the latter should be the focus of law enforcement.

When reporters or editors want me to comment on S/M becoming mainstream, I don't know whether I should laugh, cry, bang my head on the floor, or strangle them. Usually what this really means is some celebrities (like Madonna or Janet Jackson) have incorporated fetish attire into their performances or public image, and perhaps made comments that hint at their involvement in bondage or spanking. Even the faux cops in *Law and Order* or *NYPD Blue* want the viewers at home to know that they know what tit clamps and water sports are, tee hee. This shallow, sensationalistic posturing is hardly the same thing as destigmatizing sadomasochism. S/M is still portrayed as an extreme activity that results in the death of participants, or is confused with violent sex crimes. Sexual masochism and sexual sadism are still in the *Diagnostic and Statistical Manual IV* of the American Psychiatric Association.

This year, people have been arrested and charged under public sex and anti-prostitution laws for doing S/M at play parties in San Diego, California, and in Attleboro, Massachusetts. Massachusetts is the state that gave Kenneth Appleby an eight-to-ten-year prison sentence in 1980 for tapping his boyfriend on the shoulder with a riding crop. (Granted, the boyfriend appeared as a witness against him. But the law says consent is no defense to an assault charge, and this case set a precedent for defining sadomasochism as assault.) We lost the Spanner case at the European Court of Human Rights a few years ago, so it's legal for member nations to criminalize S/M. Australia has put some draconian censorship policies into place that make it very difficult for S/M literature or art to circulate freely there. The possession of many common items of S/M equipment, like handcuffs or cat-o'-nine-tails, is a criminal offense Down Under. In "anything goes" San Francisco, when a gay man was killed outside a leather bar, an ostensibly liberal weekly paper printed an article suggesting that it was overkill to charge his assailant with murder.

Sadomasochists continue to experience ridicule, job and housing discrimination, child-custody problems, and even violence if our involvement in power-exchange sex is made public. The suggestion that S/M is now "mainstream" is based on the assumption that we can expect very little from the larger society, in terms of improved understanding of or behavior toward us. Pervy people are supposed to be so excited about a rock star's latex corset-dress or a whip wielded onstage that we abandon our activism, public education, and fund-raising for legal defense. What more could we possibly want? Freedom? Dignity? Safety? Respect? Equality? How droll. How tiresome, for a vanilla majority that does not want to question its own privilege or bad behavior.

Especially irksome is the suggestion that writing about sex by and for women who love other women—and its gay male equivalent—is now obsolete, boring, or unnecessary. I cannot fathom the depth of arrogance and prudery that lies behind such a presumption. When I try to add up the sheer volume of material that celebrates, valorizes, and mandates heterosexual desire, the mind boggles. Yet I could fit a bibliography of sex fiction generated within the lesbian community into ten pages or so. Compared to what existed in the '50s and '60s, it's a deluge of sapphic splendor. But it's a long way from being a glut on the market. Once again, a sexual minority is assumed to be content with the most minimal concessions. Lesbians are allowed to live, to speak to one another, to love one another, at the most precipitous edge of society. Straight people congratulate themselves for being such tolerant angels, and wonder if perhaps they have not given "the homosexuals" too much space, too long a leash.

Last time I checked, material about homosexuality was still not a part of most sex-education curricula in our schools. Teenagers still have limited access to condoms and information about safer sex and birth control. Sex manuals for adults do not integrate information about same-sex activity, unless it is to warn women away from bisexual men who might be "AIDS carriers." Minors who want to start gay clubs or gay/straight alliances in their schools usually meet with intense opposition from the administration. HIV and other STDs are rising at a frightening rate among young gay, bisexual, or questioning men, yet it's difficult to get adequate funding to craft appropriate education or intervention. Young queers still contemplate suicide or get lost in addiction because they are isolated, treated with contempt, beaten, and rejected by their communities and families and peers. Same-sex marriage is not legal. The faintest increase in lesbian visibility, like Ellen DeGeneres's coming-out on prime-time television, engenders enormous controversy. Women who know they are lesbians still choose to get married because they can't bear to hurt their families by being honest about their sexual orientation. In other words, heterosexuality remains compulsory.

Gay-hating masquerades as good science and pious religion. Idiot sexologists like Dr. David Reuben and overexposed pundits like Dr. Laura are still going around saying that gay sex is pathological, unsatisfying, and dangerous. The Christian right continues to promulgate images of same-sex activity and gay/lesbian activism as threatening to the well-being of children. In this discourse, which threatens to erase the truth of dyke lives, there is a very important role for sexually explicit work about lesbian sexuality. The well-written and arousing stories in this book, for example, stand as evidence that lesbian sex works very well, thank you, and has nothing to do with the abuse of children. It's guaranteed to piss off the people who hate queers, because it shows lesbians deriving strength, hope, and pleasure from one another. It also threatens the hegemony of right-wing feminism, which totters on despite being crippled by separatism and Victorian ideals.

The lesbian community needs this kind of writing as a sort of compensation for struggling to survive. Erotic entertainment can restore energy and a sense of humor to weary dyke activists. Precisely because lesbians are a minority, there's an intense need for a culture that reflects lesbian needs, values, and desires. It's comforting and life-affirming to immerse yourself, however briefly, in an imaginary lesbian world. When lesbian sexual fantasies circulate in bookstores and libraries, they find their way into the hands of women who most need to see them. Lesbian porn is coming-out propaganda. It answers questions about how two women "do it," and beckons the reader to speak in tongues herself, give and receive Amazonian multiple orgasms.

Books like *Best Lesbian Erotica 2001* raise the bar for lesbian thinking about the politics of sex. They hopefully help dykes to be a little more open about their mores or value judgements regarding sex, and perhaps even help lesbians to tolerate their differences with a little more grace. In fact, lesbian erotica is good for women in general because it supports freedom for all women to make their own choices when it comes to pleasure. It supports women for taking the risks that they decide are worthwhile, and perhaps helps to create a world where it's safer to be honest about what causes us to slip and slide, shake and glide, take in and push away.

The frank voice of lesbian eroticism also serves as a corrective for the gay politicians who want to mainstream us. Of course it makes sense to point out all the things we have in common with straight people, and ask for the same recognition for our relationships and civil rights. But if we are going to be honest, we also have to acknowledge that there are deep differences. Lesbian porn celebrates the uniqueness of dyke sexuality and longing.

It was a great pleasure to work on this volume of lesbian lust, heartbreak, seduction, and romance. Tristan Taormino did an excellent job of culling the best manuscripts out of the hundreds that were submitted. It was my difficult chore to select a handful of these for publication. This was especially hard because every piece I read seemed ready for print, and I hated having to turn any of them down. It makes me so happy to see this plethora of excellent writing about lesbian sexuality! Some of my chickens, it seems, have come home to roost. The children of my spirit are all grown up and resolutely taking on one sexual taboo after another. (I hope it won't seem self-aggrandizing for me to claim elder status in the lineage of speakers of queer sexual truth. Can I be the grandpa of lesbian smut? Vindication is pretty rare; we have to take it where we find it.)

Some of these stories are rowdy and rude. Some are lovely. Some are sad. Some are scary. Some are funny. There's pussy-eating, finger-fucking, strap-on cocks, butch-femme sex, unrequited love, sexual initiation, mistresses and submissives, clit-rubbing, butch-on-butch sex, public sex, group sex, painful sex, lots of kissing, femme-on-femme sex, many wet erect nipples and wetter cunts, fisting, lingerie, sex with regret and sex with triumph. All of these voices deserve to find an audience. May they never fall silent again. May it become as easy and as fulfilling to have lesbian sex as it is to write about it.

sex hall

MR Daniel

The hallway is narrow. I had expected it to be less bare—there are no pictures on the walls, which have all been painted dark reds, slick mahoganies, and purples. I laugh to myself. The colored girls must have had fun checking out swollen pussies when they were painting this. The lights are sunk deep into the ceiling and turned down low so it's lit like a club. A house diva is wailing through the PA system, backed up by an insistent fuck-me-baby, fuck-me-baby tempo. I feel as though I'm in a peepshow.

Brown, bronze, and various sun-kissed women move past me, some with their eyes straight forward, nervous, others whose eyes seem to burn a path before them. I can feel their heat as they pass. There is a steady pulsing below my skin as I move forward, the current stopping and starting and me feeling the blood push-flow push-flow through my neck and fingers, my heart growing, forcing blood into my breasts. I pass the first doorway and hesitate. The door is open but I am suddenly afraid to be caught looking.

1

Someone behind me stops to look over my shoulder, and her fingers inquire at my leg. I can feel her questions all the way up my thigh into my stomach. I almost jump into the room, and there is laughter behind me. I catch my breath, surprised at my confusion. This morning I was so sure of what I wanted, what I felt, but now…Excitement? Pleasure? Fear?

Didn't I want to be fucked from behind, anonymous?

A voice in my ear is saying, "Look forward, baby, or I'll leave."

And, "I know you're wet."

And, "When I remember how you look I'm going to think about parting your bush, how you *almost* reached behind to guide my hands. But I told you not to move. *Don't move.*"

Hiking up skirt, pulling down panties, the snap of a glove, and a hand between my legs. Fucked in a doorway. Fingers up my cunt, feeling the space in my flesh, pushing deeper and rubbing 'til there's this cross between a sharpness and pleasure, my muscles filled with blood, taut, filling and pressing until I think I'm going to pee on the floor.

My mouth is filled with stars and they're burning their way through my vagina. They hurl through my chest and I can't breathe; sweat collects in the band of my skirt. They light up nerves, sending shocks to my clit and behind my eyelids. I hear myself salivate as she works her hand in further, I pant, my cunt pants for her and the feeling of stars.

I am high, nipples sharp from the sound of her inside me. I am straining against damp fabric, pores fucked alert, open, wanting to feel air on sweat-and-oil-steeped skin, as I brace myself in the doorway.

Bodies passing by us go quiet as another finger goes in my puckering ass, tilted to receive, and lips circle my neck, her tongue leaving a trail that ends with a mouth clamped on the back of my throat, kissing, sucking hard, until a half-moon appears. I wanna come bad, but I could stay here forever.

Can you fuck too much? Can you feel too good? Can you be so ripe that you keep bursting and swelling, bursting and swelling until a mouth bites you open again? Her teeth burn into my ass, she whips the hand out of my cunt and I feel the air leave my chest, my breasts suddenly get heavy and full. Her hand spanks my ass, my skin wet and hot, and enters me again like horses. I swear I'm gonna drop to my knees as the finger in my ass moves back and forth, teasing the rim of my anus. I feel myself coming, raging against the horses, grasping them expelling-thrusting them out as they lunge, push further inside. She holds onto me. "That hand isn't going anywhere," she says.

I feel come like hushed spurts, warm like blood, flowing out of me. I'm on my knees, my unconscious fingers take her horse hand, arching as I pull her out of me and rub her against my lips and clit. I feel like a dog, mouth open and bent over, writhing against her hand, I'm not thinking anymore, just doing what feels good. She doesn't pull away. I come again, air passes through my throat and I hear a sound like the last breath as you break the surface of water. Doubled over, breathing hard, I pull away from the finger in my ass and push her other hand from between my legs. I lick my juice from her glove, and pull the latex off. My tongue dives for the skin in between her fingers. This is how I will remember her, by her hands. She helps me up from behind, pulling up my panties stretched and tangled in my boots, her fingers spread wide feeling me up as she pulls my skirt down.

She bites my neck and says, "It's too bad you came so soon," and rubs her pelvis against the crack of my behind. I can feel her packing. Well, I'm sorry, too.

"Next time," she says, her hands firm on my hips, teasing, pressing into, circling against me, slowly. "It's underneath my black vinyl shorts, it peeks through a little cause they're short-shorts like the ones the reggae dancehall queens wear. Zippers up the sides. I only wear them here."

"How do you know you're the only one?" I ask. She can't see me smile.

"Well, if I'm not, we'll find out soon enough," she laughs, and bites the half-moon she left before. I listen to her walking away.

Boots, I guess, with heavy soles.

Of Dark and Bright
Sacchi Green

How the hell have I come to this? What am I doing here? The opening of my show, and I'm lurking high on a shadowed stairway looking down at the bright rectangles on the gallery walls, at my photographs, my visions, my studies in light and dark. And my whole, bone-shaking desire is to step back into that sun and shadow, that scintillation of sky mirrored on rippling water, that light as it strikes so harshly even the smoothest of stream-worn granite, but flows like a lingering touch over the angles of your body.

What I'm doing here is watching for you. Without any reason to think you will come, though you recognized the name of the gallery when I mentioned so casually that I sometimes show here. Or any idea of what I will do, if you do come. So much for the wisdom of age.

Nature is playing tricks on me. Not that I'm complaining; a second adolescence is a torment I'm in no hurry to escape, and my body still gets me wherever I want to go. But where does this surge of raging hungers fit into life's cycle? Where's the archetypal progression from maiden to mother to crone?

I've made it almost through the first two, not without joys, not without scars, not without clawing at the boundaries. You'd think I would have gained some wisdom in all that time, but not enough to ease me through this turmoil. Or even through the next few hours. How will I bear it if you don't come? How will I bear it if you do?

The first time you saw me, you retreated.

I should have been glad. The few days to myself had been hard enough to pry from a life of too many entanglements. No matter how graceful the undulation of your line out over the stream, how elegantly precise the settling of your lure onto the water, barely creasing the tension of its silvered surface, you were an intrusion. Good fly-fishing form, skilled hands, nice balance, but—go away, kid. You bother me.

I watched, unseen, as you moved upstream, searching out the deepest pools among the rocks. No closer, I thought. Go back. Even at a distance, even before I understood, I was reluctant to let your serene concentration be rippled by a chance encounter.

My elkhound Raksha tensed on the opposite shore, her gray fur blending imperceptibly into the rocks and driftwood. A low growl rumbled in her chest, a prelude to whatever menace might be required of her; I signaled her with my eyes to be still, since my hands were occupied with balancing stone on stone, constructing subjects for my photography. Some would become cover art for a book set on a distant planet; some were part of a sequential study of "ephemeral art" showing the effects over time of wind and water and ice; and all served my insatiable obsession with aspects of light and dark. I should have wondered at how quickly Raksha subsided, but I had forgotten, for the moment, her savage distrust of unknown men.

Then the trout struck. Your lean, intense face transformed with joy—and I knew. I watched you play the fish, draw it carefully, inexorably toward you, stoop to deftly grasp and then release your prize, the lines of your body revealing what the multipocketed fishing vest, the baseball cap over close-cropped hair, had at first concealed. But I already knew.

The stream swirling past my hips might as well have rammed a log into my crotch. A hunger raw as pain, irrational as the jerk of a hammered knee, lurched deep and low inside me. I cursed at my old-enough-to-know-better self—and in that moment of distraction my balance wavered.

One stone shifted, then another; I tried to restore the equilibrium of my construction, but the pebbles in the streambed turned under my feet. I staggered, and stones from the disintegrating tower bruised me on their way to the bottom of the river.

You heard the avalanche of rocks and looked up. In a calmer moment I might have enjoyed your expression as your gaze traveled over the surreal array of stone circles and pillars, the camera and tripod on the shore, and Raksha observing you with a lupine grin. By the time you saw me I was pulling myself up onto a wide, sun-warmed boulder, and then wishing I hadn't, realizing how mercilessly revealing my soaked T-shirt had become, how inadequate my denim cutoffs had always been. Damn it, how far into the wilds did I have to go to be spared seeing myself through someone else's eyes?

Expressions shifted across your dark-browed face like the drifting shadows of clouds on the mountainsides. I knew you were cursing the shattering of solitude, and considering what, if anything, of yourself to reveal. I saved you the trouble of deciding.

"Raksha, stay!" I commanded, turning toward the shore, knowing that she had no intention of doing otherwise. I stepped from rock to rock until I stood beside her. Then, one hand on her shaggy neck, I faced you again, smiled, and nodded in a casual acknowledgment of shared humanity.

Your answering smile was brief, startled, and lit with a sweetness you would have cursed yourself for showing. You could pass, in the right circumstances, but never with that smile. Then you turned away. I watched you retreat downstream, leaping from boulder to boulder with a long-legged, impetuous sureness that sent a frisson of delight though my skin.

So I've done it, I thought, gone completely round the bend. Fantasies, delusions...and delusions of what? I wasn't even sure which I wanted more, to fuck you, or, in spite of the scars the world could be counted on to inflict, to be you. Not that it mattered. My chances of one were about the same as of the other.

But then, in the morning, you came back.

Extension of my dreams or not, I went with it. Those dreams had left me sweaty, slippery, tangled in my sleeping bag, and utterly without relief. Raksha sniffed at my crotch with interest. I pushed her nose away and headed for the river.

Mist rose from the water into the early coolness of the July morning. I eased into the deep cascade-fed pool between the largest boulders. The current here had often swept away tension, pain, everything extraneous to pure being; but I didn't even want it to cool this fever. Some aches are to be savored.

Raksha stood above me on the bank, testing the breeze. I knew by her focused stillness when she had caught a human scent. There, across the river, half-hidden by hemlock branches, you stood, watching her wolfish form, and watching me balancing breast-deep.

This time I wore nothing but my river sandals. Fantasy, delusion, whatever; I chose to pretend that you cared. "Good morning!" I called across the rush of the water. "It's all right, I won't turn you into a stag."

You grinned, not startled this time, and came down in easy strides to the riverbank. "You sure? Might be too late. Kinda

8

feels like you already have, antlers and all. But I would've taken you for Venus, not Diana."

"Venus?" I said. "That manipulative bitch?" If this were delusion, I'd make the most of it. Your deliberate drawl and uptake on the Actaeon myth made my skin tingle; your voice, low and with just a hint of huskiness, would have done the trick all by itself.

"Nothin' wrong with a little manipulation," you said.

Damn, why hadn't it occurred to me before that this could be fun? Whatever else it turned out to be. It was a gift you offered, your willingness to play the game, to take the risk of sharing this self with me.

"Could be," I said. "Depends on the hands." I turned and waded to the shore. Slowly and deliberately I stepped up onto the flat rock where I'd dropped my towel and stood there drying myself, concealing nothing, regretting nothing. What you see is what you get. On the off chance that you might care.

You didn't try to hide your frank gaze, but there was a trace of wariness in your stance. It made sense to be unsure, yet, how much I understood, how much I intended, how crazy, after all, I might be, building towers and arches of river rocks in the wilderness. Just as it made sense for me to wonder whether my eccentricity was all that drew you.

"Come on across," I said casually. "I'll make some coffee." Without watching to see whether you were coming I stepped onto the bank and headed toward my lean-to shelter. My shorts and T-shirt still hung damply on a branch, so I pulled on jeans and the old flannel shirt that doubles as a pillow. I didn't button the shirt, just tied it up under my breasts for a little support; it's been twenty years since I could comfortably go braless. Not that fullness of flesh doesn't have ample compensations.

By the time I had the fire going under the kettle you'd found the upstream ford where, at this time of year, legs as long as yours could negotiate a crossing on rocks. When Raksha went to meet you, you took her inspection serenely in stride. I had to struggle a bit myself for any semblance of serenity. Something in the way you moved, with the sureness and grace and wariness of, yes, a stag, made me shiver in places the cool breeze couldn't touch.

I saw, with relief, that you weren't quite as young as I had thought at first. Old enough to know what you were doing, but damn, still so young! What the hell did I think *I* was doing?

"Invisible antlers or not," I said, when you were close enough, "you don't seem in any danger from my hound. Raksha seldom shows her fangs to women." Just so you'd know, in case you still wondered, that I knew. "Raksha is, in fact, a slut," I added, as she rolled on her back and wriggled for a belly-rub. "Not that I don't understand exactly how she feels."

"Always happy to oblige a lady." You bent and gave Raksha, at least, what she wanted. To me you gave a sidelong glance of amusement.

Fevered dreams notwithstanding, I wasn't about to roll over and beg. Not yet. "I'll have to bear that in mind." I turned my attention to the coffee, giving you my only cup and sipping mine from a bowl. A little pacing, I decided, might be in order, a little rational conversation beyond repartee and innuendo. Mae West, for all her subversive virtues, was never my style. If I ever had one. Still…"I see you didn't bring your rod," I said, and then, as you managed not to splutter more than a trickle of hot coffee, added blandly, "I could show you where the biggest trout hang out. Rainbows, brookies, a few salmon, now that they've been reintroduced, but those are mostly fingerlings." I untied my shirt and raised a corner to wipe the coffee from your chin. The direction of your gaze let me know that stone towers weren't all you had come to see.

Then I tied the shirt again. "Come on, if you're interested." I turned and moved downslope toward the river.

We sat on the highest rock and talked of fish for a while, and rivers, and the pair of hawks wheeling high in the warming sky. Nothing personal, nothing to distract from the place, the moment. Just acknowledgment that this place, this moment, was a bond. We had come, separately, to the river, the mountains, for the rich scent of spruce and balsam, the flow of water over stone and wind over forested slopes. These needs we had in common.

Not that the other needs receded. I wanted to lay my hand on your thigh, take your hand and press it between my own thighs to show you how every inflection of your voice, every tilt of your chin above your strong, smooth throat, every shift of expression letting beauty flash across the angular strength of your face, made the denim crotch of my jeans get wetter and wetter. It seemed impossible that you couldn't sense, or scent, my arousal; it seemed, now that you were more than a personification of my fantasies, just as impossible that you could share them.

You grew quieter, leaning back on one elbow and watching me, dark, narrowed eyes glittering under heavy lids, body a blend of stillness and tension. I wished I could catch it on film. But not now, not while my pulse accelerated and the compulsion grew to either touch you or take to the river.

Then, just as I tensed to move, you said, "So, you gonna make up your mind which goddess to be, or do I jump down there into what passes for a cold shower?"

"I don't think the Romans had a name for this one." I laid my hand over yours where it rested on your thigh. A tremor rippled almost imperceptibly through the muscle there, or did I imagine it? Your watchful expression didn't change. "I knew what I wanted," I said, "when I saw you fly casting. Such good hands."

I lifted your hand and turned it over. You didn't resist, just gazed at it as though it were some found object of only casual interest. "Think so? Too big, some say."

"Not for me." I fumbled to untie the knot in my shirt, leaned toward you, and raised your hand to my breast. "I think I can fill them," I said, as your fingers curved to cradle the fullness.

You sat up, and filled your other hand too. "Not too bad a fit," you agreed, pressing just hard enough to make me feel the weight, the heaviness increasing until it tugged at me all the way down to my cunt.

"Might be as good a fit...in other areas..." Talking was getting difficult. Hell, *breathing* was getting difficult. I pulled away with an effort. "Might be somewhere more comfortable than on a rock to find out." I stood and began edging down the sloping crease in the boulder's side. Raksha waited below, whining softly as I descended from a place her claws couldn't handle.

In a single motion you uncoiled and leapt six feet down the sheerest rock face, your landing spraying damp gravel into the river. You pulled me from my foothold and swung me around to face the water, gripping me tightly from behind. "Comfort," you growled into my ear, "is highly overrated."

Raksha began to pace nervously until she caught my mood, and scent, and understood. I pressed back, rubbing against your crotch. "Mmm...but a light touch can work wonders..." and you read my mind, or my body, and ran those strong, deft hands up over my breasts until you were stroking me so delicately, teasingly, that you forced me to strain toward your touch. Even when my swollen nipples jutted out like thumbtips, even when my breath came so fast and shrill that it drowned out the rushing water, you didn't relent, but kept luring me closer and closer to a peak that could never quite be reached.

"All you gotta do is ask," you murmured against my neck, and then, "Wonders is right! How much bigger can they get?" And you kept up the torture, and I couldn't stand to make you stop, until finally I couldn't stand not to.

I squirmed around to face you, and rubbed gratefully against the thigh you thrust between my legs as you pushed me back against the rock. "Come on, damn it, suck me, bite me, now!" I said, and pulled your head to where I had to have it; and, after a few teasing licks, you did. Hard. When you shifted from one breast to the other I could see, as I already felt, how the pressure of your hot mouth had forced my nipples to even more extreme engorgement.

By now my clit was at least as engorged, and pounding as I rode your thigh. I let go of your head and fumbled at your belt. You pushed my hands aside, in classic mode; an old-fashioned girl. I let it go. For now. You spread open my jeans and pushed them down, and I kicked them loose as you worked your mouth down across my belly and your hands gripped my substantial ass. Then you were kneeling, but as I arched my hips forward, you leaned back and grinned up at me.

"So, Goddess, what next?" Your voice was husky and not entirely steady, but the challenge was clear. You were prepared to tease me for longer than I could hold out.

"Shut up and use your mouth for something better!" Which you did, with skill and a rhythm perfectly matched to my compulsive thrusts. My clit spasmed against your tongue and teeth, and hardened again before the exquisite pangs could quite subside. The throbbing demand of my cunt shook me so hard I would have fallen without the rock at my back. I needed more than the flickering fire of your mouth. "Now," I said, "now!" and tugged at your arm, but you raised your head, just the hint of a smile on lips slick with my juices, and said, reflectively, "So that's how a Goddess tastes!"

I yanked at your arm again. "You'll find out how a Goddess curses if you don't...don't..." but you had half-relented, and brought one hand around to stroke and probe gently into my aching crotch, and it was all I could do to breathe.

"Don't what?" you said. "Just tell me what you want."

Beg, you meant—and why not? It was little enough to give you. "I want," I said between ragged gasps, "to hold your hand. All of it. Please. Right now. Please."

So you let me feel one long finger, and two, and three, too gently, too gradually, not just to tease but to be sure I knew how much I could take.

I knew. "More," I begged, demanded. "More, all of it, harder!" My slippery depths clenched around the maddening pressure, tried to gulp it farther and farther in, and then you were past the narrow point and filling me the way I desperately needed to be filled.

Your eyes were closed, your mouth firm but unmoving against my clit. All your focus, all your movement, was inside me, your curved hand probing, thrusting, working my need, pushing my ache to waves of intensity surpassing even orgasm...until orgasm struck, and nothing else had ever come close. I scarcely heard Raksha's howl above my own raw screams.

Gently, you withdrew, soaked with the flow of my coming. Gently you stood and wrapped your strong arms around me and supported me, until, not quite so gently, I nudged my knee between your thighs. "Please, I need this, too," I whispered as you stiffened, and you let me rub against you until there was no telling who rode whom. I worked your T-shirt up until I could press my full breasts against you just under your own high, tight peaks, and you buried your face in my shoulder and let my flesh muffle your shuddering release.

Raksha's cold nose on my thigh made me jump. We eased apart, and she sniffed at us, and I laughed and moved down into the stream. "Come on," I said, not looking back, giving you time to regroup, "let's clean up before she decides to do it for us."

Not that I wanted to wash away your touch, my response, even the sweet soreness. But what I did want, I got. You pulled off your clothes and joined me in the water, and somehow I managed not to stare too overtly at the beauty of your lithe, naked body. Later, I thought, I'll make you truly howl. Later.

We stayed in the river until the sun was high and hot enough to threaten sunburn. You asked about my stone edifices, and I gave you the grand tour, describing the uses and goals of my photographs.

"Light and dark," you echoed musingly. "Good and evil? Either/or? Is that what you're hung up on?" You fingered a smooth, flat pebble with distinct striations of quartz and basalt.

"More like yin and yang, solid and space, stasis and flow, each defined by the other. It isn't opposites I find compelling, but their convergence." Strange, to be standing naked in a mountain stream trying to verbalize the unexplainable. "I keep trying to catch something on film that exists only in my mind, a sort of stark, transcendent beauty that flashes at the point where opposites meet."

"Sounds like a matter/antimatter reaction," you said, and sent your pebble skipping across the pool. Then you began to assemble a construction of your own from the stones I had knocked down yesterday, and I pretended to do a little of this and a little of that, while all I could really think about was the graceful strength of your body and the residual throbbing of mine, and how I might force your own matter/antimatter to the exploding point.

Later you moved your gear to my campsite, and we shared provisions, and when the late-afternoon light was right I shot roll after roll of film before the shadows got too long for the balance I wanted. I even took a few of you, just for myself, I said, but you'd only let me do it from the back. "That's fine," I assured you, "you're just as magnificent going as coming." You looked so startled that I wondered how blind the younger girls must be these days to take what you so skillfully give but never tell you how beautiful you are.

You fished for our supper, and we watched the sunset clouds glow bright salmon and slowly fade to steel, while the cascading song of a wood thrush rippled hauntingly from the darkening forest. Then, by the firelight, we lay together on combined sleeping bags, and I challenged you.

"No hands where you don't want them," I said, "no tongue, just lie back and let me try to make you howl." Your slight frown turned to laughter when I leaned over you and pulled your hands to my breasts and added, "C'mon, how can you turn down a tit-fuck? How often do you get an offer like that? The harder you make me, the better this will work."

Your answer was to cooperate with such skill and zest I could barely subdue my own aching need for more. It was worth it, though, when I knelt between your thighs, my breasts steadied in my hands, and teased your sweet ache with thrusting nipples until you writhed and dug your fingers into my shoulders. If you didn't truly howl until after you flipped me and ground your crotch against my hipbone, you came close enough. And then, while you still struggled for breath, I drew your head to my breast and slid my nipple, still slippery with your juices, into your mouth. "That," I said, "is how a Goddess tastes."

I hear your voice before I see you, and the petulant reply of your companion. I struggle to be glad you aren't alone. I watch you move slowly through the gallery, studying the pictures, while she fidgets with her hair. Then you stop before the central work, the one that makes everyone stop. Your body

16

takes on that blend of stillness and tension I remember so well; and this time you see it, too, in the photograph before you. You lie there on a wide, flat rock in midstream, leaning on one elbow, looking down into the rushing water. Sunlight slants across your naked, smoothly muscled back and buttocks, your long, lithe legs, but your head is in the shadow of a higher boulder and your face is turned away. The arm you lean on hides all but a mere, subliminal trace of your curving breast.

Your companion pauses, says, "Ooh, sexy!" and moves on. She doesn't recognize you. No one could recognize you unless she truly knew you, truly saw you…You should be with someone who will always know you, always feel her heart jump and her breath catch at the sight of you, at your least movement, at your stillness, all through a long, long life. It can't be me, but it won't be her, either.

You lean forward to read the caption, then turn and scan the gallery. I have retreated up around the curve of the spiral stairway, but you come unerringly toward me, and your movements as you climb quickly and easily up the stairs make something lurch deep inside me.

I look into your face, watching for anger, half-wanting to see you angry, at least once—your anger could be as breathtaking as your joy—but never hurt. Though your expression is casual, detached, your dark eyes are intense. "Nice bunch of stones," you say, gesturing below.

"I'll take it down," I say, "if you want me to. You could sue me for not asking your permission, but I didn't know how to reach you." I had deliberately refused to let you tell me how to reach you, for fear that I might descend into stalking. You, sensing that my life is not elegantly simple enough to be all my own, had let it go at that.

"You might as well leave it up," you say. "Just another pile of stones."

"No! That's not how I think of you!" My throat is so tight I can scarcely breathe.

You tilt your head slightly, considering. "Where did you get that title? *All That's Best of Dark and Bright.*" You glance down briefly toward the photograph. "Sounds familiar. From a poem, isn't it?"

"Byron," I say. " 'She walks in beauty, as the night / Of cloudless climes and starry skies, / And all that's best of dark and bright / Meets in her aspect and her eyes.' " I manage a slight smile. "On top of everything else, you've turned me maudlin."

You give me that sudden, blindingly beautiful smile, and relax, and lean your shoulder against the curving wall. "So, will you be going back to get more pictures of those 'ephemeral' towers?"

"Next month, over Columbus Day." I'm still far from relaxed, but at least I can breathe again. "I was hoping you'd ask."

Your wide grin makes my heart leap. "I kinda feel an urgent fishing trip coming on," you say, ignoring the querulous voice from below calling your name.

Then you're gone, leaving me throbbing from a quick, hard, incendiary embrace. And a promise.

Sometimes She Lets Me

Alison L. Smith

Last night her back was sore, spasms from the past, a high
school injury, and I said that I'd rub it and then we could just
go to sleep, and when I finished she asked me to massage her
ass and I said yes but I could not do without kissing it, licking
that white moon. I ran my teeth along the arc of it, biting, and
her ass started to move under me.

Then she rolled over and I pulled off her shirt and she let
me touch them. They are secrets she holds separate from me,
their roundness flattened against her chest all day. She does
not like them, but I do. And sometimes, when she lets me, I
fall between them and I breathe in. The tip of my nose mea-
sures their softness and the fine, white hair rises and she gets
goose bumps.

I took one of them in my mouth last night and the dark
snail of her nipple grew under my tongue. Her pelvis moved
beneath me, moved up toward mine when she let me. The
moon was gone and the river lights outside her window
reflected like stars, as if the sky moved beneath us and she lay
on her back for me.

Her hipbones cut the air in thin circles and she tightened under me. She let me unbutton her boxer shorts. She let me take her in my mouth, press my face into her. I cupped her ass in my palms and she got hard for me. She dug her hands into my hair and shivered in the heat-soaked room and I watched her through the keyhole of her thighs.

Sometimes she lets me and when she does she talks to herself. In a low voice, she talks the fear away. Like last night when her ass was cupped in my hands and she was in my mouth and she whispered and her hips circled faster and her voice began to rise.

The dog woke, his pink tongue curling. He yawned. He circled once, twice, spread out beside us again and he watched his master's face change. He watched her call out to the ceiling, watched her back arch, watched her reach over her head, her fisted hands knocking the headboard until her long body tightened and her voice grew hoarse.

Then she begged me. She said *don't stop don't stop don't stop don't stop* and she trembled under me and her hips pitched and I almost lost her and I pressed my hands into her ass to steady her until she came in my mouth.

Afterwards, she pulled the covers up around her. She curled into their soft protection and rolled away from me. She hid. The dog burrowed under the comforter, panting into the darkness. After she let me and she fell asleep on her sore back, the sound of her voice stayed in my ears. I watched her as she kicked the covers off in the night's long heat. First her shoulders appeared, then her breasts, then the damp stain on her boxers where I had put my mouth. And I wanted to put my hands on her again, but I didn't. I just watched. The old radiator cracked and pinged in the corner and light from a street lamp bled in through the tall window and she slept and I watched and she let me.

Grande Jeté

Toni Amato

You ask for a kiss and I refuse. You ask for a kiss and I say no for all the right reasons, and come morning I wait for your sleep-soft face and a chance to say yes, oh god yes please. That evening, the thick smell of paint and a worn mattress in your studio and as your hand leads mine toward your breasts, I become harder than ever before. I become a drowning man as your hand urges mine into a salt-slick sea, and I cum harder than ever before.

The first time I dress for you, I am a teenage boy on his first date and I want to be a man for you, I want to be a man who can hold your arm there at the elbow and make you feel safe and cherished and adored. You reach out to straighten my tie and although you don't know all of what you are doing, I am undone.

You reach out to straighten my tie, there, in the hallway, and you have no idea what you have done. And neither, despite my butch-dyke cool, do I. The music is playing softly and you think I am leading as you clap out a rhythm I ache to move my hips to as I watch your woman's hands.

"Can I see it?" you ask, and I am twelve, thirteen, maybe, and suddenly embarrassed and unsure like I have not been in decades. Yes, decades, and for all my boyish ways, for all my teenage charm, I feel as though I may be falling in love again for the very first time, I feel like a baby-faced virgin boy, and I want to disappear as you handle what I have never shown outside my pants, what I have worshipped with and delivered with and sang hallelujahs with, but always from my trousers, always strapped and bound and covered by cotton and darkness.

You sit blindfolded and bound in a plush chair, a woman who has seen more of me than I knew I wanted to show. You sit willing and open for me and I begin the dance that I have mastered, and I watch. I watch the flush and the sheen and the motions of desire. I have become accustomed to knowing that I am wanted, but this time, this time I beg with hands and tongue, and everything I am and yes I pray, I pray to you and what I pray is please, please want this. Oh please want me. And you do. And here begins the dance. A dance interrupted by too many miles and too little time.

I tell myself stories, at night. I tell myself stories, now, to help me get to sleep.

It's hotter than hell here. Can't stand my own skin touching itself, can't stand the weight of even a thin sheet. I'm sweating and twisting and searching for a cool spot on the pillow and there isn't any and the truth is I'm getting restless and cranky and it's too hot even to jerk off.

The truth is, I'm desperate to fuck you. No. That's not the truth, either. The truth is, I need your body. Need your shoulders and your thighs and your belly and your back. Truth is it's very difficult for an animal to talk and what I am right now is a lust-maddened beast and I am trying to make this make sense, to make this something more than guttural noises and deep-throated grunts, trying to be a civilized human being despite the unconscious baring of my teeth. And you think it a lopsided grin, this hungry thing you bring out in me.

I have told you. I have tried to tell you that the veins beneath the skin of your breasts, the blue pulsing of your wrists and neck are a torment to me. But what I can find words to say is only a phantom of what lies down hot and heavy in my own veins and all I can do is show you and there is not space, in this configuration of our lives, there is not time for a complete showing and so the caged animal paces and occasionally growls and so here I am, working words and grinding my teeth and maybe I'll catch it this time.

It's not all sweet romance, it's not all soft and you play with fire when you tell me you remember being dragged into that bathroom.

You play with fire that I want you to swallow, entire and whole, so that I can watch the flush of flame creep across your ribs, along your collarbones. So I can see you burn the way my fingers scorch and sear at the touch of you.

It's not all tender words and longing glances, and the place you have never been to before is a place I have prowled for years but never, not once, has there been a creature like you here. You say you want to have jungle sex with me and oh yes, the jungle, and there I wait, slinking yellow-eyed through vines full of exotic birds and I will hear you coming, yes I will hear you coming again and again.

Nocturnal beast. I am losing sleep over this. Losing sleep and losing rest because when my eyes shut the dreams come and it is difficult to translate dreams into waking words but I will try because you have asked and sometimes, indeed, the hunter gets captured by the prey.

"You have no idea what you do to me," I say, later and from a distance. Wide-eyed wonder across the telephone lines. "What? Tell me what. Go on, give me words."

I am a poor poet deprived of words, a tongue-tied Romeo—
I am a woman struck speechless by desire and all the words I
know to describe this loosening of muscle, this rhythmic
tremolo—all these words are not enough. And these words are
all I have.

"Tell me."

All my years of pursuing the one who could take my defiant self and create a safe place for the bended knee I am desperate to offer—all those years of dark and mysterious places,
actors so sure of their lines, carefully orchestrated scripts and
now, here, this. Your voice. All right. I'll try to tell you.

What would I use to say the unspeakable, to tell you the
things that lay heavy on my tongue? The things that I wish
had not ever been said before and I want to make a new language, then. A language all ours, a set of sighs and murmurs
and exultant shouts. Soft groans of deep surprise and loud,
loud earsplitting shrieks of hearts torn wide open. I want a
series of clicks and tooth chatters and gusts of breath that will
tell you the particulars that are so particular. The peculiar and
the personal and I do indeed believe that this can only be said
by speaking in tongues. Strange language and insane gesticu-
lation.

In my dreams we have days and nights. Yes, long nights,
hot like these I suffer through. In my dreams there are as many
hours to the darkness as passion can create, and there is
enough of it, of passion and all its attendant desire and hunger
and need, enough to make for an eternity.

You lie on a bed of fur, soft and caressing, dark beneath
you. You lie on the skin of an animal and this reminds me of
what I become for you. More than that—helps me remember
what you need from me. Soft despite the hard wanting, the
way my muscles tense and flex with needing you. You lie on a
bed of fur and look at me, and there are myriad women gazing through eyes I watch go large and dark with the same

fierce need that moves me. You are a playful, impetuous child, a young woman discovering what your body can do for you, a temptress who knows quite well what she does to me. That one, the one who taunts and provokes and most certainly dares me. And I am desperate to please them all.

I can smell you from across the room. It's the scent of metal and blood and deep, secret places. Salt of the ocean and tang of pine needles on an ancient forest floor. My teeth ache with it, my mouth waters, and something old behind my eyes drops down. I can smell you and the memory of everything pleasurable lies just beneath that scent. I close my eyes and pull molecules of you deeply into me, the way I long to be pulled into you. Let the capillaries in my chest pass this on to every blood cell and so to the very fibers of my body. This is the first sweet step toward losing track of the boundary between us, toward forgetting where I let off and you begin.

Flooded, saturated, I open my eyes. The arch of your foot. The long curve of calf. The most succulent of all tender places resting beneath a gathering of your own fur. I need to see your belly rise and arch, need to feel your muscles tense and release. Already I can see your pulse lifting the intricacies of your veins closer to that skin, that smooth and supple skin I burn with the heat of, even here across the room.

I need this more than you can possibly imagine. Like a starved thing, too long alone and unfed, and no matter how much you give me, I know this hunger will not be abated.

I need this and I pray for self-control, for the presence of mind to treat you like a precious thing even as I lose my mind in animal ecstasy. Pray for strength and pray in thanksgiving and the words of the prayer fade away into gibberish when I reach you, when I reach down to you, kneel down before you and begin a long night of supplication and speaking in tongues.

Where to begin? A kiss, just one kiss and the fullness of your lips, the taste of your breath are enough to make me shudder. I want to kiss you until your lips bleed, until you come up gasping for air—and even this only once I've had enough. There is danger in this wanting. The continually present danger of the bottomless hungers I suffer in your absence. The hungers that are only sharpened by your physical presence.

A kiss, then. Or more like a thousand kisses in one extreme lingering. I want to feel you move for me. Feel the tip of your tongue and the smooth coolness of your teeth. I want to eat your mouth as though it were a fine, sweet fruit. Crush it and let the juices run down my chin. So easy to slip from mouth to cheek and follow that first downy caress to your ear. To that place which brings from you the shy turning of your head, the quick intake of breath.

And once my lips have made that journey, once I have mouthed a trail of desire across the delicate bones and bitten more gently than is imaginable, then I exhale. Allow the deepest of sighs to escape my lips and enter the echo chamber of your ear. Imagine it the hot, wet wind before a storm, imagine the force of murmured words—"Jesus god I want you"—able to course the distance to a place I long to be but will not go for a long, long while.

Instead, I caress the delicate contours with my tongue, the ridges and folds and the astounding contradiction of soft skin over cartilage. Between my teeth a fragile thing. Instead I burrow into a small indentation, an almost secret tender place, and drink deeply.

There is a shift, then. The last vestiges of control shatter, and my hands are creatures unto themselves. My hands that knew their way across your body from the very beginning. I want to cup the weight of your head in my palm, push my fingers through the fineness of your hair. Want to place the full grip of my desire on either of your strong and freckled shoulders, pushing into you all my want and need. Here I can feel the first soft surrendering, the first relaxation of your muscles. The giving in and letting go. If I close my eyes, I see you naked in the cool reflection of water, see the way you could float on the surface, with your body this loose, and I will myself to be the ocean, to be the steady beat of waves on a roundly pebbled shore.

Trace your collarbones with trembling fingers, run my palms over the plain of your chest, the mound of your belly, the long smooth glide of your sides and across the curve of your breasts. Undone, I am undone and there is no restraint, now. I am beyond lingering, beyond savoring and the time has come for abandon, for high winds and torrential downpour.

Business Casual

Lauren Sanders

*There is time for work, and there is time for love. That
leaves no other time.* —Coco Chanel

She was mine in the conference room on the thirty-sixth
floor. Two leather chairs jammed the door, the lights were
turned down low. Easing her onto the mahogany table, I ran
my hands along the length of her fully clothed body before
turning her head toward the windows, unveiling a theatre of
buildings by night, charcoal glass checkerboards with brightly lit squares. Between the cracks was the river, a sliver of
bridge, the outer boroughs glimmering like an old-fashioned
movie marquis. I wanted her to know how high up we were,
to feel the risk in my hands, breathe the fear through my lips.
I'd become obsessed with the spotlights on rippled black
water, the crystalline buildings wrapping their legs around us.
It was as much of a rush as our frenzy for quick, muted
orgasms. She smelled like rosemary-mint conditioner from
the corporate gym.

On good days, she escaped to the gym at twilight, just as I was beginning my day, and practically met me at the door when I came in at eleven. Other times, when I casually passed her cubicle she was buried in the corner, headphones crushing her wavy brown hair and eyes strained on her computer screen, adrift in a haze of high-stakes numerical analysis. I knew not to approach her then. She became irascible when anyone broke her spell, and there were still too many people around. We had to be discreet.

She was an investment banker at a large financial institution. I was a painter with a night job in the word-processing department there. In a manner of speaking, I worked for her.

For someone so young she had so many words. Hundreds of sentence fragments attached to bar graphs and pie charts, and she had strong opinions about how they should appear on the page. She was a perfectionist, she said, but open to suggestions. She listened when we told her what was not possible and she trusted our deadlines. Sometimes she lingered after dropping off a job, joining a conversation about a movie, play, or the political drama of the week. Nobody talks out there, she said, meaning the other bankers, her colleagues. It was important for her to separate herself. To prove she didn't belong *out there*.

Over time, I learned that she hated investment banking. She'd resigned herself to the training program to please her parents, immigrants who'd shoveled the bulk of their hard-earned salaries into the ivy-league playground she'd recently left behind. She knew how they gloated whenever they told anyone where she worked. I said I understood. My parents lived in the same rural town I'd escaped almost two decades earlier, and had always hated telling people there that I was an artist. Even the painting class I taught seemed intangible to them. But when I started working at the investment bank they suddenly had a name people recognized. Something to talk about. They never mentioned that I was a glorified typist.

She laughed at this the way she always laughed at my jokes. She engaged me in conversations about art—not in the aggressive manner of my students, particularly the little dykes with big baggy pants who followed me to the subway, demanding to know about the art world, who'd been included and excluded, what was the dominant style, how could they possibly work themselves in. No, she wanted to talk about the paintings she'd seen in museums, whether her interpretations had been correct. When I told her there was no right or wrong and offered to give her an art tour of our building, which incidentally had the most expensive collection of twentieth-century paintings and prints I'd seen outside of a museum, she said *cool*. Then she asked me if I had always known that I was an artist. Although I hadn't picked up a brush in months and was even considering dumping my studio, I said yes. This was very cool, too.

I liked her enthusiasm. Her words. The flicker in her eyes when she said *cool*, electric-green chewing gum jutting in and out of her mouth like a serpent's tongue. How eager she was to gobble up the world. I started looking forward to her e-mails and thought about her on my days off. In short, as the months passed and she marked her first year on the calendar, I developed a bit of a crush on the kid—nothing serious, really—the kind of amorous affection that occasionally crept into a relationship with one of my students and that I'd learned to keep at bay.

Until one night her presentation made the "hot jobs" board, and I spent half my shift with my forefinger buffing the mouse to create a graphic of an archer with his bow pointed at a reindeer to *imagize*—company term—a hostile raid she and a few other bankers were shoveling through the pipeline. I tried telling her there probably weren't too many hunters equipped with bow and arrow in subarctic climates, where the reindeer roam, and besides it was a cruel image. She smiled and I thought, what a beautiful mouth she has, curvaceous purple lips that seem almost heart-shaped, and commanding white teeth. What was it about cruelty that in the right face could become so alluring?

Before I began fantasizing her cultured sadism, she confessed a similar conversation she'd had with the partner who was spearheading the takeover, her boss. Apparently, she'd told him the image was a mixed metaphor. Repeating this, she shifted her weight to her left leg so her hip jutted sideways. She rested her hand upon it, giggling a bit as she revealed the balance of their conversation: naïvely, she'd informed her boss that a bow and arrow would hardly slay a reindeer, and she was treated to the following pabulum: "A hunter never questions his weapons." Her boss walked off, and that was the word.

"I was embarrassed bringing in the job before," she said. "I wanted you to do it."

"But you could have been home already."

"I'm like you, a night owl," she said, hand still on her hip, snugly encased in tight gray trousers. Ever since the company went business-casual, her clothing had been shrinking. While the men dressed down to comfortable khakis and polo shirts, and the women into flat loafers, she'd gone more contempo-rary—synthetic skins and form-fitting blouses, patent-leather platform shoes, as if she'd walked off the pages of a fashion magazine. It was her battle against the corporate culture and she waged it valiantly.

I told her not to worry. We would give her boss what he wanted.

When she came back a few hours later, I handed her the page and she burst out laughing. In her absence, I'd dug up an image of a U.S. army tank and pointed the cannon directly at the reindeer.

"Poor bastard," she said.

"A hunter never questions his weapons," I responded.

"I meant the reindeer."

"It's a she."

"But it's got antlers. Only males have antlers."

"Reindeer aren't like other deer, they both have them."

"Cool," she smiled. "I wonder if it makes them any less sexist."

I laughed, bemused by her twisted-rebel stance and ruthless determination. My students were usually shy in their flirtations, stammering bunnies afraid to stand too close or look me in the eye. But this kid was unflinching. She smiled as if she had me where she wanted me, and what killed me was we both knew it was true. I wanted to pin her down right there on my desk in the awful fluorescent lighting with an annoying pop song playing and make her put up or shut up. But my two colleagues were tapping away at their computers and there were other jobs in the rack. I handed her the real document with the bow and arrow, and when she took it her hand brushed against mine. As she left the word-processing center, the hand she'd touched started stinging. I looked down and saw my forefinger was bleeding. The little raider had given me a paper cut.

In the bathroom, I ran my finger under the tap. The warm water was soothing, but I couldn't stop laughing at myself. Flirting was an occupational hazard.

I never heard the door click open, had no idea I wasn't alone until I saw her face materialize in the mirror in front of me. She asked what happened and I told her she'd wounded me. I moved my finger from the water and held it front of her. A few drops of blood seeped through the scratch.

"A paper cut," she said.

I nodded.

She took my hand in hers, and I felt as if I were being submerged in the gushing warm tap. Slowly, without taking her eyes from mine, she lifted my finger and kissed it lightly before opening her lips around the cut and sucking as if I'd been bitten by a snake. I slipped back against the sink, letting my skin melt with every stroke of her tongue on my finger. She kept her eyes open, staring at me.

I took a deep breath. "Do they know about you out there?"

For a second, she stopped sucking and shook her head, then took my entire finger in her mouth. "Oh fuck," I said. "Fuck."

I grabbed her by the cheeks and pulled up her head. My wounded finger throbbed against her skin. She cupped her hands over mine and we stared in the rushed and inexorable manner of lovers on the precipice. Her eyes were engorged, pitch-black catacombs of desire. A reflection of my own. I pressed her back against the tiles and kissed her in the bright light. She grabbed my neck. I slid my hands down to her breasts, felt her squirm beneath me. Our kissing was ferocious.

Suddenly she pulled away. "Not here," she said.

"Then where?"

"I know a place."

Ours was a sick building. With its windows sealed shut, the same fetid air circulated through every crevice day in and day out. She got colds all winter long. I brought her echinacea tea and zinc drops, held her head in my lap in the secret room we found off the foyer on the eighteenth floor. It was like something out of an old movie. You pushed the wall and it revolved backwards. Inside was a metal desk with a small painting above it. The painting was by one of my favorite artists, an innovator of the New York school. It was pristine in its simplicity. A few colored boxes—red, yellow, blue, nothing exotic—with frayed edges bouncing off each other, as if energized by the magnetic fields between them. She said someone had left it there for us.

At last unfettered, she cried about not sleeping, about missing the gym, traveling too much, and not seeing me for days. She was being pressured to take on more clients, and with every deal she grew sicker of her own deferential conformity, her uncanny ability to make money for a system she despised. I found her moral conflict absurd, if not a bit youthful. She was playing dress-up in the last bastion of white-collar patriarchy. Though the collars were less constricting, the roles were still clearly defined. You couldn't get any further from the reindeer, I said. She cried harder.

I told her she was my baby, promising everything would be okay, and although the banalities slipping from my lips alarmed me, I knew it was what she wanted to hear. I knew it as instinctively as if she were my child. We rocked gently, her face against my breasts until longing usurped comfort and I wanted to fuck her as much as I needed to protect her. I didn't have to say it. She'd learned to read my rhythm, my body, my breath, and she was a quick study. She ripped open my shirt and played with my nipples. She adored my nipples, loved burying her face between my breasts, which made me feel more maternal and at the same time brought me to my knees in delirium, if only for a few minutes in our hidden cavern before we returned unsuspected, though a bit rumpled, to our desks.

My supervisor never questioned me. Those of us who worked grave had a tacit understanding that anyone might disappear for a while. Some people paced the halls or hiked up and down the carpeted stairwells; others, swamped by their circadian clocks, napped on the plush couches in one of the more deserted lobbies. Whatever it took to make it to sunrise.

She left before the sun came up, often skipping out just after we parted as if our assignation had been her reward for making it through another sixteen-hour day, but not without an e-mail saying "goodnight" or "miss you." In her e-mails she called me Rembrandt. She said I was the only person she could talk to. The only one who understood her. She never used the word *love*.

After being together, I was bombarded by the adrenaline of our interlocked bodies, her teeth on my nipples as she shoved her entire hand inside me. You take so much so fast, she said, as amazed by the dexterity of my cunt as I was by her ability to get me there so quickly. I never told her how good she was. I didn't have to. With her hand inside me we were both acutely aware of her cutthroat ambition. "Did you come?" she asked. "Did you really?"

"You were here."

"We can do better."

"I have to get back."

"Please, one more time. I really want to see you."

She would arrive even earlier the next morning to finish the work she'd forsaken. I would claim another migraine had kept me from my desk. Never in my life had I been such a bottom, and without an ounce of guilt.

What can I say? The kid knew how to fuck.

I blushed remembering every twist and permutation of her hand as if it were still there, like a severed limb that leaves its ghosted particles behind. The energy could remain for hours, days, even weeks.

Occasionally I went to the bathroom, turned on all the taps, and masturbated in one of the stalls, but mostly after she left I became so morose I put on my headphones and listened to country music until I cried.

At dawn I stumbled out into the cold quiet mornings and by rote ambled to the subway station. Staring at the freshly scrubbed faces, I wanted to embrace them for their tenacity. Up so early pursuing their dreams. Like her parents. I became an ethnic detective, dissecting skin color and bone structure to determine if anyone was from her country, desperate to see how she might look in daylight. I imagined her at home in bed, buried beneath the pale orange comforter she talked about. We romanticized her bed with its billowing canopy, the hotels she frequented that had two king-size beds and cable TV. She said she always ordered a porno film and charged it to the company because she knew it was what guys did on the road.

I saw her in a hotel room, lights dimmed, misty blue streams of television caressing her limbs. I saw her in the boardroom, the only woman at a table full of suits as titillated by her professional machinations as I was by her hand inside me. I saw her next to me on the walk from the subway to my apartment, promising to make me scrambled eggs with avocado slices for breakfast.

Alone in my apartment I poured a bowl of cold cereal and realized I didn't even know her phone number.

Before her I had a girlfriend. We had been dating almost a year when my affair with the investment banker began. My girlfriend was kind, beautiful, and wildly intelligent. She was a serial monogamist who fell in love with people the way she fell in love with authors, deeply and chauvinistically, devouring every sentence she could find by and about the enamored scribe, her fingers smeared with ink from rare books, diaries, and Xeroxes of academic journals. But unlike scholars who could make a life's work out of one writer, my girlfriend eventually got bored. The signs were subtle. She carried fewer titles to work, kept a bookmark on the same page for weeks, stopped visiting the library, and eventually found some nugget of betrayal she could not overlook.

The e-mail had been on my night table. It wasn't incriminating, but would have been enough to rouse the dander of any lover. When she asked who, it seemed pointless to lie. My girlfriend had fallen out of love; I'd never really been there. She called me a cheater, said I had no respect for her, and questioned my sanity in having an affair with someone at work—someone so young and wrongfully employed. I stopped listening, and instead remembered my girlfriend's wet tongue traveling from my hipbone to that spot in the back of my neck where all the nerves met, and kissing me there as if I'd grown another set of lips. We'd spent hours on her couch making out like teenagers before ever touching a button, waistband, or zipper where underneath lay another treat. My bookish girlfriend had wonderful taste in lingerie. How she could wear corsets, garters, red stockings, and lacy bras without ever looking tacky amazed me. Then again, she was the first lover whom I let light candles and rub scented oils into the crevices behind my kneecaps, the first whose pussy I lapped wholeheartedly as she mimicked on mine and somehow it never felt stereotypical. She knew how sexy tenderness could be in the right hands. She also knew how easily it could evaporate.

After my confession, she saw me as she saw her once-revered politically oppressed writer who left his wife and children for a woman half his age, moved to another country, and had cosmetic surgery, becoming a painful joke to those who believed the intellect should rule matters of the heart. Those like my girlfriend. I let her believe my moral failings had sunk our relationship. A few months later, I heard she'd moved on to her next lover. The news made me neither happy nor sad.

I stopped seeing most of my friends and started picking up extra shifts at work to increase the odds of bumping into my little banker. Insomnia set in. Even the eye masks and sandalwood I burned no longer worked. I drank red wine and watched morning talk shows, the soaps, cooking shows, and reruns of old cartoons—whatever it took to disappear inside the screen.

Then one day at the onset of spring, when sun-drenched mornings brought the rush of children lining up outside before school and dogs dragging their heavy-eyed owners through the streets, after work I went to my studio instead of going home. The last time I'd been there I was so frustrated that I hadn't cleaned anything. Most of my brushes had hardened. Paint was splattered on the walls and floor. The sink was clogged. I dug up an old canvas and whitewashed it with a roller. Then I mopped, wiped down the walls, opened all the windows, and sat silently while the canvas dried, thinking about suspended color boxes, prisms of static, and the electrified fields sustaining us.

I thought I was sick with love, sleeping as little as she did so we'd be on the same time clock. It took me weeks to see it wasn't only her cycle I was emulating. I had begun to worship productivity, becoming devout in my routine, unflagging in my work ethic, greedy in my pleasures. Unlike her, I was pleased with the fruits of my labor.

Each night in the car on the way to work I wondered whether it was a good day or a bad day, or if she'd be there at all when I arrived at the office. Her career was blossoming. Throughout the spring, they sent her on whirlwind road shows that kept her out of town for weeks, and spoke about transferring her to one of the firm's European satellites in June. When she returned, often for one or two nights before they shipped her off again, she was so worn out she could barely wheel her suitcase down the hall. She set the alarm on her watch to remind her what time it was, and swallowed antihistamines by the handful, craving the speediness as much as relief from her allergies.

One night she begged me three times to meet her in the anemic yellow stairwell, where she clung to me as if we might never see each other again. The next night she simply nodded hello, as if I were just another company perk like the twenty-dollar dinner allowances or strip clubs her male colleagues frequented on expense accounts. It amazed me how readily she could liquidate her sexuality, and how obsequiously I'd relinquished mine to the vagaries of her profession.

When she was away, I sulked through my shift, drinking stale coffee in big Styrofoam cups until I fled in the mornings, pumped-up and aggressive, ready to attack the canvases I'd carted to my studio. I was monopolized by huge territories of color, returning to the most primary forms to see how I'd slipped so far away. It had been years since I'd felt so unburdened.

At night I was still chained to her. My mind oscillated between rapturous sparks of memory and the most painful longing I'd ever experienced. Did she really stop the elevator midstream and drop to her knees in front of me with the security guard intoning through speakers *Hello, is there anybody in there? What's going on?* Did she come up behind me at the printer bay, sink her entire body into mine, hands on my tits and cunt grinding to the beat of the lasers? Did she whimper and call out my name as if our meeting were a hallowed exercise? Did she say I was the only one? Grieve in anticipation? Make me shudder with joy? The night she flew in from Tokyo, her voice cracked as she carted an armful of documents into the word-processing center and pleaded that all work be done immediately. She had to catch the shuttle to D.C. the next day. She kept her head down as she spoke and her voice in its professional guise made me cringe, her breakneck itinerary a personal rejection. My heart collapsed, at the same time increasing its missionary task, and I wondered if that was what a heart attack felt like—that sinking, speeding feeling. I brushed past her and smelled her unkempt scent, less perfumed, more doughy. She stepped one leg back as if she were trying to trip me. I wanted to smack her.

She found me in the bathroom and told me she missed me.

I didn't respond. Through a series of yawns, she said she was totally spent. That earlier she'd fallen asleep on the toilet seat, and her allergies were raging. She hadn't even been home to shower or change clothes, although she'd substituted for her silk blouse an oversized company tee shirt that tucked into her skirt in the front and made her look like a feminized Minotaur, half bull, half sorority girl. I wondered how many before me had been sacrificed at her profiteering hands.

Though I knew she craved the warmth of our secret room, I took her to the thirty-sixth floor, and without a word shoved her face against the windowpane. I ran my hand along the backs of her thighs, finding the rim of her hose beneath her skirt and pulling it down, my mouth next to her ear, hers open against the window steamed up in front of us, obscuring the buildings with their insolent white lights. I whispered in her ear, "Tell me you missed me, tell me," and she moaned, thrusting her head sideways. I pushed it back to the window so she could see the dark alleyways and slick buildings, the toxic black river beneath us. I wanted her to imagine what it might be like to fall.

She tried to break free and turn around. I pinned all of my weight against her, spreading her legs from behind with one hand and rimming her with my thumb. I talked into her ear, called her a horny little fuck, a capitalist tool, a spy. She slipped back against me, and sighed. I knew she'd shut her eyes. "That's it, baby," I whispered. "Come to me. Come home."

"I'm yours."

"Tell me again." I slipped a couple of fingers inside her cunt, still massaging her asshole with my thumb. By that time, having given over completely, she'd thrown her weight against the window, eyes tightly shut as I brought my other hand to her clit. She moaned again, said she was all mine. Told me to do whatever I wanted.

I fucked her harder than she'd ever fucked me, so forcefully she fell into a trance, enveloped by the field between us, the
streaming lights against the windowpane. She wailed, cursing
as she writhed beneath me, and with her every word I grew
larger, more powerful. Her screams echoed in the steely
canyons beneath us. I quickly covered her mouth as we fell to
the floor, and, more determined than ever—as if my taking her
demanded she come back with full force—she climbed on top
of me and kissed all the way down my stomach, undoing my
zipper with her teeth.

It was a careless move after her scream, but I didn't care.
My body had disintegrated into the resistance of our rhythm,
the energy of her tongue in my cunt, and I saw myself suspended above the city with its millions of colored boxes and
white lights, the iron claw of her mouth beneath me. I leaned
my head back into the carpet and came quietly, pushing her
head away. She slithered up my body and was about to speak
when I covered her mouth again. I wanted to remember her
without words.

If You Can Make It There, You Can Make It Anywhere

A. J. Stone

For Wyatt

It's an early fall night when the weather hovers between thoughts of summer, hot and sticky, and then changes its mind and whips into the frenzy of fall. My skin reacts, stands away from bone, supported by fine hairs, and my nipples grow hard, as if touched by a finger or a tongue. It's late. A girls' night out—my friend Nathalie and I have splurged on a new and fashionable restaurant downtown just above Wall Street, a neighborhood as sly and mysterious as the weather. Nathalie and I have known each other for years. We roomed together briefly when Nathalie first came to New York; now she lives uptown in an apartment which, until recently, she shared with Mark, her boyfriend of five years. The restaurant is thick with businessmen on expense accounts, pungent with testosterone, cocks at attention and ready to pounce. Nathalie and I gossip and drink round balloons of red wine that pop down our throats and make us as giggly as if we had sniffed helium. Two women in a room full of men, the first women most of them have seen all day apart from their dowdy secretaries or their female colleagues. Two women dressed in revealing clothing—low-cut dresses that slip and tease. A glimpse of nipple, a thigh unconsciously rubbed. Dresses of thin silk that slips into the cracks of our asses as we walk. Dresses clearly worn over no underwear. Dresses to frustrate. A few men buy us drinks but we're not biting. I have another goal in mind: the blonde sitting across the table from me. Curiosity has been an unspoken dance between us for years, frustrated by our other obligations. Suddenly, we are single at the same time.

We skirt around the tension between us, pumping it up by discussing sex, the first time, the best time, the craziest time. Nathalie puts down her fork in the middle of the main course—medallions of black cod—and runs a hand through her blonde hair. There is a moment of silence before she speaks.

"Remember the week Mark was away on business and we went out to that sushi place and got drunk on sake?" she begins.

I remembered that, and passing out on Nathalie's bed.

"When I woke up, sometime around dawn, I had a terrible headache. I downed a couple of aspirin but I threw them right up. There was this...well...trick I'd learned in college. You were sound asleep...," Nathalie falters, embarrassed, the color rising in her cheeks.

"Go on," I urged her, one hand beneath my napkin, playing with my dress.

Nathalie plunges onward. She had pulled up her night-gown and masturbated while I slept soundly beside her.

"I was so afraid you'd wake up," she says and looks at me, then adds nervously, "I have to use the ladies' room."

When she is gone, I signal for the check. I'm not wearing any underwear and I can feel a trail of liquid snaking down my thigh. Nathalie catches my eye as she makes her way across the room but I can't tell if her eyes are large with fear or desire. The eyes of the other diners follow us as we leave, their cocks thick and swollen. I can bet there'll be a lot of pounced-on wives tonight, visions of Nathalie and me beckoning forward more than one orgasm. The streets are dark and deserted and shadowed. I weave down the street, dancing to too many glasses of wine echoing in my head, my dark hair as wild as a tussle beneath the sheets. A tune goes off in Nathalie's head. She spins me and the world with me and I am thrown against a wall. A brief moment and then her tongue is in my mouth, tentative, slight, a drunken experiment, and when she backs away, amazed at her boldness, she leaves me hungry, my nipples reaching out. We walk down the street laughing and I tease her about it.

"Do you want to feel my wet pussy?" I ask her, looking at her out of the corner of my eye, challenging her. She's unable to answer but I can feel the lump in her throat. She's never done this before and frankly, neither have I, but the wine, the attention of the men in the restaurant, and her confession have made me horny and curious. I need to be touched, even if I do it myself. And, exhibitionist that I am, I want to be *watched*.

I lift my dress. Underneath I am wearing stay-up stockings. I circle my clit with my finger, beckoning her forward. First with my eyes and then, "Nathalie," I beg, my throat as thick and swollen as my cunt. She touches me tentatively, her fingers brushing my hard clit. I moan and close my eyes, then will them open. I want to see her desire, her curiosity, as she sinks her fingers into me. Does she know that I've been wet all evening, willing her to do this? Does she know how many times my finger circled my clit at dinner, my eyes creamy not from candlelight but the look down the long slide toward orgasm? Her face is closed to my scrutiny.

I want her to sink her face into my pussy and I tell her so. But she is hesitant. She has not yet found the audacity of desire. I won't push her yet, although I'm eager to have her mouth on my clit, her tongue deep inside me. I can feel an orgasm barreling down my body. I want to hear my screams echo off the canyons made by the buildings. I want windows wide open and neighbors' heads thrust out, an audience to my cries. I reach out to touch her and she backs away, but not before I have cupped my hand between her legs. Her cunt beneath her dress is swollen and ripe. She is as wet as I am and I wonder if she stroked herself in the bathroom, bringing herself just to the brink of orgasm. Nervous, she wiggles her hips from my slender hand, but not before I have pushed the front of her dress, light armor that only barely shields her naked cunt from my hand, into her. Her juices leave an imprint on the thin fabric.

I suggest a cab but they are difficult to find at this time of night and we begin to walk. She sucks on her fingers, tasting me for the first time, and I play with my nipple, hard through my dress as she watches me, unable to look away. I tell her I want her tongue on me, rough and strong. I can see that her defenses are beginning to drop and beneath her dress, her nipples are as tight as mine. At the corner, a taxi with its off-duty sign slows down for a red light and I step down from the curb.

I roll my window down reluctantly. Instantly I know these two girls are drunk; their eyes are too bright. But I'm going uptown anyway and I figure I might as well make a decent fare off it. They scramble into the back and give me two addresses.

It's late and I'm tired and I'm gunning for home and a few clicks across the porn channels before I pass out, my spent cock in my hand. The thought is enticing and I drive fast. It's strangely quiet in the backseat. And then I catch moaning. Damn, I think, two drunk girls. That's all I need, one of them sick in the backseat and an extra half hour while I have to clean it out, not to mention a little something less in my paycheck when they've got to take the whole car in for a shampoo. I glance up at the rearview mirror to check the backseat. The dark-haired girl, in a thin dress, coat off her shoulders, lies against one window, eyes half-mast, her hand lazily circling her nipple. The moans are coming from her mouth. I slow down, my cock suddenly hard and pulsing, straining to catch a glimpse of the other girl. I find her blonde head bobbing up and down, buried between the legs of the dark-haired one. I can't really see what's going on but I begin to guess, my imagination racing, as the dark-haired girl's moans direct her friend's movements. I raise my eyes and we catch each other in the mirror for a brief moment before she turns away. She must know I'm watching, listening, because she keeps looking up, her eyes seeking mine. I strain to catch her words as she begins narrating, her voice thick with lust. *Lick me, suck my clit,* she says. She pulls her dress down a little further and her nipple, pink and taut, springs free. *Oh,* a little sigh escapes from my mouth. I want my mouth on that nipple, to circle it with my tongue and bite on it and feel her clit jump against my swollen cock. *Oh, yes,* she moans, and every promise leaps out from her eyes. I'm imagining her, slick and tight, riding my cock. The cab slows as I stroke myself, pumping my cock in my fist, trying to keep my mind on driving. A red light up ahead brings my eyes back to the road. The light is green too quickly and I wish for another excuse to stop so I can use my other hand to pull at my balls, stretching the skin tightly over my cock. I search the rearview mirror for the black eyes of the dark-haired girl.

The cabdriver agrees to take us both uptown with a first stop at my house and then on to Nathalie's and we scramble into the back. I have a goal that doesn't involve a second stop but I don't argue when Nathalie pipes in with her address. I get in first and Nathalie hangs back for a moment, as shy and eager as the new girl in school who dreams of being a cheerleader, before she scoots in beside me. Then she slams the door and by the time she has settled herself beside me I've pulled my skirt up and have begun playing with myself in earnest, my head leaning against the window, one hand manipulating my clit, the other hand pulling my nipples into hard points. For a moment, Nathalie can only watch in fascination, her mouth open. And then I see her tongue, moving quickly back and forth against her front teeth, debating. I push back the lips of my pussy, my clit swollen and red between them, as an offering.

"Please...," my voice begs.

I want her kneeling between my legs, sucking at my clit—I want her so badly that I almost begin to weep. I know that I could bring myself to orgasm quickly. I also know how unsatisfying that would be.

"What do I...," Nathalie's voice falters, confused, worried about what to do in this unfamiliar, familiar territory.

I plunge my fingers into my cunt, hitting my G-spot, and for a moment there is nothing but my cunt, my fingers. I will myself reluctantly back to the present, back to the goal. My fingers are luminescent with my own juice and I reach over, slipping them into Nathalie. Her hips press into my hand. She looks at me, then down at my fingers moving in and out of her cunt and then back at me and I can see the astonishment on her face. Nothing in her experience has prepared her for this—not Mark, three nights a week, not Joe, the best-sex-ever, not even Ian, the one-night stand who introduced her to anal sex. Her hips move in circles and her clit retreats and I can feel, from the way her muscles tighten, how fast her orgasm is building. But I don't want her to come just yet. That will be later, when I have time to explore her, tease her, stretched out on my bed. Right now I want to pull her to the edge of desire, the place where all of her inhibitions disappear and there is nothing but body and want and need and hunger. She grabs my retreating hand and forces my fingers to her mouth, sucking each one slowly, telling me in silent language how much she wants me. I moan, pulsing in time to the motion of her mouth. With her other hand she begins to explore me, first tentatively, then more insistently, her fingers parting my pubic hair, pulling at the curls. Her head bends forward to examine me and I can feel her hot breath and I rise to meet her mouth. I groan, my eyes rising, and briefly meet the eyes of the cabdriver in the rearview mirror. His eyes are large and dark and I recognize the look in them and know that his cock is hard in his fist. Another moan escapes my lips. Nathalie's tongue darts out, hard and pointy, and laps at my cunt, following my fingers' lead, my pleas. My moans give her courage and she rakes at my clit with her teeth, pulling the lips down, her tongue exploring the crevices, my clit in her mouth being sucked like a small cock. She teases me, stopping and starting, knowing the rhythms of my cunt as she knows her own. I break the gaze of the cabdriver and watch Nathalie's movements intently as she inserts two fingers into me and I begin the slide into orgasm. I have only come like this a few times in my life, hovering between life and death, and when the explosions have ended, I pull Nathalie's head up and kiss her on the lips, tasting myself on her. When the cab jerks suddenly, I know that our driver has not been far behind...

I try to keep focused on the road, periodically glancing into the backseat where the dark-haired girl has locked her gaze on mine. My hand moves with her friend's head bobbing up and down and I know how warm and wet that blonde's mouth would be, wrapped around my cock. The dark-haired girl looks away and I'm frantic, trying to catch her eye. My rhythm falters for a moment. But the growing series of moans from the backseat is a command my cock cannot resist. My hips buck upward, my foot jerking on the gas pedal and I empty myself deep into my hand, the dark-haired girl's screams a call that pulls my orgasm from me in violent spasms as I turn the corner to the first stop...

"Just below the streetlamp," I tell the driver, "then you can take her..."

Nathalie interrupts me before I have a chance to finish. "No second stop," she says.

I look over at her as she springs out of the cab, already halfway up the steps to my apartment, and then I lean forward to check the fare. The driver and I study each other's faces in the light, my mouth slick with my own juice, and then he catches my eye and an understanding passes between us. I reach into my wallet and press a bill into his hand. He closes my fingers around the crisp currency.

"My pleasure," he says.

The wine whispers the Sinatra lyric to me as I scramble up the steps. *If I can make it there, I'll make it anywhere.* Nathalie pulls me to her, reaching over to suck on my earlobe. Then the door to my apartment clicks open and we are inside.

Pawn of the Patriarchy

Elaine Miller

For Aiden

> *Every woman...knows in her gut the vast difference*
> *between her sexuality and that of any patriarchally trained*
> *males—gay or straight...that the emphasis on genital*
> *sexuality, objectification...was the* male *style, and that*
> *we, as women, placed greater trust in love, sensuality,...*
> *tenderness, commitment...* —ROBIN MORGAN,
> WEST COAST LESBIAN FEMINIST CONFERENCE, 1973

I'm waiting for my girlfriend. Girl. Girlfriend. She'll be
home any second. We live together, the two of us girls.
Lesbians. Dykes. She'll be here any second, and we'll eat the
dinner I've cooked, and she'll wash the dishes, and maybe
we'll watch a movie. It's her turn to pick. We take turns.
Turn-about is fair play.

I dawdle in the kitchen, dawdle back to the bedroom,
check my face in the mirror. Yes, same face as yesterday. I idly
kick some used, abused socks around on the floor with my
bare toes, marveling at their worn-grunge glamour after only
a day's standard wear. One sock's woolen opening still gapes

with flaccid expectancy. It's been a while since we've done the laundry, my partner and I. I'm not sure whose turn it is.

I check the mirror again, in case something's changed in the last few minutes. Pale green eyes look back. I run my fingers through my hair a few times. It hangs to just below the level of my nipples, dark brown and wavy. She'll be home soon. We've been together for years, and I'm always glad to see her when she gets home. I dawdle in the hallway, pointedly not checking my watch. Any second now.

The screen door creaks in the kitchen and I look up to the sound of heavy footsteps. He walks in as if he owns the place. I sputter, taken aback and decidedly off-balance. He looks me over insolently. He looks like family. I mean, like The Family. Dark hair slicked back, eyes so brown they're almost black, he looks at me over that strong-boned nose and he smiles, slow and lazy.

I don't like that smile.

"Saw your door open," he says. "So I came in."

The accent. Subtly rounded—no jolly pizzeria accent, no fake mobster's Mediterranean mangle, but the real thing. He's still looking at me, wearing that cocky smile on his full lips. I smooth my sweating palms down my skirt and wish I were wearing more clothing than a kilt and a tank top. I wish I were wearing a *lot* more clothing to face down a strong young man fully dressed in white T-shirt, faded denim, and heavy work boots. I feel absurd in my pale bare feet, and wish for my own black boots as my red-painted toes curl against the hardwood floor.

He glances down at the motion, a lock of brown hair falling forward, and I notice for the first time how young he is. How soft the brown skin of his throat looks. How the vein that runs along the smooth cord of muscle in his neck visibly pulses. He looks a little vulnerable, in fact. Mustering my more usual, assertive self, I take a step forward—unsure what

I'm planning, but sure that I should do *something*. He steps back. I start to feel better, stronger by comparison.

"Look, I'm sorry I just barged in. I didn't mean to scare you. I just thought...I was just..." That accent again. The stray lock of hair still dangles, falling across one eye. I had no idea they made bio-guys this handsome. He spreads his strong, well-manicured hands in a helpless shrug, and smiles. The smile is boyish, charming.

I'm beginning to like that smile.

I guess he misinterprets my silent regard. Hesitantly he turns toward the door. The half turn of his body reveals something I hadn't noticed until now: a fat, long hosepipe of a cock is stuffed down the leg of his jeans.

"You want that I should go?" he says softly, accent thickening as his voice grows husky.

He's hard, I can tell by looking. And I suddenly, overwhelmingly, want to be able to tell by feel as well. My cunt clenches at the thought. I can't think straight. Fuck my dinner plans, and my girlfriend. Time to do something a little...different.

I reach out to him.

"No," I say, simply. "Stay."

I lead him into the bedroom. I don't want to seem boring, but when one is hoping for a good uncomplicated fuck, the most logical and comfortable place for it is on a large, flat, soft surface. In any house, the bedroom is where one keeps the majority of such surfaces.

He looks at the bed, looks back at me. I was right, he *is* a little shy. I answer his unvoiced question.

"Yes," I say. Not a simple yes—this is a yes imbued with the full power of my ability to say no. It is unhampered by self-doubt, a knowing yes, a clean yes. My yes is unadulterated by maybe.

"Yes," I say again, this time adding my complicated female sexuality, my lust, and an undertone of dare. There's a lot you can give with a yes. He catches it all, and we land on the bed in a snarl of lips and a tangle of limbs.

I tear at his clothes. He smells of golden-skinned sunshine and clean sweat. He tastes of danger, illicit sex, and the thrill of the forbidden. His hands rove over my body like they know it, eliciting small growls from me as my arousal grows.

I am characteristically aggressive. Leaving his T-shirt on, I finish yanking down his jeans, tugging them down muscular thighs, past the calves to his ankles, where I leave them. I know what I'm after, and I leave it up to him to twist around and pull off his boots, pop the jeans off his ankles so he's not clothing-bound. I can't think of anything but how much I want his cock.

Like him, his white cotton briefs offer no resistance, giving in instantly to my urgent tugs. His cock springs free, and he jerks and gasps as I grab it around the base, pressing firmly. It's fat and a little too long, which is *exactly* the right size.

He's not so shy now. We roll around on the bed, fighting a pleasant battle for the topographical "top" position, and after a while I contrive to lose. A strong boy like this should be made to work some, for my pleasure.

"Safe?" he pants, rubbing his hardness into my thigh's softness.

I keep getting shocks of heat as the tip of his cock touches my groin. I have to concentrate to hear what he's saying, as the gentle nudge-nudge is acting like an automatic push-button garage-door opener for my thighs.

Safe. Of course we're safe. Why wouldn't we be safe? Oh.

I point at the night table, the other reason why fucking in bedrooms is so handy. Everything is *already there*.

"Drawer," I croak.

He practically lunges over me to get to the night-table drawer, and his solid thigh presses into my cunt for several delicious seconds. I grind happily. He drops a condom on the bed beside us.

"Lube," I say further, certainly at no loss for words.

That wins me a look, as I am in the process of soaking a small section of his thigh, but he fetches the big black bottle with no comment. I already have the condom wrapper in my teeth, and am ripping off the corner to get to the contents. You're not supposed to open a condom this way. It says so right on the package. It might rip. It's not safe.

Somewhere in the tangle we make an exchange, lube bottle for condom, and he does a hasty but impressive one-hand roll-on trick with the rubber, and I follow with a palmful of lube, stroking it along his shaft as he groans and reaches for me. I'm wet enough that I don't need the lube but I like the—

Slide all the way in all the way inside right up to the center of me one smooth motion one slick fucking thrust one motion stuffed full of cock, cunt fluttering like a heartbeat, neck arched, mouth open for breath but none coming, eyes searching for an anchor and alighting on his eyes, his steady gaze, coolness of lube against hot swollen lips, delicious, don't move, stay right there, all the way in, oh yeah, yeah, yeah, my ears must be working again because we're both saying it, yeah, oh yeah...

I like the first moment to be memorable.

So we fuck. And it's looking like the second, third, and fourth moments are coming up pretty memorable too. I keep wanting to come, which is shocking as it usually takes me much longer than this, but he's big and he's skillful and he reads me like he's going to do a thesis on me. We're on a ride together, and it's anyone's guess who's driving; and I find I don't care.

Now we center almost all of our attention into a long kiss, tongues stabbing slowly, thoughtfully, drawing out small muffled moans, as he leans his whole weight into my hips and almost absentmindedly rocks into me in little inch-deep thrusts...

Now I fasten my teeth in his shoulder and curse around the mouthful of flesh, feeling the muscles in his shoulders tense as he fucks me hard, stroking all the way in and out over and over. It's the nicest possible way of getting to unlock my own private insanity, pleasure pushed higher and higher until I can't tell the inbreath from the outbreath, and I often miss several of either in a row.

Now he groans as I hold him between my knees, not allowing him fully inside, and swirl my hips in circles. I tease forever, until he swears at me, tries to push all the way inside me, frustrated by my locked thighs. Until I stop teasing.

I always want lube, lube, and more lube when I'm getting fucked. It makes me feel like superwoman, like I have the power, the feminine secret key to what all the boys are vainly chasing with their powdered rhino horn and Spanish fly urethral irritants. With lube, I can fuck all night. With lube, I am capable of vaginal feats of sexual prowess unimaginable or downright dangerous without. If lube, patience, and skill can fit a woman's whole fist inside a spot where I regularly curse tampons as being too bulky, then lube is my friend.

So I'm a lube slut, a slippery-stuff whore, but now it's getting real. His cock's big and we've been active in our fucking. I'm getting to the point where I'm feeling dry—much more of this and I'll be raw. Signaling a temporary stop with a thigh clench, I reach for the friendly, familiar black bottle. And keep reaching, left hand blindly patting down the bedcovers, Last Known Lube Location, okay...it's here somewhere.

"Lookin' for the Probe?"

His eyebrow cocks in a familiar-seeming gesture. He looks around, then expertly shifts his knees forward to bracket my hips and sits upright, cock still stuffed inside me. I squirm, gasping, as from this new vantage he scans the surrounding area, then with a grunt of dismay leans way over, making a long arm as I complain at the sudden sticky change in position.

He fetches the bottle—upside down—with long viscous strings of clear goo slanting back toward what has to be a considerable puddle on the floor. Squeezing the bottle produces only a breathy spluttering noise. Empty.

He looks absurdly guilty. "I guess it fell."

"It's okay," I muster. "I think it'll be fine. Let's just keep going."

"You're *sure* about that?" Amused at my greed, he thrusts once, very gently. I try to hide my wince. With the original lube drying up, we're well on our way to becoming involuntary Siamese twins, but damn it; I'm not done with him, or his beautiful cock.

Moving immediately to the usual resort of the lubeless, I pull up onto my elbows and try to work up some spit from a throat gone dry from panting.

"Wait," he says, as with a thoughtful look, he carefully pulls out. I squeak in dismay at the rush of cold air, and the aching, empty feeling inside, and grab for him. I try to pull him back to me—back inside me—but he leans back, stretches the elastic leg bands of his harness, and shifts the base of his cock out of the way. He locks eyes with me as one of his hands disappears briefly between his legs and reappears glistening, wet. He slides his cock through his fist a few times, then repeats the motion, dipping into his own wet cunt for the lubrication I need. He is...she is...in this moment the hottest thing I've ever seen, a dazzling, genderfucking dichotomy.

"I love you," I say to her, and she slides back inside me, answering me perfectly with her eyes and her body. I start to come, just a little, from the sudden jolt of pleasure when the harness leather squeezes my clit with the full weight of her familiar and well-loved body. And I start to cry just a little at the same time, from the *knowing,* and the passion, and the feeling of being so very well loved.

Tenderly, she watches me teeter 'twixt lust and tears, catches the moment where the lust starts to win out, and lifts my legs from her hips to over her shoulders. He pulls back, hesitates before continuing our incendiary fuck, and winks. Once again he deliberately broadens an accent that is barely noticeable in our day to day life together.

"Share and share alike, eh?"

F

Karin Pomerantz

They call me a Femme. They do, but they don't know. They don't know what happens behind closed doors at night. When you and I are alone. After the sun has set and the stars have risen. They are not there, although I'm sure they'd like to be watching. Holding their breath waiting for the next slap. The next time the paddle comes careening down on your tender ass, trying, almost with a will all its own, to bruise that toughened skin of yours. So tough and yet so indescribably soft, on such a truly delicate creature. Fragile, but so damn good at hiding it. They would love to watch you bite your lip until it bleeds. Straining and pulling on the cuffs above your head. When all we can hear is the chink of the metal on the headboard or the chains that bind you to it. And watch you screwing up your face in the most beautifully perverse manner. Waiting for you to let out that scream that may never, ever come.

They call me a Femme, but only you know the truth: that I am really only me, nothing more, nothing less, and most days nothing at all. The truth that lets you know that everything really is going to be okay, if only for a moment. If only for that one brief second when you can see the burning behind your eyes, the burning that sears through you with each stroke, curling your toes and forcing your face into the duvet. The heat of my hand on you, and the detail of my fingers and each of my rings cutting into you with every single blow.

They call me a Femme because of who they think I am, but you know the real me. The one who gets down and dirty with you, thrashes you within inches of your life until you are screaming and crying and wailing with the conflict of ecstasy and agony, and there I am looking you in the eye and making you *feel*. Something you have never felt before. Something you never thought you could understand. And never thought you'd want. More deeply, and with a greater intensity, than you ever believed possible.

They call me a Femme, but behind the doors with the white candles lit, dangling gingerly above you, tempting you with the possibility of disastrous results, my desire fits perfectly in the hole in you. The one you never thought you had. The one that makes you only a little bit uncomfortable at times. And at other times makes you wild.

They call me a Femme, they do, but they don't know what goes on behind closed doors at night, when you and I are alone. In the silence and the serenity of the evenings. After the dishes are done and the animals fed. They just don't know how I take you in my hands and feed you to the wolves that live deep within us both. They don't see what you see when you look at me. Or hear your muffled cries between the panes of glass vibrating and preparing to shatter. The way your heart beats in time with mine and your hot breath hits my face as I lay over you, in you. Balancing precariously on one hand while slapping your cheek with the other. Over and over again in an attempt to get you wailing and screaming and begging for more. But we both know that will never come.

They call me a Femme because of something even I don't understand. They call me that because it's easy. It's easy to sum me up in a word when you don't know who I really am. There are no words in the English language to describe who or what I am. What I am to you. What I do to you, and for you, and with you, and in you. There are no words to accurately describe what it is or what it means. All that exist are the blanket terms that can't even begin to describe either of us or the people we know or the things we do. There are no words—only soft sounds in the night. Whimpers and cries of fear and surprise and pleasure and agony.

Can you call me a Femme when I meet you at the door and sweep you off your feet? Or when I pin you to the wall and kiss you so hard you are gasping for air when I'm done? Or when the howl comes from deep within your throat and shakes the walls and the core of me and you and anyone who thinks they know the truth?

They call me a Femme. They do, but they don't know what happens when you and I are alone. When I get you on your knees and take you on all fours like the blinded and brazen beast you so often are, and at the oddest times. With your head thrown forward, wedged between the pillows and the headboard, and the soft end of my belt between your teeth to keep you from uttering any sound at all. As you thrust your hips back onto me and I can't possibly go into you any deeper, even though I would gladly die trying.

When I watch you from behind with your face pressed into the bed and your arms above your head, held in place by nothing but my will against yours. When you can't muster enough energy to pull your body upright and all I can see is the sweat dripping off me onto the small of your back, running down your sides and your ass, onto the sheets. When all I can hear is the beating of me against you and that sound you make just before you utter the lord's name, which you never want to do, but somehow I manage to get you to.

They call me a Femme, but can you, when I lash you to the bedpost and hold you there? In a state of suspended animation, skirting the boundaries of making you love me and making you hate me. It can always go either way with you, but I take my chances and hold you teasing, taunting, bringing you close and making you wait. Holding you bound so tightly, there is no escaping, no matter what it is that you want this time.

They can call me whatever they want, but what do you call me when I make you open that mouth of yours filled with those perfect sharp teeth that I've always envied? The ones you said were never burdened with braces. The ones that made me love you and that cause us both so much pleasure and pain. And I make you open that mouth of yours wider than you ever thought you could, and wider than you ever wanted to before. And I make you take me into your mouth. Make you suck me hard and wild like you see in the movies. The movies you used to like so much, and watched every chance you got, touching yourself and wondering when it would be your turn. I'm close to your face so you don't have to move too much to feel me all the way back in that precious throat of yours. And I wonder where a girl like you learned to give head like that. And what you want in return. And what I'm going to get for keeping your secret.

And I make the spit trickle down your chin, in sync with the spit dripping from between your legs. I could grab the back of your hair and force myself into you, deeper, but I would rather watch you squirm with the discomfort and mystery of figuring out what it is that is digging into your forehead through the front pocket of my jeans. The questions in your mind both of now what, and of how soon?

My knife like a security blanket sits idly on my person everywhere I go. It's your favorite, I know. Now. A surprise at first, but you have learned to love it as much as I do, only your enthusiasm lies in a place a bit off-center. A place only you allow yourself to go. I'm not quite let in. Not quite.

You love them all equally, my blades, all beautiful and unique like the fingers on your hands or the hairs on your head that change color every time you step outside. Your passion for them equal to, but different from, mine. The one I carry with me always, and the ones I don't. You never know which one it's going to be, or when. You have your favorites. We both do. The sounds they make, the sensations they provoke, the way they taste. You love to hear that one catch on the sheets, and you know what is coming next when you hear it hit the floor. The way the light catches it out of the corner of your eye. Or the way the cold steel feels on your fevered head.

Or when I trace the point of the blade over your belly and watch it leave a red mark, like a cat scratch, that doesn't quite cut your flesh, but could have, if you had not been so still. I hold it to your throat and tell you not to move. Sharp side out, but that doesn't matter much, even the dull side is sharper than anything that's ever touched your skin before. Even the dull side hurts to the touch and could easily cut you open if you don't listen. Even the dull side is attached to the sharp point that sits just centimeters from the softest parts of you, making you gasp for breath and hope for the best.

They call me a Femme, they do, but they don't know. They don't know what goes on behind closed doors at night, when you and I are alone. When I bring you to your knees and make you feel what you never allowed yourself to feel before. When I search your body for the answers to the questions that have lain dormant in your mind for so long. When I bring to light the unbelievable, and make your ghosts disappear. If only for a moment.

When I lay you on your back and climb on top of you. Feeling your outsides with a burning to match the one in your insides. Taking your breasts in my hand and making them fear me the way you wish you could. Searching with my fingers and my fist for something deep within you to free you from whatever it is you don't think you can take. Hesitating just one moment longer than necessary to make you see. Make you feel. And make you explode into yourself. Into a place that I can never go, filled with passions and pleasures all your own, covering the sorrow of your life and your unending question of *why.*

They call me a Femme, but what am I when your eyes fill up with tears and no one can see them but me? When you are left panting and sweating and begging me to stop? But only for a second, so you can catch your breath.

You come to me with sadness in your deep blue eyes, profound and bottomless. The pain I can see in them goes farther back into your soul than even the delight that's usually there. The smiles and laughs that obscure everything else. And you look to me to guide you through it, this mysterious ache you don't understand. You look for the answers, the ones only I can give you.

Lipstick

Aimée Nichols

It took some time for me to hear the phone. It was only because the CD I was playing, PJ Harvey's *4 Track Demos,* came to the end of a song that I heard it at all. I made a mad dash while the CD kept playing and answered the phone just as the caller was about to hang up.

"Hello?" I gasped.

"Um…is this Ange?" a somewhat familiar voice inquired.

"Yeah," I panted, "Who's this?"

"My name's Jess. I'm a friend of your cousin Ellen? I'm ringing to invite you to her hen's night next week. The twenty-fourth. You think you can make it? It's at La Maison. Seven-thirty for tea, then we go out raging."

"Uh, yeah," I replied. *Great,* I thought, *another of these goddamn things.* "Sure. I'm there. Anything special I need to bring?"

"No, just yourself. We've got it all planned out. Nice to talk to you, Ange! See you there!"

She hung up before I could muster the politeness for a good-bye. I put the receiver down and cursed her, Ellen, marriage, and the whole world. I would have to go out and be sociable when I'd rather stay at home. Pretend I gave a shit that Ellen was going to give up her individuality and freedom to be some guy's legally accepted fucktoy. Not that her fiancé was a particularly bad person, or bad at all, it's just that I could never understand why anyone would willingly put themselves through marriage, especially if they didn't have to.

But I was hardly in a position to talk. It wasn't exactly like I had a committed relationship myself.

I wandered back into the lounge room, where PJ Harvey was still massacring her guitar, this time performing "Hardly Wait": *"It's been so long I've lost my taste…"*

"Yeah," I muttered, flopping onto the couch, "I know how you feel."

Humankind in general is something I have a problem with. I often find that hen's nights bring out the worst in women. It's like seeing a magnificent lion reduced to doing circus tricks; some of the most intelligent, funny, interesting girls I know turn into giggling, fawning idiots the second a man is near, particularly if he's there as the entertainment. I wondered briefly if I'd have to feign interest in some overpumped male stripper. I hoped fervently that there would be no stripper to cause problems—a hen's night celebration is *not* the time to come out to all your cousin's friends.

For once time passed quickly, and soon the week was over and it was time to go to Ellen's party. In spite of myself, I was feeling a little enthusiastic, maybe even excited. I didn't let it get the better of me though—I deliberately dressed down as much as possible, only checking to make sure my clothes were clean and the outfit didn't look too horrific overall, and applying a little makeup. May as well pretend I was trying to make an effort. It was, after all, Ellen's night, and we'd grown up close friends. She was one of the few people who seemed to respect me for who I was—which did make me wonder why she'd invited me, seeing as she knew how antisocial I am. Token gesture to keep up appearances, I guessed. I was kind of pleased to be included though.

I made my way to the restaurant on foot, as it was within walking distance of my flat. The marks of autumn were already on the city—the leaves browning and falling off the trees, the air cooler than it had been for some months. I walked into the restaurant and realized I didn't actually know what name the party I was with was under. As it turned out, this didn't matter anyway because a very hyperactive and slightly drunk Ellen screamed "*Ange!*" across the restaurant and came galloping to meet me, slinging an arm across my shoulders. The other patrons—not to mention the staff— looked on disapprovingly, but no one said anything. We walked and stumbled, respectively, to Ellen's table, where she loudly introduced me as her dear cousin Ange and gave me a smacking kiss on the cheek. The others greeted me, and Jess informed me of how glad she was I'd come, gesturing me to sit beside her.

Ellen was a fright, dressed in some kind of veil someone had fashioned out of tulle and decorated with inflated condoms, sachets of lubricant, fake flowers, and several photos of her fiancé Sam. Poor guy. The jokes and the sexual innuendo were running high, and I felt myself retreating into my shell slightly, all too aware that I was out of place here, maybe even more so than the drunken female high jinks in this fancy restaurant.

While looking for some kind of escape, I noticed the girl on the other side of me. She looked almost as out of place as I, and although she was laughing and making jokes about Ellen and Sam's sex life with the rest of them, she seemed a little lost, a little distant. Her hair was long and blonde, and looked bleached by sun rather than by chemicals. Her skin was fairly pale and covered with light freckles. She wore a white blouse that reached down to her midriff and a black skirt. I glanced under the table and saw that her feet were covered with strappy high-heeled shoes. I wondered if she felt the cold at all.

Maybe feeling the weight of my stare, she turned to me and gave me a smile.

"Hi, you're the famous Ange? Ellen has been loudly wondering where you've been for the last half hour." I blushed, knowing that my lateness was due to my hesitation about being there. She laughed. "Your cousin's definitely an interesting person to be around. I'm Kate, by the way."

"Obviously I'm infamous around here, so I don't think I need an introduction. What dirt has Ellen been spreading about me?"

"Only that you're her 'favoritest' cousin in the world. Oh, and that you streaked at your twenty-first."

"Great. All the keep-it-in-the-family stories are going to come out."

She laughed, and for a moment I could admire her again without guilt. I noted with a little spark of pleasure that she seemed to have perked up considerably during the short time we'd been talking. She leaned across me to reach the jug of water and I could smell her, feel her vibes; hell, I could almost taste her. She gave me a smile and turned to talk to the girl on her left, and I struck up a conversation with Jess. About what, I couldn't tell you now—not only was it trivial, but I was far too aware of Kate's presence beside me. I nearly jumped out of my skin every time she moved.

For nearly an hour, we played this game. We would make small talk to each other then pretend to talk to other people, almost ignoring each other, but we were both acutely aware of each other's bodies, the heat we generated. At least I was, and

I was positive she could feel my attraction to her from where she sat; it was strong enough to be a physical force. I was halfway through eating my main course when her thigh brushed mine, and I nearly choked. She began rubbing her leg up and down against mine in slow, deliberate strokes. I wished my skin were bare so that I could feel her flesh against mine without the hindrance of clothing. I became ultra-focused on my breathing; it was becoming more jagged. My skin felt extremely warm. I glanced across at her and noticed that she seemed to be attempting to avoid my gaze, although a small smile flickered across her features. With no input from me, my hand began to slide under the table and toward her lap, seeking warmth from between her legs. I rested my hand on her bare thigh, just below the hem of her dress, and she made no move to stop me. I inched the pinky finger of my left hand under the hem of her skirt, delighting in the feeling of the smooth silky skin usually hidden under her clothing. Without warning she grabbed my hand and pushed it up further along her leg, almost so that my index finger rested against her vulva. From where my hand lay, the hot moisture of her radiated out, telling me she was excited. I felt myself begin to respond, blood rushing to my pussy and thighs, making me feel slightly lightheaded and very aroused.

She turned to me and said brightly, "I need to use the bathroom. Come with me?" I admired her style; she sounded exactly like a woman who simply didn't want to go to the bathroom alone—no hint of arousal or desire crept into her voice. No one at the table had the slightest idea, but then, at that stage, I think that if we'd said we were eloping to become circus freaks they wouldn't have cared. Amazing, the effect alcohol can have on otherwise upright and uptight citizens.

We got up, grabbed our bags like ladies, and hastily made our way to the restroom. She pushed me through the door ahead of her and pounced on me as it swung shut. Her lips were furious against mine, her hands in my hair as I ran mine down the small of her back. We began to gyrate our pelvises together, and I fancied I could feel her wetness soaking into the crotch of my pants.

"Someone might come in," I said, and dragged her into a cubicle, turning to lock the door behind us. By then she was already out of her top, and I lunged forward to assist her with removing her bra. I was rewarded with the sight of her beautiful breasts, freed and pale, the nipples erect and pointing in my direction. I began to unbutton my top and she stepped forward to help me; I let it become her job as I began to play with her small, soft breasts. She tore my bra off hungrily and took my breasts in her hands, caressing them firmly, teasing my nipples up into little monuments of lust. I sighed involuntarily, and she took this as an invitation to tongue-kiss me again. I let go of her breasts and allowed my hands to travel down her torso, then her thighs, bringing them up again under her skirt. She trembled as my fingers' light embrace moved up her inner thighs, fingertips kissing the soft skin. I ran the backs of my fingers lightly over the sheath of material between her legs and she gasped out loud. I began to rhythmically stroke her engorged lips, and she squirmed against my hand, pressing her body into mine and then jerking away again as the sensations took her. I slid my hand under her panties and she squealed, then looked shocked at her reaction.

"You little bitch!" she exclaimed, a wicked smile lighting her face and taking the edge off her words. "You're not getting to me that easily!" With that, she hastily opened my pants and shoved her fingers inside, finding my pussy wet and eager for her touch. I moaned and rocked against her fingers as they expertly found my clit, first circling and then rubbing forward and back over my responsive lips and clitoris. My fingers found their way inside her and I began to fuck her, pressing her clit with the heel of my hand as I moved my fingers in and out of her. Our bodies moved in synchronicity, tensing and shuddering as we pleasured each other. I felt so close to her, it was as if I were masturbating, and I felt all my anger toward people and the world sliding out of me.

Together, with the intensity of a lightning bolt, we came, both crying out and moving against each other in frenzied passion, not caring if the world and all our friends could hear. We began to kiss again as we came down, holding each other and shaking uncontrollably.

"I have to sit down," she gasped, and collapsed onto the toilet seat. I followed her lead and folded myself up onto the floor of the cubicle.

"You can share the seat," she told me, suddenly shy. I looked up at her.

She really was beautiful. I allowed my head to snap back to eye level, and her pussy looked evenly at me from its nest of blonde hair.

"I'll be fine. Thanks though, Kate." Her name sounded beautiful on my tongue.

"That was…incredible," she said, her gaze steady on me. I suddenly felt the urge to mark her somehow, to show my lust for her visibly on her body and, I admit, in part to attempt to make her mine. In that moment of clarity, I knew I'd found someone I didn't want to lose.

My gaze fell to my bag, and I realized I had the capacity to do just what I wanted to.

"Kate," I ventured, "would you object to me…decorating you?"

She stared: by the looks of things, it wasn't a request she'd had before. "Umm…what exactly do you mean, Ange?"

My name, though commonplace and plain, sounded rich and extravagant on her tongue. I grabbed my bag and rummaged through it, coming up with just what I'd been after—

a tube of lipstick. I drew it out and watched her eyes respond to it, first confused and then lighting up as comprehension set in.

"Okay," she said, a slow smile lifting her features. "Go for it."

I removed the lid of the lipstick and twisted the tube, pleased to discover that it was my "signature color," a dark wine-red called "Passion Splendor." I shuffled over to Kate on my knees and crouched between her legs. Tentatively I began to draw on her chest, thrilling to the vivid traces of the lipstick on her skin. I circled her breasts and down her stomach, not intending to draw anything in particular, just wanting to denote where I'd been on that pale, freckled frame. She watched as I decorated her, silent but expressing pleasure through her energy. Feeling her arousal mounting again, I started stroking her pussy, watching my fingers stroke her and how her lips passed through them. She rocked against my hand and I increased the pace of my ministrations, feeling her tense and writhe as she began to come again. Sweat ran down her body, colored wine from the makeup, and she was the most beautiful thing I'd ever seen.

We sat staring at each other in silence, neither one of us wanting to break what we precariously held between us. I wanted to speak, to tell her she was the most incredible person in the world, that she was who I wanted most, that our sex was the most amazing thing I'd ever shared with anyone, but I didn't know how to phrase it without sounding, well, pathetic. After all, it wasn't like we knew each other's deepest darkest secrets or anything.

Although she was obviously content and satisfied, I couldn't read how she actually felt about me—whether I'd provided great sex and that was it, or if there was something more there for her too.

Our peace was interrupted by one of our friend's sudden entrance into the toilets. "Are you guys okay?" asked a voice which I recognized as Jess's. "You've been ages, and Mel thought she heard crying or something…"

Terror (and I admit, a little proud thrill of exhibitionism) ran through me, but before I could think up a lie, Kate spoke.

"I…I'm a bit upset," she said, putting a slight tremor into her voice. "Ange has been comforting me. We'll be out soon."

"Are you going to be okay?" Jess was concerned. "Is there anything—"

"No, I'm fine. Just give us a few minutes."

"Done. See you soon." And the door swung open and closed again.

I looked at Kate but still could not read her. I began to feel ashamed and idiotic—she mustn't give a damn, I was probably just a cheap fuck to her. And that hurt. That hurt excruciatingly.

"Do you want my phone number?" I managed to ask. "I'm going to go straight home. I think there's a male stripper coming, and that's not my thing."

"Sure," she responded, looking a little dazed or perhaps something else. I hoped it was dazed. "Got a pen?"

"Um…no. Just lipstick." I managed a grin. She smiled back wanly and invited me to write on her. I scribbled my number, said my goodbyes, and left her in the cubicle. Back in the restaurant, I made a hasty excuse about feeling a bit sick and walked outside into the chilly autumn night.

Three nights later, melancholy, I sat in front of my CD player, looking for music that would suit my mood. The party was still firm in my mind, but I was attempting to let it go, convinced that I meant nothing to Kate.

I jumped at the sound of the phone ringing, and stumbled to answer it. Kate's voice came down the line to me, breathy but as alive as I'd remembered it.

"Hi, Ange, hope you don't mind me ringing you—"

"Of course not!" I cut in before I could stop myself. "I've been hoping you'd call." Those words didn't say it enough.

"Great! I've been thinking, I'd really like to see you again. What happened the other night feels really special to me. I could tell you felt that way too, but I was too overcome to be able to tell you. I've never had that happen before. I'm sorry if I seemed disinterested, I just..."

"It's fine, Kate. I want to see you again too. I haven't been able to get you out of my mind."

"Really?" she sounded surprised, and more than a little flattered. "Great. How about you come over to my place?"

"Sure," I said, and she gave me her address.

"Oh, and Ange?"

"Yes?"

"Bring your lipstick!"

How to Fuck in High Heels

Shar Rednour

Oh, please. I do not mean leaving your shoes on in bed while you roll around like a *Playboy* bunny. I mean you fucking someone else with your feet stilettoed firmly to the floor—or five-inch-wedged to the floor.

I have to admit it. I love that I can fuck a girl into complete ecstasy while wearing six-inch platforms. When my butch sisters are plowing into a babe, look to the floor. They root themselves in clunky boots that could hug a Harley if not a mountainside. Feelings of control and power snake through me as I go at it—no slipping as she pushes back into me, saying, "harder, harder." Yes, we all may feel that way when we have sex wearing our old jammies. But this is showing off yet another level of *mistressy*. Sexing her in heels takes incredible balance, grace, and determination, not to mention a strong back.

Fucking successfully in heels also requires quality heels. What is quality? Just something that is snug and not wobbly.

I would love to see one of those Easy Spirit commercials featuring a woman fucking instead of playing basketball.

There are a couple of ways to strap it on while strapped in heels. First off, you can kneel or lie on the bed, keeping your shoes on. But when you're on your knees, what's on your feet doesn't matter that much, so why bother? You could also end up poking holes into the comforter and sending feathers flying everywhere. Or you could rip holes into the flesh of your lust one. (That could be a plus or minus depending on your style.) Overall, the fun and point of you actually fucking in your heels (opposed to the fetish charge of you simply being in them) is lost in lying-down positions.

Another technique is for you both to be standing up, leaning against a wall. This position's success depends on your height being complimentary. She needs to be two to four inches taller than you in shoes. If she's small enough, you can just pick her up. But please be sure you *can* pick her up (or wear a weight belt). Anywhere with a sturdy bar overhead makes for a great standing-up fuck arena. You both can really get some leverage and utilize your upper-body strength. A third position is for her to sit on a countertop while you pull up to the bumper. Then there's the forgotten ladder. Cats love ladders. I love ladders. Really, unless your living space is too small, I highly recommend owning a five-foot or taller sturdy wooden ladder. I'll let you figure out those positions on your own.

My favorite position is for a beautiful babe to be bent over a piece of furniture while I'm doing her from behind. I get the full benefit of seeing her ass cheeks, sweet butthole, and pussy as I fuck her.

On to technique! Don't be afraid to move her around to where you want her. Bend her over, spread her legs until she's at the right height, where your legs are slightly spread but not bent more than just the tiniest bit in your knees. Most likely you'll have both legs between hers, but not always.

As you guide in your dick, you'll probably need to bend your legs a little. But as soon as you're in, stand up straight again and move her until you both are at a comfortable height. Make her hold still at first, when you establish the rhythm, which, by the way, you control. This sex may be about her pleasure in the long run, but that pleasure is going to come from you being a good top, and good tops exercise their control. Guide her with your hands on her hips, stroke down the length of her back, but do so without interrupting your rhythm. You can guide her firmly with your hands pulling at her hips or delicately with just a few fingers on the small of her back gently rocking her. As you get going, you'll lean forward more on the balls of your feet so that your body is straight but slightly tilted and angling against her.

If you want to do a very teasing fuck, get your dick in the right position then have her close her legs together while you push in and out slightly.

When you really get going she will most likely be pushing back into you, which could throw your balance. You can simply slap her bottom and say, "Stop fucking me back." Or you can let her succumb to her desire and simply brace yourself by putting one foot between her legs and the other back just a bit. This will keep you at an angle leaning into her.

Varying your position not only spices up the sex, but also helps you fuck longer. Even the slightest position change will draw on a different set of muscles.

Every now and then you might want to put your legs together and bend your knees a bit and fuck that way for a minute or so. This gives your back and legs some variety, which will waylay a spasm. Bending over her back to kiss her neck, bite her shoulder, or kiss her back if you can't reach her neck, is not only a sweet and intimate thing to do, but it will also give your back a cat stretch. Also, have her stand up and lean back into you for a minute. Kiss. Stroke her stomach, pussy, and chest. Call her your baby, stud, princess, or dog. Then push her back down and fuck some more.

For the most part, different positions and rhythm changes tease your partner. When she has really started rising into that pre-orgasm high, try to fuck as long as you can at that pace. Find a rhythm and stick with it. So you're going at it at a pace that works. Does she need to touch herself? You could do that yourself, depending on how your bodies are shaped. Your touch sends electricity through her body, but chances are if she really wants a good fucking, you're best served with occasional touches to her clit. For the most part, though, keep your hands on her back, shoulders, or neck. Suggest that she help herself if she wants more friction between her legs. Pump 'til you drop or until she lets you know she's had enough.

She might tire of this position after a while—not necessarily her pussy, but perhaps her elbows, back, or mind. Let her roll over onto her back where you can lie on top of her and indeed rip those heels into the bedsheets. Or, if it's your turn to be devoured, lie on your back, hook those heels behind her ears, and go for it.

The Rock Wall

Peggy Munson

Stone

We are leaning against the rock wall by the high school where
I have taken him because it's deserted. He has that board-
splitting butch gaze. He's worn his letter jacket, the one he
earned back in high school, and today he delicately wraps it
around my shoulders and says, "Do you want to be my girl?
Do you want me to be your Daddy boyfriend?" And I nod
shyly and say, "Yeah, okay." He holds my hand and we walk.

This is how it begins. It begins with something made from
stone.

The bed he has me in is firm. Daddy's callused hands are
hard. Daddy's face looks like it was chiseled off Mount
Rushmore. The wind is parting the curtains the way he brushes my hair back from my eyes. He gets serious. "Do you want
to play a game, little girl?" he asks me. I know Daddy's games:
rock beats scissors, scissors beat paper, paper beats rock.
Hands equal power. Sometimes I am a paper doll and my
clothes fold on with paper tabs, and Daddy undresses me
absently, like he's opening mail. Sometimes I am a stone

tablet, the stone on which commandments are carved. Sometimes, my legs are safety scissors, lying like dull blades, waiting to be crushed by rock. And Daddy spreads them open and they pull reflexively shut. He kisses to relax me. He curls his hand into a fist, into a stone. He slides that power into me. This simple game of hands.

But this is not just a game, Daddy-Girl. This is not just a game, Paper-Scissors-Rock. These are the scissors that cut up paper guises. This is the crane that breaks buildings. This is the fist that destroys orderly origami. This is the red paper of my cunt unfolding. This is me coming. This is how real. "Take it, bitch," says Daddy's voice into my ear. "Be a good girl. Take my fist." This is me pressed against surfaces. This is the stone that does not acquiesce. This is the statue becoming a Girl.

Quarry

Some days, I hate everything about Daddy. I hate how orphaned I feel when Daddy goes to work. I hate how Daddy can choose the simplest onomatopoeia and roll it off the tongue, so that *cock* sounds as hard as it is. How I sit all day with that word jammed in my head, cock, Daddy's cock, Daddy's hard cock, spreading out with acres of modifiers, until it becomes Daddy's hard cock that isn't fucking me. I hate it that I am so Electra. I hate it that Freud is on my shoulder and that he told me so. I hate it that I need a Daddy. I hate it that words never add up to cocks.

I lie on my back all day waiting and watching TV. I like watching teenage rock stars almost as much as anorexic figure skaters. I used to read about anorexia and about gymnasts and I would think about their discipline when the dentist was drilling pain into my smile. And I would read about how the girls didn't want to grow up and I would walk around for days with the pain in my smile and it was such good pain. And with my fading numb lip I thought of how benevolent the dentist was when he told me I was brave, and such a good girl. I hate Daddy for not being a dentist. I watch the Britney Spears video where she sings "Hit me baby, one more time" and dances around in a Catholic-schoolgirl outfit. I want to pull up my pleated skirt and show Daddy that we can end Biblical racism right here, because the devil is made of white cotton. That's what little girls are made of. This exquisite, pretty rage.

I go to therapy and I want to talk about Daddy but I don't even want to get into it with my shrink. I can't explain how my girlfriend is a boyfriend who makes me call him Daddy. Sometimes when my shrink listens to me talk he thinks about other things. I can see the Viewmaster clicking in front of his eyes. Sometimes he thinks about what I would look like naked, and how he finds the professional boundary titillating. I sit in the waiting room and think about Daddy's cock and my pussy is all wet and I decide to go wipe myself before going into therapy but the bathroom lock has been ripped off the wall. My shrink might walk in on me, or smell me. He might see what a bad girl I really am. I return to the waiting room, still wet.

I don't talk about Daddy's cock but every word I say in therapy sounds like cock and I know my shrink can see right through me. I know he has linguistic X-ray vision and that he knows I am really saying cock, cock, cock and he wants me to sit on his lap but I am thinking about Daddy. How I want the day to go faster so that Daddy will get home from work. My shrink tells me to have a good week but he is really saying cock. The double doors shut behind me, cock, cock. And far away somewhere, in San Francisco, lesbians are pouring silicone into dildo molds and not thinking cock at all. Happily distracted, they are chattering and squeezing cock after cock out of molds and thinking business. I hate Daddy for thinking business. I wish he would think about my pleasure.

I hate how without Daddy I am a book with one bookend, so I just fall and my words get crushed. I hate it how Daddy is a petty thief. Because if he steals what's petty, then what am I when he takes me? I hate how Daddy makes me sputter inarticulate phrases, so that I choke out sounds that have nothing to do with theory. I hate how Daddy makes me write him stories, because I cannot sculpt a sentence out of cock. I hate it how that word becomes so eloquent inside of me, pushing through me and out of my mouth.

I hate how Daddy's cock knows the way to hidden quarries, the watery places that were mined. How Daddy sees the drunken dives that kill sixteen, euphoric girls kissed to epiphanies on their mossy knees. Sophomoric girls getting their nipples touched on their mossy knees. And the skin scraped against sharp things, and the rustle of cops approaching, and the second before the kids run, and the hastily abandoned trunks. How he knows what to do about each truncated fuck. Of each lifetime. Daddy takes care of things.

I hate it how Daddy makes me need his cock. Because then I am a place that once held diamonds, sitting home yearning for him, waiting for a girl's new best friend. Because then I am always too ready for him. So hungry every time his key turns in the lock. So hungry for that handcuff sound of his key in the lock. So hungry for that four o'clock, drowsy, sharp sound. I hate it how Daddy walks in and feels me to see if I'm wet, and wonders what I anticipate, and then ignores me while removing his jacket. I hate it how those fingers on my pussy make me whimper like a little dog.

I hate how seconds turn to hours before Daddy leads me into the bedroom, and his belt buckle glints like it's submerged. How sweetly Daddy takes my hand and says "baby girl," and then pulls me to his denim lap. And how the things to be filled must be emptied, must be stripped. Daddy grips me and undoes me and lowers me to the bed. And I shiver because I need it. I give when Daddy pushes. Daddy pulls on my hair.

I hate how good and raw he strips me. How good it feels to be this bare.

The Rock Wall

Every night I go back to the rock wall. It is covered in moss and the rain is drizzling and I search for grips. I am ripped and mud-covered and hungry. My grasp is tenuous and my fingers are slipping. I'm tired of being a wide-eyed waif always scrambling over walls where there are more walls and more slippery rocks and more places to bruise and nowhere good to land. The rain is so irritating, the noise, the noise that's always a soft fuck when you need it hard, that's always a drizzle when you need a thunderstorm to break the air and shock the animals so they run frenzied—wild—crazed—scattershot—into spaces they never dared to go. The wall is unforgiving and I begin to slide. I land on my knees in a muddy pool and my dress is ripped and I'm old and there is no Daddy. The landing is soft. Nothing impaling me. Nothing tearing me and ripping me. No fairytale wolves, though I always thought they would be there, their dripping incisors and hunger, waiting for me to fall. There is nothing to wound me, no imaginary battles to reenact. No hole in the earth to open up and swallow me there.

Maybe I am already in the hole. Maybe I am the hole. This dark and damp place that feels like the inside and not the outside and my dress is ripped and I start crying. I hold my face in my muddy hands and my tears clean my hands and my hands smear the mud into my tears. Everything undoes everything. Nothing undoes me. Nothing does me.

Then suddenly, so dark and quick and I can't even scream, something reaches from behind and grabs me with its arm under my throat and drags me backwards, and drags me while whispering things. "Daddy's here now, little girl. Daddy's got you." He's not comforting and not scary, just unsettling, just the kind of thing that makes me all animal, all animal splitting from the pack the way the wolves want it to be, all animal confused and asking for it. I try to flail around and pull away. I try to break the grip, the wall is waiting. Doesn't Daddy understand the wall? How I need to climb it always, climb and climb and climb it? Daddy pulls my muddy body so that I'm sitting on his lap and I still can't see him but I feel his hard cock. "Daddy's got you," he says again.

I want not to want it. I want not to feel how my thighs are smeared with mud and my pussy feels smeared, but it's not, it's just mine. There is nothing between my pussy and his cock but a thin layer of fabric. And he is rubbing his cock against my panties and I squirm. I want to squirm away but he rubs me so hard and I start to want to push down onto him. I start to push down as if the fabric will just dissolve. He pushes the tip of his cock against the fabric and the fabric goes into me. And the elastic of my panties follows the fabric and pulls me, pulls my legs, into me. I'm going to fall into me. I have to fight. I try to struggle but Daddy holds me against his moving pushing cock. "Daddy, wait," I say, but I keep pushing to make the fabric go away, and I want him. "Daddy, stop!" Daddy grabs under my arms and pushes me slowly forward so that my face is down but he pulls my hips back. "Daddy wants you to take his cock," he says. "All of it. Can you be a good girl and do that?"

I want to taste the mud. The mud smells oddly like Daddy. Daddy slides my panties down my legs so I'm just there in the night air and my pussy and my ass are high up behind me. "Daddy, no," I say, but this time weakly. This time it's all reverse psychology. This time I'm not sure at all.

"Daddy can just leave you here in the mud if you want, little girl. Is that what you want?" He snarls this.

"Daddy…no," I say. "No, please, no."

"Beg for what you want."

"I want you, Daddy."

"Beg me."

"I want Daddy. I want Daddy to fill me up."

"Daddy's very hard for you. Is this what you want?" He slides the tip of his cock into me. "Is this what you want?"

"Yes, Daddy. *Please*."

"Beg me."

"I want you inside of me. Please."

"What?"

"I want you, Daddy, please." I say it with the urgency I use to climb the walls.

Daddy starts sliding his cock into my pussy and I push back onto him but he holds my hips and makes me wait for him. And the rain gets harder, the drops batter my cheeks, the rain turns everything to mud while Daddy fills me up and my hands slide in front of me for something to hang onto but there is nothing, nothing there, nothing but my hips pushing back and Daddy's hard cock and my need. And I need to hold something. I need to hold on because I am used to holding and I need the wall and Daddy pushes in so hard and I want to scream, it feels so good. My hands are fumbling forward for any handhold but there is nothing there…

"Daddy's got you, baby," he says soothingly. "Fall back into me."

Gravel

The gravel reminds me of old roads cutting between fields to deserted places, the way it clatters and then hums, keeps me unsteady. Once I cut my chin on the gravel in the Dairy Queen parking lot, holding onto my Dilly Bar all the way to the ground. I remember losing my footing, bleeding on the car upholstery, wondering if kids found reddened chunks of rock where I landed. I think about all of these things now, now that I'm old being young, riding next to Daddy in the truck. The big wheels slide over the gravel. The dark moves from beneath trees to the sides of buildings. We are near a warehouse with broken windows. And the gravel is not the kind you buy in bags at Home Depot, but stained. I get out and stumble like a tipsy slut. I straighten my skirt and start to walk but Daddy is there already, and he grabs my arm. "No," he says, pointing. "You little whore. Right here."

I look down distastefully, then up at Daddy. "Here?" I sneer. I can't believe he means it. The rock is soaked dark with things dying, bled oil and shoe rubber. I look at him again, his stern expression, then kneel down. The rocks are sharp against my knees. Daddy gives a little push on my back so I fall forward and my palms slide through the rocks. Then, when I'm on all fours, he pulls up my skirt from behind, just flips the material so that it lands on my back and I feel the breeze trying to go into me. I've got no panties on.

"Such a pretty little ass," he says. "Untainted lily-white ass. Not dirty like the rest of you." The breeze seems to follow the current of his voice and rubs the goose bumps on my ass. "Are you afraid to have Daddy's big cock in your pretty ass?"

"Maybe," I say. I feel defiant. I feel the way the rocks are cutting me and I don't move my hands.

Daddy's hands fondle my ass cheeks, spread them open, press against them so I slide forward more. He's so much stronger than I am. I let myself fall and feel the rocks against my cheek. I think of how I fell that time, when I was young, and tried to taste my blood. And how I always tried to taste my blood when I got cut. But what I liked to taste was not just mine, but also that which made me bleed. It was the thing that made the cut, the flavor mixed into the blood. It was the combination of the two, the grit that touched the cutter and the flesh. It was the generosity of both, and how my bleeding made the two combine. I think of all of this while Daddy moves his cock against the hole, and pushes hard because it's tight.

He pushes hard because it's tight, and pulls my hips against him. My face gets scraped against the gravel. My lip begins to bleed. I taste the blood and salt and earth and pain and fear and trampling. I taste the blood and all that has been done to it and lick and give it back to me. I give me back to me. And Daddy gives me, too.

"Who gives you what you need?" he asks. The natural light has fled. A streetlight shines behind his hair. I smell the tires. I smell the dew. I feel the walls that crumble into gravel. I feel the girls who must undo.

"Daddy," I say. He looks like a monument. "You do."

Inquiring Dykes Want to Know

Shelley Marcus

"You hard-news types don't have the stomach for tabloid work," my editor, Jack Tatum, told me. "I pounded the streets for thirty years before they put me behind this god-damned desk, and I know what it takes. You have to be willing to get your hands dirty, to wallow in the mud with your subject to get your story." Wallowing in the mud was the perfect analogy for Tatum. He reminded me of a pig. Bloated belly hanging way over his belt, the remnants of his last meal on his wrinkled tie. "And you need balls," he said, emphasizing his words by grabbing his crotch, "but at least you qualify in that department." He smirked. "All you dykes have balls, don't you?"

"We sure do," I answered sweetly. "You want to compare, Jack? I'll bet mine are bigger than yours."

His smirk disappeared and I watched the large vein between his Neanderthal eyebrows beat a staccato rhythm worthy of Keith Moon. Through gritted teeth he told me, "Get your ass back out on the street and keep digging. One of those bastards must have a skeleton in his closet. I never knew a politician who didn't have some kind of dirty laundry he wanted to keep hidden."

Ever since the New Hampshire primary, Tatum had been on my case to dig up something on one of the presidential candidates. He didn't care which one, as long as the something was juicy enough. The *National Scoop* didn't exactly endorse a presidential candidate, at least not in the traditional sense. Its candidate of choice was always the one involved in the biggest scandal, ensuring the paper high circulation right up until the election. Inquiring minds and all that.

I wasn't sure that Tatum was wrong. At least about me. His wasn't the first tirade I'd heard on my lack of killer instinct. Annie Yates had told me the same thing when we first met. I hadn't wanted to hear it then either, but it might have had more to do with how, rather than what, she told me. She'd been kneeling behind me, fucking me with her strap-on when she delivered the critique on my skills as a reporter, and I'd been too busy screaming into my pillow to process much of what she said.

Annie worked for *One Out of Ten* magazine, and she was the most in-your-face dyke I knew. I'd always thought gaydar was a myth, but Annie had it. Unlike a lot of members of the gay press, she disliked outing people, but she wasn't against exposing hypocrites who publicly denounced homosexuality while they secretly enjoyed gay sex. They say timing is everything, and Annie was living proof. She had an uncanny ability of being in the right place at the right time, always scooping every other reporter, including me. Our affair had been intense, the sex as exhilarating as a roller coaster ride, but Annie had put her career above everything else. That's what finally split us up. I'm not saying I wasn't just as ambitious as she was, but while Annie had no intention of settling down, I wanted something to come home to every night besides my laptop. So after a few incredible months, we went our separate ways. Annie traveled extensively for her magazine, and for a while after we broke up, whenever she passed through Chicago we got together for hot, no-strings-attached sex. Though I hadn't seen Annie in almost three years, I'd been following her career with a mixture of admiration and envy. I was grateful she wasn't in town now to see how low I'd sunk since we'd last gotten together.

When I got my degree in journalism, I never expected to be working for a birdcage-liner like the *National Scoop*. Not that I'd started out there. Two years ago I'd been at the top of my game, on staff at the *Chicago Sentinel* and on the fast track to a Pulitzer—until Jess left me and I spent the better part of a year looking at life through the bottom of a shot glass. The six months we lived together were the happiest of my life. I thought it would last forever, but for my young lover it had been only an extended stopover on a long journey. The moment someone with more impressive credentials came along, she was out the door without so much as a backward glance. Even though Jess had left me for a bigger bank account and not for better sex, the breakup had hit me hard. I used booze to kill the pain, and in record time my career hit the skids. The *Sentinel's* editor was a friend and tried to cut me as much slack as possible, but when I kept blowing assignments he had no choice but to fire me. I couldn't blame him.

I finally managed to pull myself together, but when I emerged clean and sober after four months in detox, Chicago's Fourth Estate didn't exactly welcome me back with open arms. Drunks come with a warning label, and no legitimate paper was willing to take a chance on me. So I wound up at the *Scoop*. The publisher knew my reputation BB (Before Booze), and thought my byline would add some prestige to his rag. He wasn't willing to pay much for the privilege of having me on staff, but beggars can't be choosers, so I took the job.

I'd worked the political beat at the *Sentinel,* but I'd never been a muckraker. The whole idea of digging up personal dirt on a candidate left a bad taste in my mouth. I needed the job, though, so I started digging. Taking into account that the political arena is always ripe for scandal, I expected to turn up something pretty quickly, but so far I hadn't had any luck. And considering the difference in the candidates' lifestyles, it was pretty amazing I'd come up empty.

While I was checking out both camps, I secretly hoped any skeletons I found wouldn't be in Gary Sidowski's closet. He already had my vote. A liberal Democrat, he championed gay causes, and unlike some politicians had a healthy respect for the gay community's voting power. After all, hadn't it been the gay vote that swayed the last presidential election and put liberal Bill Clinton into office? Unfortunately, Clinton couldn't keep his dick in his pants and was impeached after a sex scandal, but that's another story.

At the start of the campaign I was confident that Sidowski would win in a landslide, but now he was trailing in the polls, and it didn't look like there was anything he could do to turn things around. Most voters didn't seem ready to elect someone who didn't fit the typical politician's profile. The senator from the Golden West was forty-two years old, very handsome, and extremely charismatic. He was also divorced and childless. Two strikes against him right there. Add to that his pro-choice stance and his support of gay rights and same-sex marriage, and you were looking at a very hard sell to Mr. and Mrs. Middle-Class America. And he needed their votes. After what happened with Bill Clinton, even the votes of every gay man and lesbian in America weren't going to be enough to elect another young liberal president.

By comparison, conservative Republican Joseph King looked like he could be the model for a Norman Rockwell painting. A fifty-year-old church deacon from the Deep

South, he'd lost his wife to breast cancer four years earlier, and had brought his nineteen-year-old daughter Christina on his political stumping tour to serve as his hostess. Being a widower already gave King the sympathy vote, but all those photo ops with his devoted, motherless daughter by his side simply screamed "family values." Every time I heard him call her "Chrissy" and her call him "Daddy" it made me want to lose my lunch, but it was an image the majority of Americans had taken to their hearts. And the polls reflected it, much to my dismay.

I'd heard King spout religious platitudes and fire-and-brimstone tirades against homosexuality, making him number one on my political hit list. I would have liked nothing better than to dig up something really damaging in the deacon's background. There was only another week before the election, though, and I still had nothing.

At seven o'clock I decided to call it a day, and stopped at Rita J's before heading home. If I couldn't drown my sorrows in booze anymore, at least I could drown them in sex. The club attracted a lot of the under-twenty-five crowd, and I was hoping to find some sweet young thing to help me forget my troubles. Or a not-so-sweet one. I didn't care, as long as she was cute and she was willing.

When I saw the female figure in faded blue jeans leaning over the pool table, I was sure I'd found just what I was looking for. She must have been sizing up a difficult shot because the cue stick she held was stock-still, but her cute little ass was moving in time to k.d. lang's "Constant Craving" on the jukebox. She caught my attention right away, especially in that position. Leaning over the table with her butt high in the air, she was in the perfect position for a little anal stimulation. If this had been The Eagle on women's night, I would have taken her right then and there. I would have sauntered up behind her, swiftly lowered her jeans and stuck my tongue into her tight little asshole.

But this wasn't The Eagle. This was Rita J's, a respectable lesbian bar, and Gladys, its built-like-a-linebacker bartender, would have kicked my butt out onto the street if I'd even tried such a thing. But the fantasy was hot enough to get my juices flowing.

If it couldn't happen here, it could still happen, I thought as I started toward the inviting ass. I was working on my opening line when she took her shot, put down her cue stick, and turned around. The front of her was even hotter than the back. I've always liked them young, and she looked barely old enough to be in the bar. A petite 5'4" and slight, with boyish hips and small breasts. A short, sleek cap of honey-blonde hair. Brown eyes flecked with green that looked almost golden in the bar light. High cheekbones, and a pouty mouth just begging to be kissed. Her face had that waiflike quality I've always been a sucker for. There was something familiar about her, but I couldn't place it. A bottle of Bud Light was sitting on the edge of the pool table. She took a sip then licked the foam from her lips. I imagined pushing her face into my crotch and holding it there while that pink tongue spread my pussy lips and made my throbbing clit beg for mercy. The skintight T-shirt that hugged her small breasts proclaimed that she was *Ready, Willing, and Able,* raising my hopes for a hot night. The first two attributes were a necessity where I was concerned, the third negotiable. What she didn't know I could teach her. Besides, I've always felt enthusiasm more than makes up for lack of experience.

I was wondering how long it would take us to get to the question of *my place or yours* when something clicked in my brain and I suddenly remembered where I'd seen that face before. Right beside that of her father, Joseph King.

I couldn't believe my luck. All these months I'd been trying to dig up dirt on King, and now the story I'd been looking for had fallen into my lap like manna from heaven. It seemed too good to be true, but I figured I was long overdue for a break. This night had definite possibilities. I hastened my steps. Not only was I going to have sex tonight with an incredible beauty, I would probably get a raise.

I'll admit finding Christina in a lesbian bar really shocked me. Not because she was gay. I've been in the news business long enough that nothing surprises me anymore. But what really blew me away was the way she had transformed herself. For months the public had seen her on television and at personal appearances looking like the poster girl for Apple Pie America. She had shoulder-length blonde hair worn in a straight, simple style. Her lips were painted bubble-gum pink, as were her long, perfectly manicured fingernails. Little pink hearts dangled from her ears, and she wore a smile so perpetual I was sure her face must be frozen in that position. She looked so much the All-American Girl that each time her father asked her to join him on the podium, I half-expected to see her bound up the stairs wearing a cheerleader's uniform waving pompoms.

Here in Rita J's, looking at her shorn hair and suggestive T-shirt, I realized why she'd felt confident enough to come into the bar. No one was going to connect her with Joseph King's devoted daughter. I prided myself on being able to spot a fake, yet little Chrissy had taken me in along with the rest of the country, and because of it, I found myself looking at her with newfound respect. Of course, my admiration wasn't going to stop me from using this juicy bit of information to my advantage. Especially since now that I'd seen the real Christina King, the only thing I wanted more than exposing her little hoax was exposing her hot little body.

I walked over and introduced myself. "I'm Lindsay," I said, offering my hand. "I've never seen you here before. Are you new in town?"

"Yes," she said, taking my hand. "I'm Kit."

Now she was Kit. It made sense. A new look deserved a new name, and this one suited her. I glanced down at her hand before I let it go. Her nails were cut short, and unpainted. So the long, pink fingernails had been as fake as the long blonde hair. I found myself wondering if there was anything real about Christina King. I knew I'd have fun finding out. I suspected her small, firm breasts were real. Since she wasn't wearing a bra under the tee-shirt, my view of them was unobstructed, but being the good reporter I am, I planned to investigate further.

"So, you've just moved to Chicago?" I asked.

Kit shook her head. "No, I'm just visiting. My father's here on business and I made the trip with him."

That certainly clinched it. Here on business with her father. It was the truth, just not the whole truth. Kit eyed me with interest, but absolutely no sign of suspicion. She obviously had no idea I'd recognized her.

The heavenly k.d. was gone, and Melissa was inviting her lover to sleep while she drove. "This is my favorite song," I said. If Kit was like most dykes I knew, she loved Etheridge's fiercely romantic ballad. When she nodded, I took the beer out of her hand and placed it on the table. Then I pulled her into my arms. "Dance with me," I coaxed.

Kit didn't offer any resistance as I moved us onto Rita J's small dance floor. I held her close as we danced, letting my hands wander down to grab her asscheeks. Oh yes, I noted as I felt her nipples harden under the T-shirt, definitely real. Business first, I told myself, but it was easier said than done.

"Do you work for your father?" I asked, trying to keep my eyes on the prize.

The question seemed to take her by surprise. "No," she said cautiously. "I'm just helping him with a project, but once it's over I'll be free to do whatever I want."

If Kit thought that was true, she was living in a dream world. When the election was over and King became president, it would be the beginning of four long years for Kit. People watching every move she made, making it impossible for her to be herself without jeopardizing her father's public image. If her father was behind her All-American Girl masquerade, I couldn't help wondering what misguided sense of loyalty had made Kit agree to play along.

Suddenly I began to see my exposing her as a noble thing. Once I outed Kit, she'd be free to live her own life. I did feel lousy about what I was going to do, but I rationalized that her freedom would be worth everything I put her through. She'd probably be grateful. I felt a stirring in my crotch as I imagined all the ways she could thank me.

Kit's hair smelled of herbal shampoo. I buried my nose in it while we danced. I bent down and placed my lips on hers in a gentle kiss. When she returned the kiss, I cupped the back of her neck in my hand and held her while I kissed her harder, more demandingly. She responded by opening her mouth. The fresh taste of beer sent a shock of déjà vu through me and I sucked her tongue into my mouth.

Wanting desperately to explore her ripe, young body, I danced us toward the rear of the bar to a dimly lit area near the back door. Gladys, busy behind the crowded bar, never saw us leave the dance floor.

I kissed Kit again and slipped my hands under her T-shirt, filling my greedy hands with her breasts. I worked them roughly, stroking and squeezing. Testing her, I pinched the small, hard nipples. Kit moaned into my mouth. Giving in to my need to taste her, I broke from the kiss and lifted up her shirt. I placed my mouth over her left nipple and suckled it. Kit began to purr.

Any ideas I had of Kit being inexperienced disappeared when she unzipped my pants and stuck her hand down inside my silk thong bikini.

"Let's go somewhere private," she said as she fingered my wetness. Her voice was filled with lust. I thought things were happening way too fast, and way too easy, but I was too horny to question how good my luck was still running. Groping each other, we stumbled out the back door.

I didn't especially like sex outdoors. It brought back too many bad memories of drunken quickies. But I was too hot to argue when Kit insisted we do it in the alley behind Rita J's. It was dimly lit and deserted, and considering how I was planning to expose her and hopefully cost her father the election, it seemed almost appropriate.

For a girl from the Bible Belt, she had no inhibitions. Once we were outside, she grabbed me, kissing me savagely and grinding her delicious body against mine. She tugged my pants down to my ankles and roughly pushed me up against the building. The coarse brick surface scratched my bare ass. A small triangle of silk was the only thing that separated me from Kit, and she ripped it off. The cool night air chilled my naked pussy, but Kit dropped to her knees and quickly warmed it with her mouth. She blew on my outer lips, sucking each in turn into her hot mouth. Catching strands of my dark brown hair between her teeth, she tugged on them. Her heated breath was turning my cunt into an inferno.

I tangled my hands in her short blonde hair to hold her in place and prevent her from stopping, but I was kidding myself if I thought I was in control of anything that was happening.

Her tongue parted my pussy lips masterfully and slid inside me. I growled at the contact. She licked me with long, slow strokes, leaving no inch of my flesh unexplored. After a few minutes of her tonguing, my clit was swollen and aching for attention, but Kit wouldn't give me any relief. She teased me mercilessly, licking circles around, but never touching it. I thought I'd go mad. I took my left hand from her hair and tried to finger myself, but Kit caught my wrist. When I tried to use my right hand she caught that wrist, too and with incredible strength, she pushed both my arms out to my sides and held them there.

"Please!" I begged, my voice hoarse with need. I felt her smile of victory, then she gathered the hard little button into her mouth and squeezed it between her lips. I let out a strangled cry—and went over the edge!

I felt weak in the knees. Heat flooded my body and I shook violently. So violently I was afraid I was going to pass out from the sheer intensity of the orgasm. Kit released my wrists and I bore down on her shoulders as my body continued to shake. My knees buckled and Kit held me around the waist to keep me from falling. Finally I stopped shaking, and, limp with pleasure, I rested my head against the wall. When I could speak again, all I could manage was, "Mmmmmm."

"Say 'Pussy'!" a cheery voice trumpeted.

A bright light exploded before my eyes, momentarily blinding me. I was dazed, but even in my confusion, I was sure I knew that voice.

"One more for insurance," the voice sang out.

Again the light exploded, but this time I closed my eyes. When I opened them again, the white spots had disappeared and I could make out the figure clearly.

"Annie?" I gulped, unbelieving.

"In the flesh," Annie Yates declared. She looked at me with a lecherous grin. "Though at the moment, that particular phrase does seem to describe you more than it does me."

"Jesus, Annie," I said, my face flushed with embarrassment. I reached down and pulled up my pants. "What the hell are you doing here?"

"Working, of course," she replied, slinging her camera over her shoulder. "Same as you."

"I'm not working."

"Really?" she said, her eyebrows raised. "You could have fooled me." She looked thoughtful. "I was wrong about you, Lindsay. I never thought you'd go to such lengths to get a story, but tonight you proved me wrong."

The story. Kit. With all the distractions I'd forgotten about her. The poor kid would be devastated if Annie used the photos she'd taken.

"Kit," I started, but she wasn't standing near me anymore. She was standing next to Annie Yates.

"Call me Chrissy," she said in a cold, detached voice.

"You can't let Annie use those pictures," I told her. "If you do, everyone will know you're gay."

Kit looked at me as if I were a defective child. "That's the idea, Lindsay. Once everyone knows Daddy's Little Girl is a dyke, they'll see him for the hypocrite he is and his political career will be over. Then I'll be free of his control for good."

"You set me up," I said indignantly, then realized how ridiculous the accusation sounded. Hadn't I planned to do the same thing to her?

"If it makes you feel any better, girlfriend," Annie told me, "you weren't the target in our little scam. Kit went to Rita J's planning to pick up a woman—any woman—and get her into a compromising situation. I was waiting out here to get it on film. Until I saw you two race out the back door, I had no idea you were here. And once Kit started eating your pussy, the plan had moved too far forward for me to stop it."

"I'm so glad it wasn't personal," I said sarcastically.

"It never is," Annie smiled. As an afterthought she added, "I'll be in town for a few more days. Maybe we can get together? For old times' sake?" When I didn't answer she shrugged. "Suit yourself. Let's go, Kit."

I watched them disappear into Rita J's, but I didn't follow. I knew I'd wind up with a glass of vodka in my hand if I did.

The new issue of *One Out of Ten* hit the stands the day before the election. Annie's a very talented photographer. There was no mistaking me in the 8 x 10" photo, bare from the waist down, a slightly dazed expression on my face. There was no mistaking Kit, either, kneeling between my legs, her cheeks glistening with my juices as she faced the camera.

To my surprise, Joseph King didn't drop out of the race, but he got so few votes it was embarrassing. I thought about telling Gary Sidowski he had me to thank for his victory, but figured it wouldn't do much for my career to bring up how I'd done it.

I left the *National Scoop.* To be honest, I was shown the door. Jack Tatum congratulated me on finally getting my hands dirty with the King story, then fired me for letting Annie scoop me on it.

He actually did me a favor. After the story came out, my phone started ringing. Some of the legitimate Chicago papers suddenly became interested in me again. I even heard from my old editor at the *Sentinel,* wondering if I'd consider coming back to work for them.

I'm still weighing my options, but I think I'm going to take the job I was offered by *One Out of Ten.* My sudden notoriety didn't bother them, and I think working for a gay publication might be just what I need to turn my career—and my life—around.

Maybe the next time I get caught with my pants down, I'll be wearing a smile.

Monica and Me

Rachel Kramer Bussel

I think I've found a way to convince the ever-luscious Monica Lewinsky to come back to my hotel room with me—at least, I'm counting on it.

I've been fascinated with her ever since the news of her affair with Clinton first broke. I mean, he's the president—it's not just the everyday person who can get access to being in the same building as him, let alone down-and-dirty under his desk.

In all the hubbub over the legal maneuverings and the moral outcry, it seemed like everyone had forgotten that Monica is indeed, despite it all, just a young woman, and one who obviously has a very sensual side. But that's obvious, not only from her actions with Clinton and whoever else, but by looking at her and hearing her talk. Her lust extends to life— she's lively and excited, girlish and sweet.

I'd followed all the drama and the minor tabloid stories, collecting Monica facts in my head, trying to piece them all together to create a whole person. But I needed more—I needed to see for myself what she and I had in common, whether the sparks I envisioned in my head would truly explode when we met.

I booked a room at the Paradise Hotel as soon as I knew that she would be coming to town for a book-signing. The only really fancy hotel in town, this will provide me with extra chances to casually "bump" into her. Of course this will require lots of preparation and a bit of luck, because I'm sure, with her looks and fame, she has people trying to get close to her every day.

The day of the book-signing, I go to the store as soon as it opens and browse for a little while, thinking I would look too much like a stalker if I were the first person seated in the audience, but also wanting to get a seat up front. I've primped myself into a sexy but not overpowering outfit: a low-cut blouse with a tight silver jacket over it, short black skirt, and sexy black stockings with glittery silver lines sparkling here and there. I also added some shiny silver eye shadow and applied enough black eyeliner and mascara so it actually looks like I have eyelashes.

Completing the outfit is my recent indulgence purchase: open-toed maroon high heels with a patterned design. I don't want to scare her away, but I need her to notice me.

She reads briefly from her autobiography, tearing up once or twice, but more often looking coyly at her audience, knowing that most of them are here because she has captivated their libidos even more than their need to gossip. She licks her carefully painted lips, every action carefully constructed to make us pay nonstop attention to her body. She's flirting en masse, and I'm ready to seduce her right then, but I bide my time.

As she finishes and people line up for autographs, I graciously allow the other attendees to go ahead of me. After all, I'm not *really* here to get my book signed. She looks up and I pierce her with my gaze, brown eyes on brown, not letting her look away until she must turn to the man in front of me.

"Miss Lewinsky, I have great faith in you and am behind you all the way," he says as she smiles and asks his name.

I bet he'd like to be right behind her, but that will be my position later tonight. He steps away and she gazes up at me, looking around for my book.

"Hi. I left my book back at the hotel, but it's very important that I get it autographed."

She looks at me, not saying anything, but a slight smile hovers around her lips. "So, are you going to go back and get it?" she asks with a bit of a smirk.

I stare right back at her, letting her know that I'm open to whatever lascivious scenario she's concocting. "Well, I can't go get it right now, I have a few appointments, but, well—I just *need* to get it signed," I end up whining, desperation making my voice climb. All my acting lessons have been distilled into this moment.

She tells me that she'll be signing for a little while longer, and that if I come back in half an hour maybe she can arrange to meet me later. I have no choice but to trust her. I wink at her and head out the door.

I breathe a large sigh of relief at having actually made contact, and stroll around the block, frantically trying to come up with a plan B to get her up to my room. I walk a few blocks and then head back, realizing that my half hour is almost up.

Despite twinges of uncertainty, I have a feeling she'll still be there and will talk to me.

I see how starved she is not just for good sex but for some real attention to Monica the person, not just Monica the intern. Yes, like everyone else I follow the stories on her in the tabloids, but I'm more than just a groupie. I sense in Monica a kinship, a kind of sisterhood, if you will, that will make our union tonight special beyond either of our dreams.

I reenter the store and see her in the back, talking to the manager. As I walk toward her she turns around and smiles, beckoning me to where she's standing.

I wait a few steps away, not wanting to intrude on her conversation.

She finishes talking and takes my hand in hers and leads me into a back room. We sit down at a little table where she's stored her bag.

"So, what hotel are you staying at?" she asks me.

I stare at her, so caught up in being close to her that I can barely answer.

"Well?" she teasingly persists.

"The Paradise."

"Oh great—that's my hotel too."

I'm still gazing back at her, starstruck, awestruck, and lust-struck all at once.

"Come on, let's go," she says rather matter-of-factly, standing and grabbing my hand.

"What do you mean? You're just going to go off with some stranger? I could be anyone!" I halfheartedly protest.

"Well, then tell me your name."

"Rachel," I say.

"So now I know you—let's go!" she repeats, this time more forcefully.

We walk out of the store and toward the hotel.

"Don't you have, like, people who are traveling with you? A chaperone?" I ask.

"Usually, but this time I wanted to be on my own. I've gotten used to the crowds and I can pretty much handle it. I don't usually attract people like you, who are sweet and normal."

"Thanks," I reply.

We walk the rest of the way in a comfortable silence, each of us surreptitiously trying to sneak looks at the other.

When we get to the hotel we both pause, staring at the ground and then at each other, not sure how to approach the topic of where to go. Finally, after an absolutely interminable silence, I say, "Do you want to come to my room for a bit?"

"Yeah, I do," she says softly, suddenly growing shy.

Alone in the elevator, I take her hand, holding its soft flesh in my own rough one. I squeeze her hand and she squeezes back.

I open the door to my room and we're greeted by the many offerings I've brought here to tempt her. I've arranged for the room service carefully, noting her likes and dislikes: champagne, strawberries, and chocolate have been delivered on elegant silver trays that show she's worth it. I don't want this to be like the Clinton affair for her. Despite her protestations that she had the first orgasm of that relationship, I'd venture to guess that her pleasure wasn't at the forefront of Clinton's mind.

I, on the other hand, have her delight as the goal of my evening. I know that Monica is really a bad girl lurking in the fancy outfits of her richer, more genteel peers. I want to unleash that bad girl, let her show her true colors.

She looks a bit stunned, but then takes it in stride. I don't know if this exactly meets her expectations, but I do know that she wanted to come back here with me.

"This is a nice place, isn't it?" she comments, sitting down on the bed.

I give her a glass of champagne. She takes it and giggles as she slips out of her heels. I'm trying to figure out how I should play this: slow and languid or rough and dirty.

Maybe a little bit of both would work.

We talk about her day and the book-signing, and she tells me how tough it's been for her. "People always want, want, want from me—they want my time, my name, my money. They act like I'm some superhuman force rather than just a normal girl."

She looks as if she could cry, and while I do want to get to know her better, I don't want her to dissolve into misery. I motion for her to scoot closer to me and I start massaging her shoulders and back. She sighs and relaxes her muscles, letting me squeeze and shape them, vigorously tending to all the places that feel too burdened, too knotty. I reach under her shirt and work my hands into her skin, manually telling her that I want to please her, to do for her.

As I knead harder and harder, digging my knuckles into her shoulders, pushing my thumbs into her back, she releases an "mmmm" and starts to lean into me.

"More," she says, and I squeeze as hard as I can.

Now I'm giving her skin little pinches, knowing their sting will stay with her for a few seconds. I can tell she's getting excited by the way she's squirming around, like she wants to take her clothes off but doesn't quite know how to go about it. I move over and she lies down across the bed. I run my fingers across her lips and she kisses them.

"You are so gorgeous, do you know that?" I ask her.

She responds by taking my index finger and biting it gently.

"I guess you do," I say as I start to take off her top. As I lift her shirt, I see a gleaming lacy-black bra underneath. Her full breasts are cozily couched there.

"Touch me," she says, opening her eyes and staring back at me as she had at the bookstore.

Her eyes bore into me, giving me a taste of her soul, her passion, the things that she now has to hide behind a steely gaze to protect her media reputation. For whatever wondrous reason, she is letting herself go with me.

Instead of complying with her request, I tell her to get comfortable in the nice, soft queen-size bed, and that I'll be right back. I sneak off to the bathroom, where I've hidden my stash of sex toys. I'll bring only one of them back to her; my purpose in leaving is mostly so that she'll get nervous and question my next move.

I want her on edge, unsure, my actions unreadable.

I walk back in and dim the lights. She is sitting up in bed, eyes closed, sipping her champagne, a dreamy smile on her face. I wonder what she's thinking about.

I walk over and kneel on the floor in front of her. She turns her brooding gaze toward me, her mouth hovering over the champagne glass without drinking. She dips her tongue into the champagne, then leans down and slowly slips her tongue into my mouth. She teases me, lingering around my lips and then slipping away.

"I know how much you want me," she says wickedly.

Of course she knows; I'm kneeling in front of her, practically panting with lust.

"You can have me...I just want to have a little fun first," she says.

I give her a quizzical look.

She spreads her legs and brings them around me, pulling me closer to the bed. Then she leans down again, places her glass on the floor, and kisses me. When I say kissing, I mean really, deeply *kissing* me, as if kissing alone were the entirety of sex. She puts her hands on the back of my head and positions me to her liking, then somehow slides her mouth to mine and does the most amazing things with her luscious soft lips.

She feels like a pillow, like silk, like pure sweetness.

She tastes gorgeous, and her aggressive side is a complete turn-on.

She swirls her tongue around mine, gently licking and stroking, turning her head this way and that.

We kiss like that, frantic and needy, consumed by our mouths, for a long time—twenty minutes or so—before we both stop to catch our breath. She sits up with her eyes closed, still in that blissful desire-soaked world. I choose that moment to take advantage of her position, tying a silky black blindfold around her head. I see the look on her face as she realizes what I've done: startled, surprised, a tiny bit scared, but even more excited. She knows that finally someone is unlocking her deepest fantasies, and that she doesn't have to pretend anything with me.

"How does that feel?" I whisper in her ear.

As she starts to answer me, I slip two fingers into her mouth and she sucks on them. "Shh...you don't have to answer that; I just wanted you to think about how the blindfold feels covering your eyes. You're going to have a really delicious time tonight if you do what I tell you to, OK?"

She nods her head and makes a small whimpering noise.

I decide to tease her a little by making her guess what I'm doing. In preparation for tonight, I've bought some of her infamous *Barbara Walters* lipstick, "Glaze" by Club Monaco—I got one as a gift for her and one as a gift for me. I open mine and start decorating her lovely body, swirling the plum-colored makeup onto her nipples.

"What are you doing?" she asks, not really expecting an answer. Her nipples harden.

"You're my canvas and I'm painting you, all of this gorgeous pale skin of yours, and your pretty nipples," I tell her. I make them nice and dark, juicy-looking, then snap a Polaroid to show her later. Then I lean down and rub my lips against her nipples, giving new meaning to the words *lipstick lesbian*. I squeeze her round, bulging nipples between my fingers, pulling them tightly until I hear her gasp.

"Do you want me to stop?" I say in my most teasing voice.

She shakes her head no.

"What was that? You have to speak if you want me to hear you."

"No, please, don't stop," she begs me.

I keep pulling, drawing her nipples toward me, squeezing them just about as hard as I can for a second or two. By now she's frantic; her nipples have become gateways to her cunt. She reaches up to touch them and I observe her technique. She rubs the edges of her short nails against them, scraping and pushing, giving a little jolt each time her hard nail rubs against the even harder surface of her nipple.

With the lipstick I draw a line down her cleavage, down over her stomach and toward her pussy. I replace the cap and then rub the slim tube up against her pantyhose. I lay it flat against her and rub it back and forth over her clit, getting her even more worked up. I keep pushing the lipstick against her, wanting to touch her for real. She pushes back in rhythm, already aroused despite still being dressed. When she seems on the brink of coming, I stop.

I walk over to the counter where the champagne is chilling, picking up the bottle in one hand and palming a few ice cubes in the other. "Open your mouth, sweetheart," I tell her, then slip a cube into that sexy pink hole.

By now her lipstick has almost all worn off, but I can still detect its traces on her soft lips, which are getting flushed and big in her excitement. "Now spread your legs for me, Monica," I instruct her, liking the way she instantly obeys me.

I lift up her dress and press my fingers against the fabric that encloses her pussy—it's wet and thick. I push the fabric against her, making her feel her own dampness, making her even wetter. She wants to talk but has to finish with her ice cube first. She sucks it greedily, eager to tell me all the naughty things she wants me to do to her.

I don't let her, though, since I already have enough naughty ideas in my head to last all night. I give her another cube to suck and tell her she's being a very good girl and will be rewarded for her patience. With that I climb over her and push my knee hard up against her cunt. She pushes back with all her strength, needing as much contact as I can give her— and then some.

I take her wrists and hold them above her head, leveraging myself against her body, rocking softly against her stocking-covered pussy, on the edge myself. If I don't pause for a moment to regroup, my carefully formed plans will go out the window.

I take off the blindfold and she looks at me quizzically. I tell her we're going to play show-and-tell. She knows what I want to see first. Now it's my turn to sit up against the nice fluffy pillows and relax.

I tell her to bring me a glass of champagne and then to stand by the bed. "Lean over," I say gruffly, wanting to make sure she knows that there are no other options. "Lift up your skirt for me, honey," I tell her, wanting my own glimpse of the Monica-thong. But Miss Lewinsky has her own plans—she pulls her dress up and slowly starts to peel down her stockings to show me that she is, alas, not wearing a thong.

And she's not wearing any other undies either!

No, the only thing I'm seeing now is her round white ass, looking so fucking gorgeous that it's all I can do not to grab for it right away. I let her finish her little show for me.

She pulls the black stockings all the way down to her ankles and leans over farther so that I can also see a little bit of her bright pink cunt poking out underneath. By now I've forgotten all about my champagne and I'm staring breathlessly at Monica's ass, wondering what she'll do next.

Now she moves around and spreads her legs even farther apart. I can see the way her ankles are stretching the elastic of her stockings, the contrast between their darkness and her pale skin. I can't contain myself any longer and I reach up and bring her ass closer to me. Her skin is cold and beautiful, tender, soft.

I kiss her ass softly at first, then take a little bite and hear her intake of breath. I bite harder, knowing that she's eager for me to get to the heart of who she is. Knowing that I'm so near to her warm pussy is driving me crazy. I lean back and push her forward a little, then give her a nice slap on the ass.

I can see my bite marks and the red stain left by my hand. I tell her how sexy her ass looks. She doesn't say anything, but turns her head to look at me with deep longing in her eyes. I lift her up and pull her on top of me.

"Hmmm, you're so beautiful. I love how full and soft your body is. I've dreamed of being with you and here you are. What do you want me to do, Monica?"

She closes her eyes and turns over onto her back. "I want you to fuck me," she says, surprising me with her language. Even though it's been obvious all night that that's what she wants, I'm still a bit taken aback.

"With what?" I ask her.

She takes my hand, licks the palm, and says, "With this."

I put two fingers in her mouth before moving down to her pussy, covered with its dark, curly pubic hair. "I'm gonna give you what you want now," I say as I slide my fingers into her warm, soft cunt.

She moans as I enter her and she pushes herself up off the bed. "How many fingers are you using?" she asks me, so caught up in her heat and my hand that she's almost talking to herself.

"What do you think?" I counter.

"I don't know," she pants, barely able to speak.

"Two," I whisper into her ear, and I like how she squeezes me even more tightly as I say the word. I push and push, wanting to go as deep as I can, wanting to fill all of her. I press my stomach and hips into her, pushing her against the bed, and put two fingers of my other hand into her mouth.

I want to feel all of her reactions to my touch. I slide another finger inside her and she moans. "Three," I say directly into her ear. She is pushing against me, wanting to turn over so she can look at me. She's so beautiful, so big and lustful and open and soft, I can't resist her request. I let her turn over and I gaze into her eyes, letting her know that I'm enjoying myself as much as she is.

I push harder, faster, deeper than I think is possible, and she is ready for me. Now I have four fingers inside her.

Her breathing quickens, her eyes close, and she is pulling at her skin, her hair, the sheets, the bed, anything to hold on, to try to prolong the ecstatic agony of her orgasm, but she can't resist. The shudders start inside her and her thighs shake and her pussy gets even tighter around my fingers.

I coax her on, whisper to her, brush a finger over her G-spot, make it last as long as I can. After about twenty minutes, she's done, and she looks at me with such sexy tiredness, relief, and delight that I want to stay with her forever. I hug her and lie down next to her on the bed, taking in her warmth and her scent.

We lie there for a while, holding each other, drifting in and out of luscious sleep. I get some of my energy back and decide it's time to test her infamous skills. Telling her to touch herself and wait for me, I get up and go into the bathroom and come back festooned with a nice sturdy harness and a rather large cock. I've never really been much for strap-ons, from either side, but this seems like a moment to just go with the impulse.

As I walk toward her, her eyes seem to bulge—I'm not sure if it's anticipation, trepidation, or a little of both. I smile reassuringly at her, letting her know that I really mean all this in fun, even if it won't seem that way in a few minutes. I pull her head toward mine and kiss her roughly, then push her down toward my bulging red cock and tell her to swallow it.

"Yeah, baby, I know you're good at it, I know you'll give me what I want," I tell her as I see her lips part and start to take in the tip of my silicone extension. I start to understand why so many dykes are into strap-ons. The sheer power of standing against the bed while she kneels in front of me, doing my bidding, letting my cock go deeper and deeper down her throat until it starts to cause her discomfort, makes me feel special—high almost.

Her lips suck and then push down against my dick, practically causing my clit to spark. When it seems just unbearable, I pull her off me, get rid of the strap-on, and push her back into place, needing her tongue on my clit that very instant. She seems startled at first, unsure, but I think she picks up on the fact that she doesn't have to be all that proficient to satisfy me once I'm so worked up. Her tongue takes to my cunt in a pleasantly unexpected way, lapping and licking and discovering all its contours and crevices.

After the pressure from the cock her soft tongue is such a delightful contrast that my come is soon dripping down my legs. She licks some of my juices off me and kisses me, then curls up against the pillows and falls asleep.

I know that I could treat her better than the Bill Clintons and Andy Bleilers of the world. They were married men full of their own concerns, out to use and discard her without taking a moment to notice who she was beyond what she could do for them. I want to give her back a sense of joy in her sexuality—the joy that exudes from her every pore when she's with me. I knew when I first heard her story that not only does she have a lot to give as a lover but she can take pleasure as well.

I envision the two of us living together and gallivanting all over the world, taunting everyone with our sensuous escapades, shoving the media's hypocrisy back in its face. I picture her happy, glowing, free to pursue her own interests and desires. And most of all, I picture her next to me, just like she is now. She sleeps through the night, occasionally reaching for me, once even waking up and touching me, knowing right where to put her fingers to make me instantly wet. I grind against her and come on her fingers, unsure if she is asleep or awake.

In the morning she wakes up and grins at me slyly. I've seen a side of her that few people have. She gets up and puts her clothes back on, telling me she has to go to some meetings and that we should stay in touch. I give her my card, walk her to the door, and kiss her lingeringly, almost pinning her to the wall. Then I realize I have to let her leave.

If she wants to call me, she will.

I haven't heard from Monica since then, but I think about her often. When I see that she's going to be on TV, some big interview, I smile to myself, because I know more of her secrets than will ever be told to some reporter. I wonder whether she thinks of me, if she'll give me some secret signal during the broadcast, if when they ask about her sexual appetites she'll remember our wild night together. I hope so, because I certainly do.

If you're reading this, Monica, I have more tricks up my sleeve.

Lots of them.

Splitting the Infinitive

Jean Roberta

I'm standing in my office waiting for Didrick Bent, the one I think of as Dim Bulb. I don't like to be kept waiting. As long as I have nothing better to do, I glance at myself in the mirror on the back of my office door. I am only 5'3", and I have placed my mirror so that my face is perfectly centered in it and taller people must duck to see themselves in my domain. I would rather stand than sit, and I prefer to see other people below me—I suppose I picked up this preference when I began teaching English at the university ten years ago. I like the legend that Emily Brontë died standing up. Like any great work of fiction, this story probably contains more truth than fact.

I am not a vain woman, but I find comfort in my own reflection. I like to know how I appear to my audience. My long chestnut hair, turning to gray, is coiled and pinned at the back of my head. The overhead light picks up the silver at my temples and gives depth to my large brown eyes. I reapply the burgundy lipstick that dramatizes my full lips, and powder my small nose to cover the shine.

I am wearing my white silk blouse without a bra because I see no need for it; my breasts are still "assertive," as my first woman lover used to say. When I dressed this way as a teenager in the 1960s, the men who called themselves my brothers treated me like meat. Now my students are disconcerted when they realize that they can see my nipples, but they must control their tongues as well as their hands. A tenured position is better than a suit of armor.

My black wool skirt and the cotton petticoat under it brush against my boots as I pace. My wide leather belt emphasizes the contrast between my small waist and my full hips, and it can also be used for other purposes. I am beginning to simmer with anger at Didrick's lateness, which is not surprising. She is the spoiled child of misguided professionals who have always given her expensive toys to substitute for their attention. I suppose they think that a university education is equivalent to the sports car they gave her for giving up her post–high school slacker life and moving back in with them. They, and she, have no idea with whom they are trifling.

The hesitant knock on my door may be meant to appease me, but it's the last straw. The purpose of a knock is to attract the hearer's attention, is it not? Brushing one's oversized knuckles lightly against the wood as if testing it for splinters seems as pointless as daydreaming in class.

When I pull the door open Didrick is already blushing. "I'm sorry I'm late, Doctor Chalkdust," she gasps, seeing my look. She lowers her head in my presence, which somewhat compensates for the fact that she is a good six inches taller than I am. At age nineteen, she could be called a baby butch or a tomboy brat. Her short sandy hair always looks like it's just come out of a wind tunnel. Like most young women, she is a bundle of contradictions. She obviously spends too much time trying to look as if appearance doesn't matter to her; she desperately wants other people to accept her as a cool dyke who knows the score. In her own language: *as if.*

"Didrick," I intone, trying to keep my temper on a leash, "you're in serious danger of failing this course. Do you know that? I've gone out of my way to help you pull up your socks and start learning how to express yourself, and you respond by wasting my time." I could drive her away from me forever, and she knows it. Perhaps this would be the ultimate way of hurting her.

She doesn't know how to start apologizing or explaining herself so she begins to stutter. "I thought—I thought, I mean I used the Spell Check on my last essay, and I thought it looked all right—." This kid is not a cyberpunk or cyberslut; she is a cyberfool who expects a machine to do the thinking for her. Her words make my hands itch.

I sigh. "I thought we could start by discussing that wretched essay, but I see how badly you need a reality check." She knows what this means, and she is already breathing hard. Her large hands are shaking and in another minute the crotch of her jeans will become visibly wet. I'm not willing to wait that long. "Take off your pants, Didrick," I tell her, "and keep my name in mind."

"Yes, Doctor Chalkdust," she answers, not daring to look me in the eyes. She has seen the diplomas on my office wall often enough to know that my first name is Athena. She also knows that for her, that name is unspeakable.

She steps out of her bunched jeans and man-styled underpants. Her long, muscular thighs and firm young ass gleam pearly in the office light. I know that she is embarrassed when anyone sees the triangle of curly light-brown hair at her crotch, and this knowledge makes me smile. "You know what to do," I warn. She is as slow as molasses today.

Quivering slightly in fear or anticipation, she bends over my desk and rests her head on her folded arms. I've decided to use my eighteen-inch wooden ruler because she finds it more humiliating than other means of correction. I will have trouble resisting the urge to break it over her lazy butt.

The first smack makes a satisfying sound and she jumps. The second and third dangerously stimulate my temper instead of soothing it. Against my better judgment, I want to see blood and hear the unwilling scream of a young rebel who has lost her mask. She is already whimpering, probably more from fear than from pain. For a slow learner, she has an uncanny ability to read my moods.

She also seems able to send the heat from her swollen clit into mine, and I can't (or won't?) block it out. Like everything else about this big colt, her reactions to me seem beyond reason. I would rather die than tell her this aloud, but her energy slams into me with a force that I can barely contain. In Portia's words: "my little body is aweary of this great world." When I was growing into womanhood, we were never told that we could channel the tides.

I'm not satisfied, not even close to it, but I know how dangerous it would be to go as far as I want to. In reality, I am at her mercy. I can see that the edges of my ruler have raised some little welts on her very red cheeks. She will heal from these minor wounds much sooner than my career would heal from the coup de grâce she could give me by telling someone over my head what takes place in this room. Too many of my colleagues have heard about the office renovations I had done last summer. Does anyone know that I had soundproof insulation put in, or why? Didrick can afford exposure no more than I can, but whether she can carry our little secret to the grave is another matter. After all, she told me her whole life story (admittedly not a long epic) during our first session.

I slide the ruler back into my desk, but she knows better than to move without permission. I can't resist running my right hand gently, slowly, over her hot cheeks while my left holds her hips in place. She flinches from my compassion as much as from my discipline. "You stubborn little girl," I murmur into one of her freckled ears. "How long do you think you can keep this up?"

I put my hand firmly on her neck to keep her down and to let her know that I'm here, I'm not going away, and I'm not going to lose faith or let her lose hers. A humble pencil on my desk attracts my attention. I reach for it as if I were planning to write a list of her grammatical sins on her back with its sharp little point. I withdraw from her just long enough to anoint the pencil with baby oil from a bottle on my desk. Then I find the small, puckered mouth between her butt cheeks and slide the eraser in until four inches of wood are embedded in the site of her punishment. She groans, and an uncontrollable shiver of pleasure seems to run all through her. Reaching between her legs, I find her cunt lips so wet that a little more attention will probably make the juice run down her legs.

The pointed end of the pencil looks like a little tail, and I wield it so that it dances in spirals and figure eights inside her, stroking walls of flesh that were never explored this way before I touched them. When I draw the pencil out it will be smeared with her shit, and she will blush to see it. I imagine running a steel pole into her hot, pulsing guts and raising her off the floor with it. I imagine her bleeding and crying—but never, never resisting me, even in her innermost core.

"Doctor Chalkdust," she whispers, begging. She needs to come soon, but she will hold off until I give her my blessing. I am tempted to find out how long she can last, but that test can wait for another day.

"Come for me, baby," I tell her, running the sharp burgundy fingernails of my right hand over her bursting clit. She jerks violently, trying to suppress a childish yell as the pencil probes her at an unexpected angle. Her thin veneer of machisma has melted away, leaving her face covered with tears. She convulses helplessly as I draw the pencil out of her and pull her down to the floor.

While she is still open and panting I pour oil into my left hand. Then I push each of my small, slick, well-manicured fingers into a cunt as wet and heaving as an ocean cave. I form a fist inside her and let it rock her the way it wants to.

She is afraid of exploding out of her skin. I know that she is ashamed of her needs and her ignorance but she is terrified of the possibility that in an instant I can change her into someone she doesn't recognize. Education is about transformation, and she feels as confused about that as all my other students do. I wonder if any of the others have dreamed of writhing on my fist in anguish and relief, screaming my name in the silence of their half-formed minds.

"Didrick," I call her, almost singing her name to the rhythm of my fist and her hips. "You have to give me more. I know you can." Her heat is rising up my arm, which is aching. Nonetheless, I won't stop until I'm finished. I know that this strong young animal plays on the women's basketball team. I picture myself fucking her in the gym, surrounded by her amused teammates. That would be a suitable penalty for writing another essay like her latest masterpiece.

She is crying, shaking, and gasping louder and louder, as if she is about to start howling like a wolf. I know that she wants to please me and is terrified of failing. In class she watches me when I call on my most articulate students for answers, and her face is an open book. I suspect that she wants to kill Reginald, my wannabe pet, who keeps inviting me to watch him rehearse with the other young Hamlets in the Shakespeare Club. Alas, poor Didrick—know ye not a budding queen when he poses before ye?

I am kneeling over my hapless pupil, who hasn't had a chance to catch her breath since her last climax. Now she seems about to erupt like a volcano. "Not yet," I warn her, pressing her cervix. "I'll be very angry if you come now."

My threat comes too late. Her hot cunt clutches my fist over and over, and the more she tries to control this greedy mouth, the more it talks back in its own way. My right hand checks out her clit and my gentlest stroke sets off a new wave of contractions. I suddenly wonder what she would look like giving birth.

She is soggy with spent energy, gratitude, shame, and guilt. I can see her bracing herself for a few strokes of my belt. I usually give six for disobeying an order. "I—I'm s—sorry," she snivels. "I couldn't help it, Doctor Chalkdust."

I feel generous. "Ssh," I soothe her, petting her head. She reminds me of a racehorse colt in training. I feel blessed to have such a powerful female creature under my control. "This time I'll let you make it up to me instead of punishing you, Didrick," I offer, "but stop blubbering or I'll change my mind."

She glows, and her blue eyes almost reflect an image of my body under my clothes. I want to shed all of them, but I can't allow her to be covered more modestly than I am. "Take your shirt off," I tell her. I know that she takes pride in her muscular arms, but the heat of my gaze on her small breasts makes her uncomfortable, so she grabs the hem of her tee shirt and pulls it roughly over her head as if to get the process over with as quickly as possible. Her pungent sports bra soon joins the pile of her clothing on the floor. I smile at her innocent pink nipples and she forces herself to seek approval in my eyes.

Without a word, I walk to the antique chaise lounge that stands in a corner of my office near the floor lamp with the ivory silk shade. I turn on the lamp and it casts amber light on the midnight-blue velvet that will soon receive my bare skin. "Turn off the overhead, Didrick," I tell her casually. She rushes to obey, and we are left in an intimate circle of light. The books on my shelves watch us from the darkness like discreet mentors.

I sit. "You may undress me," I offer, "beginning with my boots." She kneels at my feet and studies one small, creased leather boot as she carefully pulls the laces out of their holes.

After my boots are neatly placed, side by side, under my desk, Didrick raises her head and gasps as she sees my hair flowing over my shoulders, released from its pins. "You may bury your face in it when you get there," I tease. She blushes, and looks flustered as I stand up and slowly, deliberately, unbuckle my belt. She looks relieved when I hand it to her in a coil, like a sleeping snake, to place on my desk.

I turn my back to her, shaking my hair over my shoulders. She reverently unbuttons and unzips the back of my skirt as if it could easily tear. She is moving too slowly. "Hurry up, brat," I warn her. Her fumbling fingers pull the skirt downward and I must remind her to pull the petticoat down with it to save time. As I step out of the fabric at my feet, she waits awkwardly.

I remain standing for a moment so that she can take in my black satin panties and the matching garter belt that holds up my stockings. When I sit down, I gesture impatiently. She begins shakily unbuttoning my blouse. She removes the sleeves from my arms as gently as a loyal maid, but as she glances at my breasts, she can't keep the predatory gleam out of her eyes. I am reminded that I am making myself vulnerable to a newly ripened incarnation of the Amazons of old, a novice warrior who doesn't yet know her own strength. As I watch her, she drops her eyes as if sheathing a weapon that might give nightmares to a sheltered soul. Her chivalry pleases me even as it makes me see red.

"Sometimes you want to take me hard, don't you, honey?" I demand. As usual, she doesn't know what to say. "You can tell the truth, baby," I whisper in her ear as she kneels at my stockinged feet. She mumbles something and I tell her to repeat her answer.

"I want to satisfy you," she says bravely to my face. "If you'll let me, Doctor Chalkdust," she adds quickly.

I chuckle as I slide my panties down with one hand then kick them off. I gesture in a way she recognizes. She fastens her mouth on my left breast like a leech, sucking steadily as if she could pull the milk of knowledge out of my hard nipple. "Ahh," I sigh as one of her big hands envelops my right breast. Her mouth and her hand speak to my hungry pussy, and I can hardly sit still.

"I want your fingers, Didrick," I insist. "Now." I seem to be filled with boiling lava. I am so close to coming that my touchy clit could not stand any direct attention. I don't want to be tickled now. I want to be plowed.

She pushes two long fingers into me and begins to pump, slowly at first and then faster. A third finger, not wanting to be left out, finds room inside me. With her head against my heart, she fucks me tirelessly. Like a devoted knight in service to her queen, this child strokes me harder and deeper than anyone else I can remember.

Didrick, Baby Dyke, you move me more than I'm willing to tell you. I don't expect my heart and my mind to change much in the future. Why must yours?

Thank the Goddess for soundproof walls. I hear my own animal sound as if from a distance while large quakes and smaller tremors run all through me in quick succession. She stays deep inside me until my breathing has steadied.

I kiss the top of her head. "I have to be home soon, baby," I murmur into one of her protruding ears, "and so do you." Penelope is usually too tired for what she calls "lovemaking," but she is a good cook, and she no longer asks me to explain my absences in detail. After twelve years together, we are probably getting as much from each other as we can reasonably expect.

Didrick doesn't want to move. "Doctor Chalkdust," she asks, desperate to hold my attention for a moment longer, "did I split a lot of infinitives?"

The child can be trusted to screw up her priorities. Luckily for her, this topic no longer makes me feel rabid. "Yes," I laugh, "but that's one of your minor problems. I'm more concerned about your dangling modifiers and misplaced punctuation, paragraphs that are all over the map, and your argument as a whole." I sigh. "Didrick," I advise her as patiently as I can, "you need to learn how to think." I can't keep the sarcasm out of my voice.

She can't look at me because I have hurt her. She tries to hide her tears from me, and the sight of her wet gaze makes my cunt tighten. "You're so smart," she gushes. "I don't think I can ever—"

"Sshh," I silence her. "Never say *never*. I'll let you rewrite that essay. If it's still not clear, you'll rewrite it as many times as you need to. Until your logic would persuade the devil to change his mind."

Didrick's smile is part hopeful, part skeptical, and part sassy. "I've never been good at putting words down," she confesses. As her friends would say: *duh*. "Do you really think I can fix it that good?"

"You'll fix it *well*, honey," I threaten, "or you'll face the consequences."

She looks dangerously close to the psychic state I think of as her bottom trance. I stand up at once. "Turn on the overhead, Didrick," I remind her briskly. The circle has been opened.

As we both put on our clothes and prepare to face the outside world, split infinitives strut through my mind: to soundly thrash, to thoroughly fuck, to helplessly wriggle, to sweetly beg, to piercingly scream, to stubbornly love, to boldly go where few (or many) have gone before. I remember that rules were made to be broken, and that to fully live is to dance on the edge of a knife.

Didrick, you are my offering to the Goddess I serve. Don't bring my judgment into disrepute by messing up. "You have to come in again this week," I tell her. "Come here at one o'clock sharp on Wednesday to work on your essay. You'll be here all afternoon."

The brat can't hide her pleasure. "Cool," she grins. "I mean, yes, Doctor C."

How I Learned to Drive

Gitana Garofalo

I was an eleventh-grade baby butch when I learned how to drive. It was Erica who taught me. I didn't know terms like "butch" back then. I didn't know much of anything, but I knew I liked Erica.

As most farm kids do, Erica learned how to drive early—cars, trucks, tractors—and by senior year she already had her own car. She transferred to my high school for her last year and we got to know each other quickly, as the teachers frequently mistook us for one another. How Erica—athletic with straight black hair, and a grandmother on the reservation—could be confused with me—heavy, unathletic, and with skin several shades darker—was a mystery. Perhaps, to them, all girls who preferred jeans to skirts and cut their hair short looked the same. This wasn't new. I'd grown up being called boyish and mistaken for my younger brother, Carlos.

"Maricela, don't you like boys?" he asked me that fall. We were sitting outside, slapping away mosquitoes and putting off homework and chores.

"Sure, I like boys," I replied. I liked boys—boys like Erica. Erica, with her no-nonsense way of moving; Erica who drew wild cartoons in the margins of her notebook during study hall; Erica who ran on the track team and whose long, slow grin made my stomach do a back flip.

I spent the whole first week of school practicing how to say *hi,* but Erica beat me to it.

"Hey," she said, setting her tray on the scarred cafeteria table across from me.

"Hey," I gulped, suddenly losing my appetite.

"What's up?" she asked, not looking at me as she opened her milk carton.

"Uh, not much." I replied, kicking myself for sounding so stupid.

Erica looked up to say *hi* to a couple of passing teammates and then turned back to give me her leisurely grin. I glanced down at my sweaty hands curled on either side of the faded yellow lunch tray.

"Got any special plans for the weekend?" she was pushing her food around the plate. I noticed she wasn't eating either—a good sign.

"Not really," I answered, and then, clearing my throat, "Hey."

"Yeah?" She looked up.

"I was," I paused, "um, it's like, I was wondering," I stopped again. In my head this had all gone so smoothly. "Listen, would you teach me how to drive?" I blurted out, my face flushing and a trickle of nervous sweat sliding down my back.

"Sure, why not?" she replied, taking a swallow of milk. I slowly let my breath out in relief.

"But why didn't you just take driver's ed?" she asked, curious.

"I had to work after school and last summer so I never had time."

"Will you have time now for me to teach you?"

"Oh, yeah. I'm not working this year and anyway I just need some pointers and practice." My heart was pounding in my throat.

"Cool. When should we start?"

We used the parking lot behind the old grain elevator. Erica was a good teacher and it was so much better to be learning from her than from Mr. Shields, the driver's ed instructor. She was separate from all that, from my old life, and fast becoming the most exciting part of my new life—a life that would belong just to me, the me who was friends with Erica, who would have a driver's license, and someday live someplace far away like Duluth or Detroit.

We didn't become instantly inseparable with long nightly phone conversations or notes passed in the halls like other girls in our school. But we sat together at lunch and during last-period study hall and drove every day after school. One hot fall Friday we skipped school to practice for my driving test the next day. Getting into the car I noticed that something had shifted. Every word lingered a moment longer, the smell of Erica's shampoo clung to me, and her hand kept bumping mine.

Erica told me to try parallel parking so I collected my thoughts and shifted the car into reverse. We both turned to look over our shoulders and found ourselves face to face. Hitting the brake, I stared at her as we hung there—suspended only inches apart—hovering between backward and forward. Erica's eyes darkened; my lips parted; we leaned forward and kissed—a tentative lopsided kiss, but way better than in books or the movies. She pulled back and grinned at me. I blushed.

"Let's skip the rest of the lesson and go to the beach," I suggested before I could think about what I was saying.

"Okay, but I get to drive."

I nodded, staring at her lips and her cheek, and the curve of her ear partly hidden by the old baseball cap she always wore. We switched places, drew our seat belts over our chests, and pealed out of the parking lot with a squeal of tires. We flew down the deserted highway—a wavering tarmac mirage—away from town and toward the lake, the beach, each other.

We found a good place to pull off the road and hide the car and then scrambled under low gnarled trees and through dense undergrowth to reach the sandy beach. It was completely deserted—no houses or people in sight. I sat down and pulled off my sneakers so I could bury my feet in the hot sand. We both turned our baseball caps backwards and walked a short distance until we found a sheltered bowl of sand that was protected on three sides but open to the lake.

Sitting and watching the endless expanse of water, the whitecaps crashing into shore, we were awkward and silent. Glancing at each other, we leaned in at the same moment to kiss, but bumped noses so hard we pulled back laughing before trying again, more carefully this time. We kissed for a long time, then I put my hands on her shoulders and pushed her back onto the sand. Erica reached up to take my hat off and tangled her hands in my curls before pulling me on top of her. I was anxious at first, afraid that I'd be too heavy for her, too fat, but then she was dragging me down for a kiss that made the bottom drop out of my stomach and every worry disappear. Emboldened, I slid my knee between her legs to press up into her.

"Can I touch them?" I asked, both shy and eager, as I pushed up her sweatshirt. She nodded and gasped as I drew my finger across one nipple then the other. My mouth followed and, without thinking, I drew the fabric-covered nipple into my mouth, sucking and then gently running the ridge of my teeth over first one then the other. Erica moaned and arched up into my mouth while thrusting her hands under my T-shirt and running them over my sports bra. She looked up at me for permission.

"Leave it on," I said.

She nodded, but didn't take her hands away. Instead, she began pressing my breasts into me, rolling my nipples between her fingers. It was my turn to gasp and arch. I sat back and pulled my shirt over my head, throwing it aside.

"Take your shirt off?" I asked.

"You do it," she replied, lifting her arms so I could pull her sweatshirt over her head and remove her bra. Inhaling her scent, I nuzzled into her warm salty skin. Her mouth was on me again and I lost track of where I ended and she began. I'd always hated my breasts, but in Erica's mouth they felt different—hard, urgent, strong, alive—a hidden mirror of her own naked chest.

Then she flipped me. Stretched out below her, my hands caressing her shoulders, circling her neck, tracing the curve of her back, cupping her buttocks, I spread my legs to allow one of hers in between. We began to rub against each other, wet seeping through our jeans, breath coming in hiccuping pants as we built momentum. Erica, her face beaded with sweat, moved even harder. I thrashed my head from side to side, as if saying no but meaning yes, and cut my cheek on a clump of sharp beach grass. Blood trickled into my mouth; blood rushed from my brain down to my pussy; blood throbbed at the tips of my fingers which were tugging at the fly of Erica's jeans. She pushed my hands away and continued to rock and rub her leg between mine. I began to shudder, my pelvis bucking, taking Erica with me—the undulations of my body bearing her up in the air. I was exploding, breaking the surface, and crashing harder than the nearby waves.

Embarrassed, I hid, shutting my eyes and worrying about how I looked—sweaty face, jiggling stomach, bouncing breasts—stupid, fat, ugly. Softly Erica kissed my shoulder, neck, cheek, and, finally, my mouth. I opened my eyes and looked at her. Holding my gaze with hers, she pulled off her jeans and boxers, leaving them pooled in the sand. Erica's legs, darker than her torso, but not as dark as her arms, surprised me. Everyone in my family had uniformly dark brown skin. Seeing so many gradations of color on one person was like seeing a new kind of body.

Lying on her side next to me, Erica kissed me and slid my hand between her legs. All I could think was how incredibly warm and silky she was inside. She was wet too, making it easy to slip my fingers into her. I started rubbing, first in circles then back and forth. Erica spread her legs, opening up to me and breathing, "Yes, yes, yes," into my mouth. But then she put her hand over mine.

"Stop for minute," she whispered. I stopped, but didn't pull out. I didn't want to stop touching her in this new and electrifying way. Instead we kissed slowly and I held my hand still, all the while aching to turn her inside out the way she just had done to me. Then Erica started to move my hand. Gradually she let go as I kept up the same motion, following her lead—quick then slow—marveling at how she looked strong and raw, distant and vulnerable. Erica came with a series of jagged movements and rough growling grunts. Unlike me, she didn't hide after coming. Instead she snuggled close to me where we lay on the warm sand—wet and woozy as newborn animals.

Slowly the day came back into focus. Looking around, we laughed at the mess of tangled clothes. After shaking the sand out of everything and getting dressed, we lay down again, my body spooning Erica's, our heads resting on a folded sweatshirt. She dozed off, her body twitching from time to time, but I remained wide awake. Curling closer around her, I savored the new spaces in my body and knew that I was ready for more than tomorrow's driving test.

Back in the Saddle
Skian McGuire

Weegee whisked the sheet off her latest masterpiece. "The client said she wanted something different, and not just a vibrator," she said, and looked at us expectantly. Shiv and I stared at it—openmouthed, in Shiv's case—then looked at each other.

The contraption looked like a cross between an old motorcycle and a weirdly futuristic vibrator. There was a saddle seat with handles on either side. The sissy bar had been fashioned into a well-padded upright panel. The whole thing was wired, with multicolored lines snaking to the floor.

"Jeez," Shiv said at last, "what's wrong with her own hand?"

Weegee blinked.

"It's hard to forget whose hand it is, I guess," she answered, far more mildly than I expected. Shiv wouldn't have been invited to the unveiling at all except for the fact that she was my houseguest. Between evictions, Shiv usually ended up back with me. Lucky for both of us, my own landlord was pretty easygoing. She just needed somebody she could call on at a moment's notice to admire the latest product of her ingenuity.

I reached out and cautiously stroked the part that looked like a saddle.

"That's not leather, is it?" Leather would be hard to clean. Besides, it didn't really feel like leather, unless it was some expensive kind I'd never met before. You couldn't put it past Weegee.

"No, it's a new kind of elastomer. Wait a sec." Weegee turned around and started typing; there was a computer on a cart behind her that I hadn't noticed when she ushered us in here. "Watch this," she said, still facing the monitor.

"Well, what about somebody else's hand then?" Shiv continued undeterred, "What is she, some kind of recluse amputee?"

Now it was Weegee's turn to stare. Hell, I wouldn't have thought Shiv knew those words, either. I shrugged. Weegee rolled her eyes and went back to typing.

The black leatherlike stuff was definitely getting warmer under my hand. As I watched, a small lump appeared in the middle of the seat. Next thing I knew, a blob the size of a largish cucumber had sprung up, gleaming obscenely in the fluorescent overhead light.

"Gyaah!" I yanked my hand back, the dinner-table scene from *Alien* flashing through my mind.

"Whoops." Weegee hit a few more keys. The blob subsided gradually. "It doesn't do that if there's somebody on it."

Beside me, I heard Shiv swallow hard. "*On* it?" She looked a little green around the gills.

Weegee shot her an impatient look. "Well, *yeah*. What'd ya think?" She hit another key. This time the blob grew slowly. Soon, a smaller, skinnier blob appeared right behind it.

"Hooo-ah," I said softly, reaching out to touch it again. I ran one hesitant finger up and down the larger projection, then laid my palm flat on the seat in front of it. There seemed to be a gentle swelling there, too. The whole thing was a little tingly to the touch, as if it were vibrating very, very faintly.

"What do you mean," I asked carefully, "it doesn't do that if there's somebody on it?"

Weegee came over and knelt by the machine. "Look," she said, pointing at the base of the saddle, "this isn't just a polymer skin on an assembly. The seat here is a macrocomponent itself, imbedded with hundreds of tiny hydraulic cells and thousands of electronic sensors. I've been working on this for *weeks*."

"What, on your coffee breaks?" Shiv quipped. We both knew how Weegee worked; she could knock off a rough draft for something like a 3-D holographic projection TV design before breakfast and have the rest of the day free for the really important things, like state-of-the-art sex toys.

Weegee ignored her. "It senses weight; it knows whether there's somebody on it. That automatically limits the speed of probe formulation. Failsafe. Foolproof."

"Probe formulation?" Shiv repeated.

"It detects resistance." Weegee went on. "And nonresistance. That is to say, the places where something *isn't*."

Shiv and I both looked at her blankly. She stood up and looked back at us with a pained expression. "You know," she said finally, "holes." She turned back to the computer and tapped in a few more commands. The blobs disappeared into the not-quite-shiny, not-quite-matte-black surface.

"The sensors detect weight, resistance, temperature, and galvanic skin response, here," she went on briskly, pointing to the saddle, "and here." She pointed to a pair of what looked like handles, one on either side of the saddle. "Here, too," she said, pointing to another pair of handles at the top of what was once the sissy bar.

"Your old Kawasaki?" Shiv asked.

Weegee blushed. "I don't fabricate things I don't have to." She pushed a lever on the base of the saddle and the sissy bar tilted further back. "There are no sensors in that, just in the handles." She pushed another lever and frowned. The whole thing tilted back and things that looked like footrests swung into a higher position.

"I've been trying to make it user-posturable for prone or supine, but I don't think it can work that way. Not comfortably, anyway."

Shiv looked at me for a translation. "Back or belly down," I said. "I think."

Weegee pursed her lips. "So," she said, "I think I'll have to do a second one for prone. Oh, I almost forgot." She framed a rectangle with her hands around the place where the probes protruded. "This area here," she said, pointing with her chin, "also detects moisture. So," she said brightly, "do you want to try it?" Her eyes were locked on mine.

Shiv had already taken a step backward, and her eyebrows had disappeared up under her head wrap. I closed my mouth. We both turned to look at the not-quite-closed drapes, which were all that screened this glass-walled conference room from the rest of Weegee's bustling R&D department.

"No, no, not *now!*" Weegee jingled a set of keys. "After hours!"

"Oh, God," I muttered. Did she really think I was stupid enough to go along with this? "Later, Weegee. Later."

I could hear Shiv's voice behind me as I headed out the door.

"Do you, like, have a user's manual?"

I dragged her out of there.

It was another week before Weegee came knocking on my door. According to my small wild-eyed friend, both the prone and the supine models were now ready for product testing. "So...what do you say?" She bounced a set of keys from hand to hand.

"What, do you think I'm nuts? Besides," I added, "I don't even know how it works."

"Oh, that's easy. You just get on. It boots up automatically. The voice menu asks you a few questions, you answer them. From there on, the device responds to your body readings to provide the optimal orgasmic experience. Or you can run it from the demo program."

I just looked at her.

"Well, here," she said dropping the keys on my hall table on her way out, "think about it. Now that the Wiltron project is done, there won't be anyone in the shop until Monday at eight. You've still got the keycodes, right?" Of course I had the keycodes. Keeping an eye on the place was part of my rent. The three sets of numbers were jotted on the back of my wall calendar, as always.

"Yeah, yeah, yeah," I told her. "But, look, I really don't—"

She cut me off. "So maybe you'll have a bored moment." Bored moments were not something with which Weegee was personally familiar. She was closing the door behind her when I remembered what I wanted to ask.

"Weeg," I called out. The door swung back open. "Have *you* tried it?"

"Elena and I have been putting the devices through their paces while we worked the bugs out, of course. Oh, that reminds me. There have been a few minor alterations on the Mach 1 since the day you saw it. There are some elasticized straps on the handles, now. A few velcro bands, here and there. That sort of thing." She cleared her throat. "You know."

I looked at her, puzzled. Was Weegee getting shy about bondage in her old age? "Elastic? Velcro?" I asked. "Doesn't Elena trust you anymore?" Sheepskin and little padlocks were more Weegee's style.

"It's really meant to be used alone, you know," she said huffily. "I didn't want anybody getting stuck, alone in a deserted work—ah, alone, ah, anywhere."

"Ah," I said, grinning. "And how is it, all—," The door shut with a thud. "—alone?"

Not that I really wanted to know.

I didn't get home from the bar until nearly four. It took the managers four tries to count the cash drawers and come up with the same figure before we could make the deposit that night. I hadn't even flicked on the lights in my apartment before I spotted the alarm readouts flashing like a Christmas tree just inside the door.

"Shit," I muttered. I didn't need this. I forced myself to calm down and decipher the damn thing; after all, if there had been a real break-in, the whole board would be flashing and the place would probably already be crawling with cops. Sometimes a power failure can make some of the secondaries flash red. Sometimes a tremor will set off a motion detector. No big deal.

"Shiv?" I yelled into the closet Shiv uses as a bedroom. I didn't mind waking her up. Live in my apartment and *mi job es su job*. "Shiv!"

Her bed was empty.

The indicators pinpointed Weegee's R&D section, but the primaries hadn't been triggered. Probably not a real break-in—yeah, tell that to my pulse rate, I thought, running through the other possibilities in my head. "Shit," I muttered again. No choice but to go look.

The elevator door slid shut behind me as I juggled the flash-light to wipe my sweaty palms. "Okay, okay," I muttered, trying to steady my hand enough to tap in the code.

A bank of fluorescents lit up the area just inside the door, but nothing stirred. The usual clutter of machines and high worktables, stools, and rolling computer carts loomed in the dimly lit reaches. Was that a glow coming from one of the conference rooms? I took a deep breath and moved out of the circle of light.

The door was ajar. As my heart quieted down to normal, I thought I could make out the sound of distant, tinny music. I dismissed the notion of an industrial spy equipped with a boom box. Maybe Weegee hadn't gone away for the weekend, after all. Maybe she and Elena had had a fight; it would be just like Weegee to drown her sorrows in work. Or maybe, I realized as a grin spread over my face, in some late-night "product testing."

Good thing she hadn't troubled to close that conference-room door, I thought as I tiptoed toward it—I hadn't even thought of grabbing the keys on my way down here. Oh, this would be well worth the panic I'd had before. I suppressed a chuckle. The glow, now that I could see through the door, was a TV on a cart. Bad music from a soundtrack that sounded like it was recorded underwater could only mean one thing: as I quietly pushed the door open, I noted the huge straining cock filling the screen and the mustached mouth riding up and down on it. Fag porn—Weegee's favorite. I tried to suppress my grin as I turned to face my little friend and her newest toy.

Blue light flickered across naked legs straddling the ink-black saddle. Blue light shone greasily off the scuffed black Wellingtons that were hooked into the stirrups. My eyes followed the expanse of white skin—long, skinny legs, bent at the knee, a scraggly edge of dark bush above a crotch-obscuring bulge that looked like a saddle horn, the gleaming zippers of a biker jacket framing a rail-thin torso, big hands with long, skinny fingers cupping two nearly nonexistent tits, kneading, squeezing the nipples. The narrow face, blank and slack-jawed for once. The ever-present bandanna.

Shiv.

I shook my head in disbelief. Did she expect me to cover for her if the alarm brought the police?

She hadn't heard me come in. While I watched, she let go of her nipples and grabbed for the handles overhead. Her face contorted and her hips bucked. On the screen, the mustached hunk was now on all fours, smiling back at the blond, who was guiding his enormous dick between the hunk's butt cheeks. Without a second thought, I had my cuffs out and ratcheted one on Shiv's knobby wrist.

"Hey!"

I grabbed for the other wrist before she could yank it away. In seconds, she was trussed fore and aft, thanks to the straps Weegee had thoughtfully provided. I snugged the last one around Shiv's boot and came up to find her grinning at me. A low hum came from the Mach 1, and Shiv's eyes slowly closed. Her hips began to move again.

"You asshole." I rubbed my weary eyes. I nearly pissed myself for *this?*

"Yeah," she gasped, "cunt, too." She sucked in a hissing breath and started rocking harder.

"Christ." I swung around the machine, looking for a switch. "I'm serious, you shithead. How do you turn this thing off?"

Shiv was gritting her teeth and grunting. The smell of sweat and pussy and leather filled the small room, which suddenly seemed much too hot. I straightened up, lightheaded, and looked down at Shiv's pale belly, undulating. The teeth of the jacket zipper sawed against her rigid nipples as she moved. I licked my lips and tried again. "Shiv, you can't just wander through the building. If you'd just told me—"

Shiv let out something halfway between a grunt and a groan.

"Shiv!" I barked, "Where's the fucking switch?"

She arched her body and went stiff, jerking as she came. I clenched my teeth, trying to ignore my own heavy breathing.

At last, she opened her eyes and looked up at me, all innocence. "I dunno," she said, "I just told it to start." She shut her eyes again suddenly, with a look of concentration. The Mach 1 whined softly; somewhere deep in its guts there was a muffled clunk like something changing gears. Then Shiv gave a high, braying, annoying laugh I knew all too well. "Here comes number three!" she choked out.

"Well, tell it to stop!"

She threw me another wide-eyed look. "Tell it yourself." She breathed out hard and began very slightly, very gently, to squirm.

"If that's what you want—," I said, reaching for the lever Weegee had used. It took hardly any muscle to tilt the backrest almost horizontal. I pushed aside the jacket and took Shiv's nipple between my fingers. "—You can leave the driving to me." I squeezed hard.

Shiv winced. "Shit," she breathed, "I can just tell it—"

I covered her lips with mine. Her tongue pushed into my mouth, and I felt her groan deep in her throat as she pushed her body forward against my hand. My cunt flooded.

"It's a goddamn shame you didn't pick the other one to try," I growled, coming up for air. "If you were belly down, I'd beat your ass ragged."

"Promises, promises."

I turned on my heel. Shiv's demented giggle followed me out into the workroom.

It wasn't hard to round up the things I wanted. Shiv actually opened her eyes and stared at me when I slapped a strip of duct tape over her mouth. Was that a look of panic? Fat chance. Gleeful anticipation, maybe. Oughta just shut her down and leave, let my shitbird buddy stew in her own juices a while, that's what I ought to do. I sighed. I do like my fun.

I trailed the ends of a bundle of twelve-gauge wires down the middle of her belly. She shivered and squirmed against the probes.

"Ticklish?" I knew she was. Her eyes narrowed. She tried to hold still while I danced the strands back and forth over her ribs, but it was no use. She struggled against her bonds, and garbled sounds that were surely curses came from under the tape. Not that she was trying to get away; her half-closed eyes fluttered and her pelvis pumped.

"Do you want me to stop?" Now I could see a hint of panic. She shook her head from side to side, emphatically.

I chuckled. "You know what to do if you want me to stop, right?"

Shiv nodded vigorously.

"Not that I ought to." I pressed her knees as wide apart as they would go. "I ought to teach you a lesson." I smacked the wires down hard. Shiv sucked in a hissing breath through her nose.

First the right thigh, then the left: I kept up a steady rain of blows until the plastic-coated wires started to slip in my sweaty hand. Behind me, grunts and growls had risen to a fever pitch. I turned to see technicolor jism spurting across the screen; when I turned back, Shiv's body was tensed, waiting. Dark eyes watched me warily from above the duct tape.

"I've got something for you," I told her. I fished an ice cube out of a styrofoam cup and pressed it against her left thigh. "Ah, now you're paying attention." I slid the melting ice from knee to belly until it was gone. Shiv pulled her leg back hard, away from the cold, at first; by the time I'd fumbled the third cube onto her skin, her muffled yelps had become something else. I ran the melting ice across her writhing belly until a puddle glistened in her navel. I pushed her jacket out of the way and rubbed the slick ice on each of her rock-hard nipples.

Droplets glinted in Shiv's dark bush; a sheen of wet gleamed off the plane of her belly and the swell of her small breasts. Her chest rose and fell; her head arched back. I couldn't resist; I ran my tongue along the line of her throat and fastened my mouth on her for a good hard suck. That would be hard to ignore tomorrow. Shiv didn't mind. She turned her face toward my head and nuzzled against my hair.

Feeling my way to the right spot, I snapped an alligator clip on one rigid nub. Shiv's skull knocked into mine as the jolt of pain hit her like an electric current. I had to brace one forearm across her and bring all my weight to bear, just to get the other clip on. She was thrashing so hard I started to worry about the velcro straps around her boots. She was glaring at me and roaring under the duct tape; I took pity on her.

"Do you want to yell now?" I ripped the tape from her face. Her scream cut off in mid-bellow, her breath taken away; tears squeezed out of her tightly shut eyelids.

"Oh, God," she breathed.

On the screen, the bandido's ass rode up and down on the blonde's stiff cock, the sun catching his halo of golden pubic hair every time the bandido lifted off. Deep in the Mach 1, something shifted gears, and Shiv sagged against the back rest.

"Oh, God," she said again, deeper and more emphatically.

I bent to kiss her, quick and light. "Yeah, babe," I breathed, "It's me between your legs, fucking your ass." My hand pressed down on her belly, damp with sweat, tensing and moving. "Is it big? Is it deep?"

I brought my hand up and brushed against the alligator clips. She winced. "Answer me," I ordered. "How big is my cock in your ass?" I lifted my hand.

"Jesus, it's big. Christ, it's huge."

I smiled and laid the flat of my hand just above her mound, pressing against her taut abs as she arched. She was grunting deep in her throat, hips rocking, grinding against the saddle horn.

"Oh, shit, I'm coming, oh, shit, oh, shit," she murmured. Her eyes were screwed shut. "Oh, *yeah!*"

I grabbed the bobbing clips and yanked them off. Shiv screamed. I did my best to suck the moving targets of her nipples into my mouth as Shiv stiffened and arched and yelled. At last, a shudder ran through her, and she went still. Gently, I caught the edges of her head-wrap between thumbs and forefingers and tugged it into place on her forehead. I bent to kiss the damp cloth.

Beneath us, the machine still hummed. I scrambled for the keyboard. Behind me, Shiv smacked dry lips and cleared her throat, whispering something I couldn't quite make out. Hurriedly, I ran down the menu with the mouse pointer. Where the hell was the "escape" button? The Mach 1 whined.

"Program off! Program off," Shiv barked, "oh, shit! Off!"

She was shivering with the chill of drying sweat. I unlocked the cuffs. She pulled her jacket tight around her.

"Where are your pants?" I asked her; it had just occurred to me to wonder if she had come all the way down here without them. I heaved a sigh of relief when she stretched one bony finger to point, Jacob Marley–like, into the dark corner behind the TV, now showing nothing but blue screen as the video automatically rewound.

"Let's get you home," I told her as I helped her down from her mount. "I'll take care of this stuff," I offered generously, waving a hand at the disordered conference room. I escorted her back to the elevator to see her off. "I'll be along in a bit," I told her as the door closed. "Don't wait up."

I locked the R&D entrance behind me. I regarded the Mach 1, now cold and silent in the bright blue glow of the TV. The small room still smelled of sweat and pussy. I rubbed at the sticky film on the black surface. "What kind of cleaner does Weegee use?" I wondered aloud. "Probably keeps some handy, huh." I scanned the small room. The video box lay face down on lower shelf of the cart. I bent to retrieve it. *Back in the Saddle Again,* I read, leaning back, hand on hip, to check out the blurb. My elbow connected with something, and I turned to look.

I'd hardly noticed the thing before, distracted by the show already in progress. The Mach 2 was just as sleek and black as its older sister, a little higher off the ground, and instead of a sissy bar at the back, it had a handlebarlike arrangement in front that made me think more of a crotch-rocket than Weegee's old scoot. Foot pegs stood out from its lower skirt, with what looked like loops of rubber hanging from them.

I hit the "play" button.

"Steady, now," I said, after my chukkas and work pants had found their way to the same corner Shiv's had. I planted my bare right foot on the peg and slung a leg over. "Steady, girl." The smooth surface was already starting to warm. I felt something shift as the saddle started molding itself to my shape. On the screen, tumbleweeds rolled outside a corral fence. Somewhere, a horse whinnied.

"Giddyap," I said.

Water Music

Elspeth Potter

It was snowing when they finally climbed out of the Jeep after six long hours. "What is this place?" Cara asked, plunging her hands as far into the pockets of her biker jacket as she could manage, and stomping her boots in the frozen mud of the road. Snow collected quickly on her dark flattop haircut, and there was nothing in sight but trees, trees, and more trees. She didn't mind wilderness, but she hated being cold—not that she would ever admit it to anyone.

Why was she doing this? Going on a mysterious trip with her martial-arts instructor? Had she lost her tiny mind? Was she that desperate, or was Mariko that beautiful? Not to mention the intriguing hint of tattoo ink she'd sometimes glimpse as Mariko shrugged on a robe in the changing room...Hell, she wasn't even sure if this was a date or not.

It seemed like a date. Mariko had asked her to go for a drive after afternoon class. A surprise, she'd said, for her favorite student. And Cara, wanting to impress Mariko with her adventurous nature, had said yes. All she'd been told was that there would be food and a place to sleep. A place to sleep *with* Mariko? James Dean wouldn't ask that question, Cara reflected.

"There's shelter over here," Mariko said, playing a flashlight over the snowy ground ahead. Her sleek wool coat and equally sleek bobbed black hair sparkled with melted droplets in the reflected light. She wore snug red leather driving gloves that matched her scarf, and polished black boots that clung to her muscular calves. "My uncle owned this place. You can't see the whole thing; there's another path that goes uphill to the cabin." As Cara trudged behind, Mariko added, "Once I held a party out here—"

"In the snow?"

"No." A shabby-looking wooden building stood before them. Mariko pushed the door open—it creaked—and Cara followed her inside.

It was hot. "Great," she said. "First I freeze, then I melt."

Mariko pulled on an electric light and looked up at her, the chain still clasped in her gloved hand. "You don't like your surprise? We can go somewhere else if you want."

Mariko's politeness intensified Cara's embarrassment. "Oh, very funny. Would you really drive me home all that way if I asked?"

Mariko's eyes met hers, steadily. "Yes."

Cara looked away. The heat came from steam that rose in leisurely tendrils from a pool of water. The air had a strange mineral smell, nice after the biting air outside. "What are we here for, anyway?"

Mariko's face turned a weird hue. With a shock of surprise, Cara realized that her instructor was blushing. Mariko said, "The whole idea is to sit in the water. Without any clothes on. I thought you'd like it."

"Oh," Cara said. "I knew that. Sure. That's great. Thank you, Mariko." She lightly rapped her boot heel against the rock floor, then bent down and inspected the water. Looking around for hooks, she found them embedded in the wooden wall. Cara slipped off her leather jacket and slowly began to unbutton her denim shirt.

"It's very relaxing," Mariko said behind her. There was a small jingle—the Jeep keys being set down. Mariko said, "I'll go and get juice from the cabin."

"Thanks," Cara said, putting her boots on a bench so that water wouldn't get slopped into them.

Mariko returned a few minutes later carrying bottles in a string bag and a pile of towels that must have come from the cabin. Civilized accommodations, it looked like. Cara watched from the corner of her eye as Mariko stood next to her and stripped quickly, shivering, her nipples in tiny hard peaks. Undressed, as dressed, she looked sleek, like an otter or a seal. Cara felt more like a Labrador retriever, muscular and stocky, tending to scratch at the wrong times. Yet in bare feet, they were precisely the same height. "I'm going in," Mariko said, and Cara watched her gingerly dip in her toe.

Cara couldn't look away from Mariko's smooth, muscular back. Huge green-and-blue wing tattoos adorned her like paintings on porcelain, and were much larger and more elaborate than Cara had suspected. The feathers flexed with slight movements of Mariko's shoulders. Mariko glanced back as if sensing Cara's intense gaze.

Cara stared at the floor, stripped off her underwear, and went down the steps carved into the rock, trying to imagine herself covered up to hide the blush that seemed to go down to her feet. The water was hotter than she'd expected, but to her aching muscles the temperature was exquisite. She sighed deeply as she sank in up to the neck, sitting on a ledge across from Mariko. In a few moments she was sweating and understood the reason for the cold juice. Cara took a long swig from her bottle. The icy cold was a magic contrast to the steaming water.

What had she gotten herself into? Why couldn't she just proposition the woman and get it over with? It had always worked before. But somehow Mariko was different. So why couldn't Mariko get her act together and do the propositioning? Then everything would be easy.

Mariko settled in a little lower and rested her head on the edge. Then she sat up, reached for one of the folded white towels, and tucked it under her neck. "Perfect," she said, staring up at the ceiling.

Cara took another swallow of her juice, watching Mariko through half-closed eyes. She felt absolutely limp.

"You've been staring at me, Cara."

Surprised, Cara sat up a little. "No, I haven't." She grinned and said, "Not that I wouldn't."

Mariko didn't answer her feeble attempt at flirtatious humor. "Earlier," she said. "In the gym. At my tattoos."

Cara hesitated, but curiosity won out. And she had to make a move sometime. "Can I see?"

"I don't see why not." Mariko waded over to her and turned around, as matter-of-fact as if they'd been fully clothed at Tigress Defense. "Go ahead."

Carefully Cara traced her fingers over the wings, marveling at the gradations of color. Mariko's skin was soft. Suddenly shy, Cara let her hand fall. "Thank you," she said.

Mariko shrugged and sat down next to her, her side against Cara's. The unexpected skin contact was electric. "Have another juice?" she asked.

"No, thanks," Cara said, glad to have something to say, flustered from having Mariko so close to her. You win, Mariko, she thought, with an imaginary salute. She slid her arm around Mariko's shoulders and pulled her a fraction closer. "About the juice—there's an outhouse, or something?"

"Or something," Mariko said, reaching up and brushing her fingers through Cara's damp hair. "There's even a real shower."

Quickly, Cara said, "How long do you think it will take before we parboil?"

"Days," Mariko said. This was definitely a pass. Mariko worked an arm around Cara's waist and passed the other over her breasts, circling the nipples. "Isn't this interesting?"

Deliberately, Cara slowed her breathing. "Yes."

Mariko dragged her fingers through the water trickling down Cara's sternum. Cara tensed. Mariko licked her own fingertips, reached up, and touched Cara's mouth. Her hand dropped and lazily circled on Cara's left breast. A small gasp escaped Cara when Mariko flicked the nipple with her nail.

"Do you want to—," Cara began, her voice unsteady.

"Hold still." Mariko stood up and curved her palm against Cara's neck, then resettled in Cara's lap, facing her. Cara braced Mariko's muscular waist with her hands and leaned forward to trace her mouth over Mariko's forehead then slid down to her lips for a long, slippery kiss. Cara identified the growing ache in her stomach as hunger, consuming hunger that blotted out her mind. It was so strong it seemed to blot out her mind.

Mariko was making her crazy. Cara pulled back, gasping for breath. Mariko began to nibble on the side of her neck, and a small sound caught in Cara's throat.

"Slow down," Cara said, eyes shut, neck arched into Mariko's mouth. A long moment later, she sat up and could think again through the haze of hormones.

Cara grasped Mariko's waist and stood, slipping off-balance for a moment until she found her feet. She gave an experimental lift. "Edge, sit on the edge, here."

"Tell me you want me, Cara," Mariko said, her eyes glazed, her hair in wild tendrils. She looked as if she were about to attack Cara in a flurry of limbs. She looked impossibly desirable.

Cara needed a full minute to control her breathing enough to speak. "Mariko," she said, low in her throat. "I want you."

Mariko held Cara's gaze for a moment more. "Your voice is so beautiful like that." With one smooth movement Mariko lifted herself and sat on the edge of the pool. Water cascaded down her body in a sheet.

Cara kissed a spot just above Mariko's knee and murmured into her thigh. "I want you," she repeated. Mariko's scent mingled with that of the steaming water and the leather smell lingering on Cara's own flesh. "Tell me I can have you."

"Yes," Mariko hissed, gasping when Cara kissed a feverish path across her inner thigh. "Talk to me."

Mariko couldn't possibly know what it did to Cara when language became sex; she couldn't let Mariko know how turned on she was when they'd only just begun. "Can't do two things at the same time," Cara growled, parting Mariko's labia with one long wet stroke of her tongue. Mariko made a choked sound and Cara felt momentary triumph. "You're mine now," she said.

"So—so I—make you crazy, right?"

"I knew you were out to get me," Cara said, replacing her mouth with her hand and lightly stroking Mariko's labia. She kissed Mariko's abdomen and spoke quietly against her damp skin. "It's true, isn't it?"

Mariko was unnaturally still for a long moment. "Oh...I felt that inside..."

"Yes, you're making me crazy. Why are you doing this to me?" Cara said, then resumed her finger's gentle circling, nearer to Mariko's clit. "I can't stop until you're not so...not so...hot and wet and making me want you."

"Yes," Mariko gasped. "Don't stop."

Hardly conscious of what she was saying, intent on watching Mariko's reactions to every minute shift of her index finger, Cara said, "I'll win."

"At?"

"You'll come first."

"No," Mariko replied, the effect somewhat spoiled by a drawn-out moan.

Cara's fingers were dripping. She took a deep breath and smeared the back of her hand with Mariko's slick fluid, then coated her palm. Mariko looked down at her and slowly nodded, her dark eyes huge. Cara slid a finger inside her, biting her lip as Mariko's vagina sucked gently at it. She took another deep breath and closed her eyes, then slipped in two fingers. Then four.

"Hurry up," Mariko groaned.

Cara grinned, her cheek pressed against Mariko's thigh. A fantasy come true. "No."

"Bitch." Mariko's moan took the sting from the word.

Cara moved her hand gently, her own body calming down as she concentrated on Mariko. She maneuvered her wrist, allowing her fingers to curl under.

"Hurry *up.*"

"Why, when this is so much fun?" One push. With a soft feeling of suction, Cara's entire fist slid inside. Mariko encased her hand in hot, slick muscle.

Mariko gasped out an exclamation in Japanese and dug her wiry fingers into Cara's hair. A slow smile crawled over Cara's face. Experimentally, she flexed her fingers a fraction of an inch and was rewarded with a parallel reaction. "Is this all right?" she asked softly.

Mariko's response was unmistakable, though Cara knew no Japanese. Cara rotated her wrist first to the left then to the right, then pushed gently. "Like that, Mariko?"

"Yes," Mariko moaned. "Just—just—"

She looked as if she were dying, if dying could look like art. Gently Cara twisted her wrist again, judging Mariko's elasticity, then pushed rhythmically. At the third repetition, Mariko moaned softly.

"Relax," Cara murmured, slowing down. "Relax."

Mariko moaned again.

"You're mine, you said you were mine. You have to do what I say."

Again, Mariko called out in Japanese.

"Let me have you," Cara purred. Once. Twice.

"No—"

Three times. Four.

Mariko made no sound as she came, but her inner muscles contracted with crushing force, trapping Cara's hand. Cara breathed raggedly with pain and satisfaction. "Let go," she rasped, trying to command, but Mariko probably couldn't hear her, was beyond such control anyway. Cara waited, panting, until she could pull free of her, then cradled her hand against her chest, sinking into the water. Mariko slid down next to her, and curled into Cara's side. Cara stroked her back and nuzzled at her ear.

"Well," she said, then couldn't think of anything else for long moments. Finally she asked, "After that, do I win something? Free lessons, maybe? Just kidding."

Mariko didn't—maybe couldn't—answer. Cara smiled and stretched under the water, contemplating her success with lazy pleasure.

Finally, Mariko said, in a voice that sounded slightly drunk, "Ohhh, Cara. There's a cabin. But..."

Mariko's hand wandered over Cara's stomach and began to circle on her hip under the water, rekindling dormant arousal.

"Here," Cara said. She wasn't sure what else to say. Then Mariko's mouth was closing gently over hers, languid, a wet and sensuous kiss. The urgent need Cara had felt earlier in the evening had evaporated; she relaxed into Mariko's embrace, tingling to the tips of her fingers and toes as if she'd drunk champagne.

"Slowly, Cara? May I?"

Not feeling like speaking, Cara nodded. She closed her eyes, letting Mariko push their bodies away from the edge. They stood in the center of a world of water and steam, surrounded by a vaporous mineral smell now fragranced with musk.

Water lapped like hot fingers at Cara's hips and buttocks and mons as they rotated slowly, shifting from foot to foot like dancers. "Lean back," Mariko murmured, in between kisses on Cara's neck. "Lean back into the water. I'll hold you up. Lean back."

Cara's feet didn't want to leave the bottom at first, but then Mariko's strong arm curled around her waist and she floated, the water startlingly hot against her scalp. A long sigh escaped her.

"Like class," Mariko said. "Feel your body. You'll float."

"I had a crush on my first swim teacher," Cara murmured. "She wore a purple bikini. But now it's wing tattoos, all the way."

Mariko laughed, and Cara blinked open her eyes and smiled back at her. Mariko said, "This is my ultimate slow seduction, and you're telling jokes? What a woman."

"I didn't know martial arts would be like this."

"Only if you're very lucky." Mariko cocked her head to one side. A strand of dark hair clung to one high cheekbone and sweat had dewed her thin upper lip. "Do you want me to make love to you or not?"

"Oh, I suppose you can go ahead." Cara began to laugh softly, drunkenly, and Mariko giggled helplessly against Cara's belly until she began to sink. Sputtering ensued, and desperate clutching that dissolved into more laughter.

When both had caught their breath again, Cara said, "I'd like to lean on the edge."

"Perhaps you should," Mariko said. She splashed over to the pool's rim and retrieved a towel. "Here, put this under your neck."

After a few moments, Cara was arranged comfortably with her head on the edge of the pool, the rest of her body buoyantly reaching for the surface. She reached over her head and gripped the smooth stone, aware that the gesture showed off the tone of her triceps and pectorals and lifted her breasts wantonly.

Mariko stood between Cara's ankles. She sank to her knees and maneuvered Cara's legs over her shoulders, massaging the insides of Cara's thighs with firm, strong strokes. Cara felt sound building up within her and let it out slowly as a soft moan. Mariko's head lowered and she nuzzled Cara's labia apart. Tiny waves created by the motion of their bodies mimicked the dabs and flicks of Mariko's lips and tongue.

Cara's hips writhed upward, unable to control the whimpering sounds any longer. Mariko's lips closed over her clit and tugged. Cara crested, riding the pleasure as if moving through a long tunnel. When she became aware of herself again, she was sitting on the underwater bench wrapped around Mariko like an octopus, panting.

"Wow," Cara said when she could speak.

Mariko smiled and kissed her.

Cara grinned back, sharklike. "I liked my surprise."

"Good. Do you want to surprise me next time?"

Cara reached up and caressed Mariko's soft, smooth cheek, lingering on her jawline. "Not a surprise," she said. "It'll be sunny, scorching July. You'll wear a backless red swimsuit provided by me, and we'll borrow my Aunt Beverly's swimming pool while she's in Vegas, and there'll be inflatable pool toys."

"And until then?"

"We can keep busy, can't we?"

Mariko settled in next to Cara on the bench. "Yes, I think we can manage that."

Dress Pinks
M. Christian

The funny thing was that the day—until about half an hour
ago—hadn't been half-bad.

Rosy had gotten up at—for her—a respectable ten, and
leapt into getting showered and primped: good shampoo,
excellent conditioner, moisturizer, gentle glides of the razor
along her legs, practiced sweeps of her brush to give her black
hair just the right amount of lift. After, she carefully crawled
into what she called her dress pinks—even though the whole
outfit was just black and off-whites. Most of the time she
looked at the simple black, calf-high skirt, business-high heels,
taupe hose, satin blouse, and austere jacket with more than a
little distaste—but that morning she felt like she was getting
ready for inspection, and barely suppressed a snapped salute
when she checked herself out in the mirror before heading
out.

That afternoon Mr. Perez had actually liked the cover and
layout treatments, going as far as to say *"Bueno*—exactly
what I was looking for!" What suggestions he'd made had
even made a certain amount of sense, and wouldn't take more

than an hour, maybe two, to tweak. After the meeting down-town at the offices of *Si!* magazine they'd all gone to dinner at Plouf—a couple of glasses of a gentle white wine and the handsome Latino businessman had even hit them up for working on some designs for *Si!*'s sister mag in Argentina.

Heading back to her car, weaving just a little bit from the good wine and the heady success, she smiled and congratu-lated herself on a job well done. Though, as usual, she couldn't help but wonder how much of her job-well-done had arisen from her talent as a graphic artist and how much had been the cool professionalism of her (metaphorical) three-piece business uniform.

Walking down the dark streets—click, click, click on her not-too-high, but high-enough, heels—Rosy smiled: usually the rule was to imagine the audience in their underwear, but she always seemed to bring a springy sense of humor to her presentations by relishing the ridiculous façade of her hose, heels, and silk blouse when, after all, she'd been wearing an old Glamour Pussies tee shirt and threadbare, but comfort-able, panties when she created the designs Mr. Perez had gushed over.

After all, she thought as she wandered down Dore Alley just after midnight, I'm in the business of images—I'm natu-rally a canvas for a particularly effective one.

It was about that time—turning from the narrow alley onto the larger river of Folsom—that she realized she couldn't find her car.

In a blush of anger and embarrassment, she stood on the empty street and ran quickly through what she'd left in the battered old Cougar. Right there. Definitely right there—she remem-bered the overflowing trash can, the *Guardian* news rack, the lighting store (which was still very well lit) across the street—it was definitely the right corner: all that was missing was the car.

Luckily, Rosy's inventory didn't turn up a lot to be worried about, except for the car itself: an old coat, a five-year-old Thomas Bros. map, an ashtray still overflowing from Louise's pack-a-day habit. If anything, it was that damned disgusting ashtray that she suddenly longed for the most. Louise hadn't been the best girlfriend she'd had—far from it, in fact, her pack-a-day had been just one of her whole parade of self-centered and more than a little repulsive personal habits—but she'd been in Rosy's life for almost five years. Five years of toenail clippings in the bed, ancient dishes in the sink, moldy sandwiches in the fridge, and morning breath that could bring down light aircraft. But, still, Louise had been hers and she had been Louise's—it wasn't a fancy, three-piece relationship, but it had been a smoking, fuming one. They had melted together, flowed through many a long weekend, only crawling out of their heavily rolling orgasmic ocean when Rosy had been forced by 8:00 A.M. to crawl into her dress pinks and wander off into the real world to earn their living.

"Oh, fuck," Rosy said, not for the car (because it was a piece of shit), not for the cigarette butts that were all that was left of Louise (because that was done for, and the ache was really starting to close up), not because she had to walk home (it was only eight blocks), or that she had to get up early (she didn't), but because there was just something profoundly lonely about that eight-block walk without anything to look forward to in the morning, and without even the hollow reminder of a past love to keep her company.

"Well, that's a bitch," said a voice nearby. "Isn't it?"

Should have expected it, after all: Folsom and Dore, the leather paradise for a whole generation of gay men. "Damned straight," Rosy said, turning and smiling at the voice.

For someone who'd lived in the city as long as she had, Rosy didn't claim many fag boys as friends. Maybe it was because she'd met Louise very shortly after moving to the city from her old home turf of Miami and they hadn't left their little Mission flat unless they had to—but, more than that, Rosy suspected that after coming out to herself she just didn't see the attraction in men. It was as if after allowing herself to love women, she didn't have time for anything else.

"Yeah, a royal one," she said, huffing out a good deep sigh as she looked again at where the car had been parked. "Not like the thing was worth stealing."

"Had it happen to me once. A piece of shit but it seemed everyone knew how to get in and take it for a spin. Had it ripped off half a dozen times the first two years I was here."

Looking at him, though, Rosy could feel a bit of attraction—a gentle fluttering down in the pit of her stomach—and that bothered her. He was young—almost boyish in fact, something she knew was pretty rare for a hardcore leatherman. Ash-blond hair cut into a severe crew, showing off his very squared and elegantly shaped skull, and a wispy mustache. He wore his uniform well—a revelation that almost brought a giggle, but did bring a smile, to Rosy's lips as she realized that she was still in her own severe dress pinks. He wore tight, tight, tight leather chaps, thick-heeled calf-high motorcycle boots, a muscle-contouring black vest, and even a small cap. He looked like a recruitment poster for *Drummer,* a center spread for *Mach,* a living totem of the spirit of Mr. San Francisco Leather.

"Well," Rosy said, shaking herself slightly, "I'd better get to a phone and call it in."

"Who knows," he said in his deep but still remarkably musical voice as he moved back, giving her space to step up onto the curb, "maybe it just got towed. Happens all the time."

"I can only hope," she said as she started to walk away.

Half a minute later she realized she had no idea where the nearest phone was, and turning around she was shocked—and again felt that fluttering deep in her belly—to see him smiling broadly. "There's one over this way," he said, gesturing in the opposite direction. "Here, I'll show you."

It seemed so perfectly natural to take his arm when he offered, and together they walked off down the street. Even though she wouldn't have admitted it, on the arm of the leatherman her day had actually begun to look up.

"You don't seem freaked out—that's good!" he yelled into her ear.

Rosy shook her head, not wanting to bellow over the thumping disco. She definitely didn't feel...well, uncomfortable wasn't really the right word. She felt safe, certainly, but she definitely wasn't completely at ease, either—she was, at best, distracted.

Looking around, she smiled again to herself: only in San Francisco—a business afternoon, a towed car (thank goodness), a short walk, and then an evening spent in a leather bar.

Rosy would have liked to think her leatherman charming, but the fact was she could barely hear him over the heavy-beating disco. It was hard to be charming, she discovered quickly, when your wit couldn't be heard.

But Rosy was able to tell that—deep breath, deep breath, deep breath—he was (ahem) kinda, well, sorta, um...damned sexy. The first admission that she actually found him attractive had rushed over her like a kind of panic—the same kind of panic that had grabbed her just a few hours before when she realized her car was gone. Rosy didn't have a indecisive past; she liked to say that she was a born lesbian: no clumsy proms trying to feel attracted to the boys, no waking up in the middle of a marriage to hunger for another woman's lips. None of that. Boys, to Rosy, were like some distant land—she knew where it was on the map, but didn't really care to visit.

Until her car got towed, and she found herself in the presence of the leatherman. Maybe that was it, she thought, mulling over him as she sipped her Coke. Was she really attracted to him or to the leather? He was almost too perfect, a dead-cow icon, a Tom of Finland deity: gleaming leather chaps, vest with those merit badges of boy-sex S/M clubs, even the little leather cap. He was like a thirty-three-cent stamp for hot leatherboy sex.

Seeing him made Rosy feel like she had a hot, hard leather fist up inside her. It was an unexpected and—yes, at first—shocking sensation, but the desire she felt rolling around in her body was strong enough to quickly and firmly shove that hesitation aside.

The only thing she really regretted, staring at her icon, was that her own dress pinks were so stiff and emotionless. Although she'd never wanted it before (but that night seemed a night for first times) she wished she had a collar on.

As she had been thoughtfully and—yes, she had to admit it—hungrily eyeing him, the leatherman had been looking at her as well. He said something. Over the pounding of the music, she couldn't make out what he'd said. She leaned forward and yelled, "What?!" at him.

That's when he said it. Simple enough in an everyday context, but for Rosy in her power suit and he in his incredibly sexy leather, it meant a lot more—a lot that Rosy suddenly realized, fully, she was willing to go along with: "Do you want to go to the bathroom?"

That's how Rosy, who'd never even kissed a boy, ended up being led by a leatherman into the dinge and tile of a SOMA S/M bar.

"Did I say you could kiss me?"

No, he hadn't. He hadn't said anything, actually—dead silence had followed them, not a word, not a command, since the door had closed behind them. Surprisingly, the bathroom had been empty—a fact that she didn't puzzle over till later. He could clear a room by just wanting to use it.

Even though Rosy felt submission blooming within her, she didn't have the tools to deal with what was happening. She just had Louise and half-a-dozen girlfriends behind her. She knew the mechanics of boy-girl (what there was of it), and had a pretty good idea of what could happen to her in the tiny, moderately dirty bathroom, but didn't know the first steps to the dance. It had just seemed natural to turn and try to kiss those strong yet soft-looking lips.

Quicker than her own pounding heartbeat, he had her long brown hair in one knotted fist, pulling her head back. "Listen, slut, you're mine—you do nothing but what I tell you. Got that?"

She didn't know what to do—fear bubbled up from down deep, and—even more shockingly—anger. A part of Rosy wanted to shake him loose, gut-punch him, and walk proudly out. But another part of her...she was wet. That was it. What was getting to her? Was it his cock? Was it the possibly of a good, old-fashioned (aghast, 'straight') fuck? Surprisingly, Rosy was able to look deeply into herself and answer "no." So what was it, then—what was it that was making her simple, professional panties so damp?

Then it was there—simple and straightforward. In a little voice that sent shivers of delight and excitement through her body, she said, "Yes, Sir."

"Good, slut—very good. You're a good slut, aren't you? A hungry slut. You want it, don't you—you need it. You ache for it. Right, slut?"

"Yes, Sir—I do need it."

"Good, because you're going to get it."

One of his slender—yet very strong—hands reached up to her blouse, cupped her right breast. Before she could get ready, his fingers skillfully flicked over the swell of her breast till he found her already-hard nipple. The squeeze was powerful, even though it was partially expected: with a gasp, Rosy gripped his strong arm and felt her knees quickly give way under the wave of pleasure spiced with pain. When her voice returned it was a high squeal: "Yes, Sir."

Again his hand found her hair, again her head was jerked back, but this time rather than growling his displeasure, he traced the lines of her tight neck muscles with his thin fingers. "Good—very good: sluts should always recognize themselves."

His other hand found her breasts again. The powerful squeeze brought tears to her eyes. Again, strong fingers to her aching, throbbing nipples. The pinch this time was even stronger, but somehow controlled: it was a precise generation of pain pushing toward pleasure...or was it the other way around? Mixed up with endorphins of all kinds, Rosy couldn't tell anything, anything at all beyond the burst of sensation—except that she wanted more.

Distantly, she heard buttons hitting tile, metal partitions. Distantly, too, she regretted the loss of the blouse—but not the cause. She arced her body forward, offering him her breasts.

He took what she pushed at him, scooping first the right and then the left free of her business-style bra. Bare to the warm air, and the even hotter atmosphere, of the bathroom, she groaned from their release and whatever else he was planning for their torment—and her pleasure.

His bite was quick, sudden, shocking, frightening—but, like his fingers, not the predatory tearing of a beast. It was as if his perfect little teeth were precise instruments for the delivery of agony. Just behind the plump nibs of her nipples, he gave her quick stinging bites—before retreating just a little to slowly, ponderously, grind his jaws together. The steady progress of his bite pushed Rosy even farther from the cool tile wall she was leaning against—and increased her grip on the side of the sink she had grabbed to steady herself. The hiss that escaped her lips was like a crack in a boiler—hot, shrill, and unstoppable.

She knew she was wet...no, Rosy was absolutely sure that the simple business panties under her dress pinks were soaking wet. She was always like that—a base primal lover.

His fingers reached down and pushed up—hard—her no-nonsense black skirt. A firm pressure reached her through her taupe pantyhose and right through the pedestrian cotton of her panties. The contact was a shiver that blasted up through her body, an inexorable skyrocket that straightened her spine and escalated the velocity and pitch of her hiss.

A part of her that had been resting just below the surface opened its eyes, growing from groggy to ravenous. Something tore, parting under an unstoppable force—his fingers ripping through taupe pantyhose. Rosy took a breath, expecting the next step, waiting for it, wanting it.

As the thin veil of nylon parted, the leatherman spoke, "Good, slut—very good. You want it, don't you, slut. You want it bad. You need it, you need it like you never needed anything else in the world. You need this, slut—you need it now...don't you?"

She knew that the rules dictated that she say something, open her mouth and play the role she was supposed to. But Rosy was excited and her cunt was wet, so all that emerged from between her tight lips and clenched teeth was another notch to the shrill hiss. But her heart was in the right place—and in her mind she was The Slut, his slut, his plaything, his toy. "Yes, Sir" might not have escaped her lips, but it certainly was loud and clear in her mind.

In the next moment he found out how wet she was—a discovery that changed the timbre of her sounds to a bass purr. She felt his fingers expertly part her damp underwear and find the slick folds of her cunt. Gentle at first, but then with more and more insistence, he explored her cunt: the plump lips, the tight, slick passage up inside her, the pucker of her asshole, and—deeper purr—the throbbing point of her clit.

There, he stopped—"That's you, slut, that's you right there. That's where you live. Right there: and now I've got you"—and right there he really started. He was more than a leatherman, more than her Master, he was a finger artist. Feelings rushed up through her. Not a skyrocket, no strange little metaphors this time; the simple fact was what kept ringing through her mind: "My Master's finger on my clit, my Master's finger on my clit." She was right in that magic spot she suspected but never realized was deep inside herself: Rosy the slut, Rosy the toy, Rosy the object of his powerful will.

It happened almost before she was aware it had started: a quivering, shaking body-rush of exaltation that took even more strength from her legs as it brought brilliant flashes of light to her eyes and a thundering pulse to her ears. As orgasms went, it was good—not the best—but there was something else there, a kind of awakening. Not to him, but rather to Him—to her position and his power. It wasn't the sex that blasted through her but rather the fact that she was on the receiving end of his strength.

When her legs stopped shaking and she felt she wasn't going to drop down to the cool tiles in a quivering heap, she breathed in deeply—one, two, three, four—and managed to focus on his (slightly) smiling face. "There was never a question," he said, "in my mind: good slut."

There was something missing, there was something she had to do. It was part of the act, part of the ceremony. She knew it was wrong to speak without being spoken to, but she had to complete the act—to place herself firmly in the world to which her leatherman belonged: "Can I suck your cock, Sir?"

"Yes, slut, you may," was his smiling response—pleased at some subterranean level by the eagerness and correctness of her desire.

Cool tiles this time under her knees, torn pantyhose riding up the warm, damp seam of her ass, breasts wobbling, tender nipples grazing the coarse material of her open jacket. There—in front of her, the altar of her leatherman, her leathergod: slick black chaps over too-tight jeans. A bulge of power just inches from her face. "You know what to do, slut," he said from above, thunder from on high.

Actually, she hadn't a clue. Vibrators and toys, yes, but never touching those other lips. But this was the new Rosy, and this was something she had to do for him—it was part of the rules. Slightly quaking fingers to his fly, a slow, steady inching-down. She'd hoped that he'd help at some point, give her pointers or at least shrug himself free from the jail of his pants. No such luck, though—he stood, a leather statue, above her and didn't move, didn't say a word.

So she had to do it all. Hesitant fingers in through the metal-toothed opening, a gentle dig around. Ah, contact—not too soft, not as warm as she expected. A careful pull—not too insistent—feeling the fat head slide up and then, oh yes, out. Out, out, out—her first sight of her Master's dick, her leather-god's cock.

A moment of shocked silence.

A very long moment. Longer than any moment in Rosy's life. A record-setting moment.

It ended with a smile. "It's a wonderful cock, Sir," Rosy said, kissing the tip of the long dildo, tasting a little cotton lint and much plastic. "It's fantastic, Sir," she said as she opened her mouth to take in the tip.

As Rosy licked, kissed, and sucked her plastic cock she basked in the warmth of what she had discovered: not that she'd been ready, willing, and able to suck a leatherman's cock; not even that she'd realized how much joy there could be in being a powerful figure's plaything, his slut; but that sometimes the wrapping, the uniform, is the best thing about what's inside.

Her name was Jackie. She lived in the Mission. She was a musician by choice (which was important) and a word processor out of necessity (which wasn't important). She was also Jack, and Jack was a leather...man, boy, person? Jack was leather, a gravely tone, and firm commands. Jack was a pair of chaps, a leather vest, a white T-shirt, and a little black leather cap.

Outside, in a light drizzle, they exchanged phone numbers. Before parting—Jack on a throbbing motorcycle and Rosy by cab—they kissed: soft lips and a hesitant but electric touch of tongues.

"Another time?" said Rosy.

"For sure," said Jackie.

"Be sure and bring Jack," Rosy said.

"Oh, I will—you just bring the slut."

The Stars in Her Mouth
Thea Hutcheson

In the dream leads are attached to my body, breasts, my feet, my mouth, my ears, my sex, my fingertips, my navel. When the first one disconnects, I am horrified, understanding that as they go, so go my feelings. They fall away and the horror fades, replaced by numbness. When the final one, in the middle of my forehead, my sacred third eye, drops away slowly, I feel a tiny twinge of regret. The view pulls back and I see myself hanging limply in gray mist. Distantly I know that I must find a way to reconnect the leads or I will fade into the mist. "Help!" I try to scream; only a whisper comes out. I am terrified to think no one can hear me.

The alarm rang and I rolled over as I do every morning, shut it off, and got out of bed to make coffee and breakfast. I was still making a whole pot. Angrily, I scooped out the extra grounds and got a ladle to remove six cups of water from the reservoir. I turned on the coffee maker and went out for the newspaper.

I laid the paper on the table and poured a cup of coffee. I really should cancel it, I thought, realizing as I did that habits do die hard. I lifted the cup to my lips. I'd been making a whole pot of coffee every morning since I was five. All those years of habit, now for nothing, like the rest of my life.

"You have the rest of your life," I said, parroting my aunt. "You should be planning how you're going to spend it. The house will sell quickly and you and the other kids will divide up that and the retirement account and you'll move. You're lucky, you know. Your second cousin Bonnie was the youngest and her parents died when she was forty. You're only twenty-three. Go live the rest of your life."

Except that I'd discovered I didn't know who I was when I wasn't making coffee or beds or dinner. I pulled idly on the rubber band around the newspaper. *Plink, plink, plink*. It sounded loud. Ordinarily, the kitchen was busy with cups clinking, silverware clanging against china, the sounds of cooking, and I knew what I was supposed to be doing.

Right as I was about to lapse into another round of tears, I remembered that I was supposed to call someone to fix the air conditioner. Summer had just begun and the air conditioner was broken. Now that Dad had followed Mom into Shady Rest, I was going to have to do something about this on my own. I ripped the rubber band off the paper, snapping myself on the fingers.

Cursing, I thumbed through to the classifieds. I folded the broadsheet in quarters so I could manage it, and got a high-lighter and the cordless from the telephone table in the dining room.

As I scanned the paper I rubbed my forehead right on the place where that third eye had been. Brandon's, Brothers, Brewster Mechanical—there were thirty of them at least. I shook my head, closed my eyes, twirled the pen over the service ads, and stabbed.

I opened my eyes. "Thompson Heating and Cooling." I read, rubbing a sudden tic in the middle of my forehead. "Expert heating and cooling solutions, emergency service. Every problem is the right size."

I shrugged and picked up the phone. The answering service took my name, phone number, and address and promised to send someone out before lunch. I congratulated myself. If I could just solve all the rest of my problems that easily. I read the paper while I finished my coffee.

I had just polished off a second cup of coffee when the doorbell rang. I went to the door and looked out the peephole to find a woman in a light cream sleeveless dress, the gauzy kind you twist to dry. I had been expecting a man.

I opened the door. Before I say anything, she stepped in. She had olive skin and curly dark hair like mine, only hers was pulled back with combs. She had a tattoo on her forehead, a beautiful brown eye that matched her other two except that its colors were brighter, more intense. Rose outlined her mouth, and swirling, graceful lines covered her hands, her fingertips. I backed up. She stepped forward. I moved into the living room. She followed.

"How may I help you?" She stared at me, my hair pulled back tight to keep the curls smooth along my head. Her eyes trailed down across my breasts and my hips. She met my eyes on the way back up and smiled. I smiled nervously.

She spoke. "You called for help? Here I am."

"You're the service tech?" I looked her up and down. The dress was gauzy and, where it caught the morning light, translucent. She looked at me, eyes crinkled in question, mouth quirked in humor.

"Well," I said, turning away from the sight of her legs reaching up into the shadows of her dress, "let me show you where it is." I turned, grateful for an escape. This woman made me uncomfortable, as if she knew too much—about me and about everything else. I held the back door open and she walked outside, her eyes warmed by the smile playing at the corner of her lips.

I pointed out the air conditioner just off the patio. She walked up to it and I followed. She had more tattoos on the backs of her arms and spirals around her elbows. I could see that her ankles and feet were covered in more lines.

She began to laugh. I stood looking at the sinuous lines that flowed over her. Finally, she turned back to me, flicking her pale dress to keep it from the dust. She eclipsed the morning sun. And for a moment, as I stared into the darkness of her face, her tattooed eye blazed like a beacon and there were stars in her mouth.

Then she stepped toward me and spoke. "Frankly, I think *you* need more help than that old thing."

"I beg your pardon?"

Somehow she was now in my space and brushed a stray hair away from my forehead. I stared into the eye in her forehead. It was exquisitely done and I saw how the muscles of her forehead made it seem lifelike. I was impressed with the artist's skill.

I couldn't think what to say. She smelled faintly of patchouli and I wanted to close my eyes and breathe it in. I stepped back, hearing one of Mother's favorite lines. "You're impertinent," I said.

"Sometimes it takes that." She smiled at me, head cocked.

"Takes what?" It was hot and I wanted to go in and have some tea, except that I couldn't quit staring at that eye.

"Impertinence, sometimes downright stubbornness. Personally, I prefer fun; it makes it more mutual. You look hot. Why don't we go inside and have some tea?"

I almost said, "All right," but shook my head instead. "I think you should go." I turned and gestured toward the door, intending to usher her through the house and out the front door.

"Okay, but if I do, who will fix you?" She glanced slyly back at me as she walked into the kitchen. I'd swear that eye in the middle of her forehead winked at me.

"Fix *me?* I don't need fixing. I'm fine."

She stopped and turned to look critically at me. She shook her head. "You don't sound fine to me."

I walked into the living room. I thought of myself floating in the gray mist of my dream.

"What do I sound like to you?"

She leaned forward slowly and at first I thought that she was going to brush another lock of hair away. I watched her lips coming at me. They were full and firm, bright red lining the edges, fading to a flush that followed the curve of them down into her mouth. I could see a coy hint of tooth from behind her top lip and then her lips pressed mine softly. I was surprised and it took me a moment to take in the implications. I pulled away and licked my lips nervously. They tasted of honeysuckle.

"Did you like that?"

I couldn't think of anything except how her lips felt when they yielded to mine. "I don't know," I finally said.

She grinned at me. "Well, that's a start. Shall I do it again?"

I knew I should be nervous. I could hear Mother shrieking, "Hail Marys, Hail Marys," over and over again, yet I couldn't take my eyes off this woman.

I reached my finger up and lightly traced the rose line around her lips. She stayed very still and stared straight into my eyes.

"Did it hurt?" I asked.

"Life hurts sometimes; it passes, and look at what you have."

"Lines?"

"Experience."

I lowered my hand and leaned forward to kiss her. My heart beat loudly in my chest from the knowledge of what I was doing, and quickly from the shock of it. This time she parted her lips, allowing me to explore. I closed my eyes as I slipped my tongue in and darted it back out again.

"Did you like that?" she whispered as she lightly stroked my cheek.

I thought about it. "Yes, though not the way you mean."

"And how is that?"

I paused, red as her lips. "Turned on."

"Is it bad to enjoy pleasure, a gentle touch?"

"No, it isn't bad. That's what I mean. Your lips are so soft. I never knew they were so soft."

"Would you like to touch my breasts?" She turned to and fro so that I could admire them from both sides.

I blushed and looked away while my hand, of its own accord, touched her gently. Her breast was firm, just larger than a handful. I could see a spiral that led right to her nipple, which poked impudently into the gauzy material. It and the aureole were smudged with the same red as her lips.

She leaned into my hand. I touched the red nipple, kneaded it lightly, smiling when it hardened between my fingers. She closed her eyes. I reached up to my own breast and felt the nipple harden against my fingers.

She opened her eyes and smiled. "Do you like doing this?"

I considered. I loved exploring her shape. It was beautiful and I loved the feel, the smell, the softness of her skin, the way her back arched as she leaned into my touch.

"Yes, but not the way you mean."

"Right now it doesn't matter what it means." She stepped up to me and her arms slid around me very deliberately. I concentrated on experiencing the moment, feeling her fingers as they pressed against the top of my hip and the muscles of my shoulder. I explored the sensation of her nipples and breasts pressed against mine. It was unlike anything I'd ever known. Hugs at our house only involved the body from the shoulders up.

She kissed me and I kissed back. I was acutely conscious as she undid my braid. It obliged as never for me, loosing itself in a cascade across my back. She clenched a handful of curls and her lips began flicking mine lightly. Her tongue darted into my mouth and filled it, sliding along mine, trying to draw it out.

I was warm, my face flushed, and I sought to press tighter, flatter, closer against her. The cleft between my legs felt at once loose and tight. We played hide-and-seek around each other's teeth. I raised my hands up and took out her combs. We pushed our fingers through each other's hair. She eased me down on the couch.

"Do you want me to take off my dress?"

I was languid from her kisses. "Yes, take it off, please. I want to see." I said, smiling at my naughtiness and eagerness to see the lines on her legs, her soft thighs, her belly.

"Positively brash," she said, nodding approvingly as she lifted her arms. The dress pooled at her feet.

In my mind, my mother screamed, "Hail Mary, full of grace." I was caught in the intricate lines flowing like script over the woman's shoulders, down her back, up her throat, around her navel, and across her hips, finally pointing down to her sex, flushed with the same color as her lips.

She offered herself for my inspection. Her body was firm and young and as she turned I saw the same patterns repeated on her knees, feet, and toes. "Full of grace," I said softly. I beckoned her to come closer and I wondered whether the red of her sex was from my touch or from ink. She opened my thighs as she knelt between them. Her touch was electric and I shuddered.

She unbuttoned my dress to reveal high breasts, firm belly, the line of my panties. Her fingers were cool and her nails long enough to trace lines as she touched me: nipples, fingertips, belly, mouth, eyes, toes, elbows, ears.

"So beautiful, so alive," she whispered. "Can you doubt you are alive? Can you doubt that you could live? To live, one must know one's self. If you never discover yourself, you only survive. Will you live or not?"

She kept staring into my eyes. I met the gaze of that third eye and saw, in this moment of profound truth, myself alive.

She kissed me and I surrendered to her, willing to accept, wanting what she offered. I moaned as she put her arms around me, crushing me to her. My hips felt loose and I pressed against her. She thrust her hips and the cleft between my legs thrummed against the pressure. Each time she pushed forward she created desire and each time she pulled back she left terrible longing. My deepest center clenched tightly, making pleasure sing a long note that trailed off, only to begin a step higher as she met my hips again.

I let my hands ride her buttocks and opened my eyes. Her face was beautiful in concentration. Her lips were parted and I could see stars in her mouth. As I looked I realized it was the universe inside. As I wondered how that could be, I caught a glimpse of myself in the pupil of her third eye. I saw that I was vibrant and strong. I could go out into the world and find my way. As I stared at my reflection in her sacred eye, I realized we had the same face. Yes, hair, almond-shaped eyes, cheek-bones, supple mouth.

At that moment, she thrust hard against me and I fell over the edge, my orgasm a waterfall against her hips and down our legs, cascading to the floor.

I could feel my sweat, the pulsing of the blood between my legs. She lay against me and I stroked her hair.

"Why do you have the universe in your mouth?"

"Everyone has the universe inside. They just have to find it."

"Why do you look like me?"

"To the universe we all look the same because we're only different combinations of the same thing."

"The same thing?"

She kissed me and stood up. "The universe, we're all part of the universe."

She stood. Her skin was flushed and her mouth and sex were brilliant. The black lines on her skin were shiny with sweat.

I watched her as she pulled her dress over her head. It swirled down to settle itself.

I wasn't sure what to say. "Thank you."

She smiled. "I heard you."

"I was afraid no one would."

She hugged me and kissed me on the mouth. She held my face in her hands. "To me it was as loud as a baby in the night, and just as immediate. Go find your life."

I slipped my dress back on.

She picked the combs up off the floor and dressed her hair in the mirror over the sideboard. She pinched her cheeks, bit her lips, and smoothed her dress. She walked to the door and smiled back at me before she stepped out, closing it behind her.

There was a knock at the door and I hurried to answer it, thinking that she couldn't possibly have forgotten anything.

A man in a grimy uniform stood on the porch. I looked around him to get a glimpse of her, but saw no one up or down the street.

"Well, did you call about an air conditioner?"

I reluctantly pulled my eyes back to him. "Yes, it's out back. Follow me."

I led him to the back door and pointed to the right. He moved past me into the bright sunlight. I retreated into the house and shut the door. I could smell our sex as I cleaned up the living room.

The house went up for sale with a new air conditioner. I found a little place with a balcony overlooking the lake in a park. It has the most fabulous bathroom with a huge tub where I light candles and pour in bath oil and practice pleasuring myself.

The oil glints in the candlelight and makes me think of the stars in her mouth and how they're in me, too. I slide into the warm, wet embrace of the water and touch myself, learning who I am. Someday I'll go out into the world and find the rest of me.

Blood

Susan St. Aubin

I never liked blood until my periods ended, not the moldy-leaf smell, not the cold-iron-railing taste, and certainly not the dark-muddy-river gush. I never wanted sex during my period, when orgasms seemed to rip through me, making me bleed all the more. Only when my blood stopped flowing for good did I miss the whole essence of it, the thickness, the metallic scent, the black-red color of old tomato sauce left too long in the can.

Without blood, my skin grew whiter and thinner along with my hair, as though both were clarified. My feet felt like they no longer touched the sidewalk as I floated along streets where I felt invisible, and my senses grew more acute. I could hear the pounding babble of radios plugged into someone else's ears as though I were a god aware of every thought; I could see the sun seep around the edges of my dark glasses and smell the ripeness of peaches or the cheesy sharpness of sour milk drifting from the door of a small grocery.

The scents of other women began to attract me more than usual, especially the blood scents I hadn't wanted before. Like a vampire, I could tell instantly if a young woman I passed on the street had her period, and would turn around to track her, soundless as a hunter until I chose to reveal myself. One day, a woman passed me wearing a long green coat that brought out the rose highlights of her mahogany skin. I smelled her blood on the wind, along with a cinnamon tang I hadn't noticed in other women. Her unique smell made me turn around to follow her because my hunger for her youth, her beauty, her spicy blood left me no choice. Was it true that the blood of beautiful maidens could keep vampires young forever if they bathed in it and sipped it like fine wine? Was menstrual blood the same as live blood? Was I creating a new myth, Countess Dracula on the trail of the moon's red tide?

Though I was on my way home after a long day at work, I got on the streetcar after her and rode back downtown, where I tracked her through small lingerie shops and up the escalators of large department stores, wandering from women's sportswear to hosiery. I knew what I wanted, but what was she looking for?

"Do you have it in red?" she asked a saleswoman while I pretended to go through tights on sale, feeling my heart rush. What in red? Stockings? A garter belt? Redness overcame me, the dead scent of it flowing behind her clear, questioning voice.

Because I was a shadow she looked through, a woman made insubstantial by age, I was able to follow her unnoticed onto the streetcar after she left the last store. She went to the back while I stayed up front behind the driver, where, in my seat for the aged or infirm, I felt as invisible as a vampire in a mirror, though I could still smell her. As we approached my usual stop, I knew without looking that she had moved to the rear exit. I left by the front door, letting her follow me down the street, knowing which way she wanted to turn by the scent she released when her body shifted direction.

We passed the apartment building where I lived and continued for three more blocks before turning onto a quiet street I hadn't noticed before, a street lined with big trees and wood-shingled bungalows with large front porches. When she stopped, I continued for several paces before turning to watch her open a picket-fence gate with paint peeling off in white strips, then walk slowly to the sagging front steps. I wanted her to stop and see me with a will so strong that when she reached the front porch, she turned to wave at me, calling, "Well, you'd better come in since you've followed me all this way."

Although I'd walked ahead of her, she knew when she was being tracked. How could I resist such a frighteningly smart woman? She waved again as she walked across the porch to the front door, then put her key in the lock, turning it, opening the door, holding it open for me so I could enter the dark hallway before her. A vampire can only go where she's invited. First I saw smoke that turned out to be sunlight from a small window illuminating the dust in the air. At the end of the hall was a sitting room where shadowy brown furniture emerged from the dark walls: a couch, a large chair, lamps, bookcases. I turned around to see her grin as she leaned on the doorframe.

"Nice place," I said.

"It will be," she answered. "I inherited it from my aunt and only moved in last week, so I haven't done anything with it yet."

Not even dusted, was on the tip of my tongue to say, but I didn't want to sound like her aunt.

"My name's Gemma. I've seen you around. You work at the university, don't you? In the library?"

I nodded.

"I see you on the bus, too," she said. "You live around here?"

"A couple of blocks away," I answered. I was ashamed to admit that without the scent of her blood at its peak, I hadn't noticed her, and now that scent so overwhelmed me I could barely hear.

"I'm just finishing up a graduate degree in social welfare," Gemma was saying. "I'm working on my thesis, so I'm in the library a lot. Periodicals, that's where you work."

She was right. My mouth was so dry I had to lick my lips before I could swallow. She took off her coat and pulled her sweater over her head, ruffling her short springy hair. I followed her down the hall into the living room.

"It's stuffy in here. This house definitely needs ventilation." Gemma pushed back dark, dusty curtains to open a window while I inhaled her earthy scent and watched her shadowy breasts move beneath her white T-shirt. She stood by the window shaking her sparkling dark hair at me until my knees felt so weak I sank into the chair behind me, my hands sliding on the leather arms.

"Would you like some tea?" she asked.

Tea could mean anything: herbal, caffeine, even marijuana, though she was too young to know that old slang. Tea might be what her aunt would have offered.

"I'm a coffee drinker, myself," I said.

"Good, I'll make a pot."

There's a concept from the past, I thought to myself as I followed her back into the hall and entered the kitchen. A pot, not hot water poured through a paper filter, but a real pot of coffee, black, grainy, rich as blood. The kitchen had faded wallpaper with a design of teapots barely visible, and a collection of appliances I hadn't seen since my childhood: a white-and-green Mixmaster attached to a pale green glass bowl; an electric cooker, ancestor to the Crock-Pot, built into a white metal cabinet on wheels; and an old aluminum coffeepot, a percolator with a glass bubble on top, the brown liquid filling it and falling, filling and falling until the coffee was ready.

Gemma poured two cups and got out the milk, which I declined, asking instead for sugar.

"I don't know if...Belle must have had some." She rummaged in a cupboard until she found an old box of lumps, probably stale. I added four to my cup.

"Belle—Aunt Belle—didn't eat sugar, but she did keep some for guests. It wasn't good for the teeth, she said, and when she died, she did still have every tooth in her head."

She sat down across from me, adding milk to her cup, but no sugar. "I'm not good at this hostess thing," she said with a shrug. "I've never had a house, never had to worry about coffee or sugar."

I looked around her time-capsule of a kitchen. When I took a deep breath, I could take in her rich odor with my coffee, the way you can sometimes taste your lipstick in your food. I wondered if Belle had really been her aunt. There was something hidden in the way Gemma said her name, but she offered nothing but coffee that day, so I had to leave after I finished my cup.

There were other days when we talked, though without the scent of her blood the meetings weren't memorable. We had lunch at a café near the university, we had fresh mint tea at my apartment, and one day she even invited me into her bedroom (did she spend nights there with Belle?) to view two swatches of possible material for curtains and a matching bedspread. When Gemma asked which I preferred, I chose the red and purple paisley, picturing her brown nude body stretched across it, but she was quick to tell me she preferred a blue-and-white dotted swiss because it would brighten the bedroom.

That day she told me she was going to France and then North Africa for most of the summer, her treat to herself for getting her degree. She wouldn't be back until mid-August.

"Send me a postcard," I said, but she never did.

The next time I saw Gemma was at a neighborhood swimming pool filled with screaming children during one of those early September heat waves. I went only because I was desperate for the feel of cool water against my skin, but the noise and the glare of sun on water and concrete soon gave me a headache. I lay down on my towel on a patch of dried grass shaded by the building next door and closed my eyes. After a few minutes, I smelled her on the hot breeze, like a fish-rich pond or a field of new-mown hay, along with the sharp, sweet tang that was hers alone. I rolled onto my side and opened my eyes to the sight of her sitting on the edge of the pool in a red bikini, her hair and skin glistening with rosy highlights in the sun. She was talking to two other young women who stood in water up to their knees at the shallow end. I was too far away to hear what they said, but one of the women put an arm around the other's shoulder while they all laughed. I shut my eyes, still inhaling her, my headache cured by her scent, which seemed to have come closer, enveloping me like fresh water. When I opened my eyes, I found her standing above me.

Gemma crouched down, murmuring, "Hello there," as though she'd never gone away. "I've been thinking of you," she added.

When she put her towel down beside mine, I sat up.

"I hate public pools." She stretched out on her stomach, her head turned toward me. "So full of damned kids you can't even swim."

I ran a hand lightly over her bottom because her bathing suit looked like raw silk. It was.

She dug her toes into her towel, turning her head toward me as she closed her eyes. "Funny how darkness seems to make the noise go away."

I, too, sensed the buzz of the pool receding as I bent over her and there, in the open, kissed her lips. Gemma didn't resist, though there wasn't much of a response, either.

"I'd like to get away from here," she sighed, "to some-place cool."

I thought of her old house, protected from the heat by trees and thick walls. Her eyes opened, then she smiled up at me as though she knew what I was thinking. "My house isn't far," she said. "Let's go over there."

I agreed, trying to recall the mythology: if a person invites a vampire three times, does she belong to the vampire forever? But what was this vampire game I played in my mind? Hadn't my kind—old, white—been draining her kind—young, black—long enough? Did I want nothing but to drink, to take? She invited me, I told myself as I followed her, and my myth continued: a vampire can go where she's invited.

We walked down her street of old houses, each one with a narrow strip of grass or garden in front to break up the con-crete and asphalt, each with a pine or maple tree beside it. The odor of cut grass rose between us, making me want to take her hand, but I didn't until we reached her front walk, when our hands seemed to meet by mutual consent.

In the cool, dark living room of Gemma's house, dark pine boughs pressed against one window, blocking out the sun, and the drapes, now a clean light blue, were pulled shut on the other. As the hot, sticky day fell away from us, we became cool enough to touch more than hands. I stood behind her, burying my nose in her hair, inhaling the rich scent at the back of her neck, swallowing it as though I could drink her.

She turned to peck my lips, quicker than I'd have liked. "Lemonade?" she asked.

In the kitchen she poured two large glasses, which we drank in silence. I'd forgotten I was thirsty for anything but Gemma until I swallowed that home-squeezed juice. After I drained my glass, she poured me another.

"There's a lemon tree out back," she said. "Big old thing, been there forever, and loaded with fruit. I don't know what to do with them all except make gallons of lemonade. Now I know why Belle was famous for her lemon meringue pies—she had years of practice."

Her body was as smooth and solid as the oak kitchen table where we sat drinking, where I traced a cut in the wood with my finger, then put my hand on hers to trace the smooth, long tendons, turning her hands over to reveal pink palms and delicate wrists pulsing with life. My hand against hers was old parchment, a historical object drained of life, yet as eternal as old ivory gloves behind glass in a museum.

She let me touch her hands, her veins, opening her life to me. I stared into her eyes as I lifted one wrist to kiss it, right where her blood ran close to the surface, wondering as I did so whether I could be a real vampire, whether I could sink my teeth in right now to drink her, even though this blood wasn't the blood that drew me to her.

Unsafe, whispered the realist still conscious inside me. Blood carries diseases, carries AIDS.

Vampires don't get AIDS, I told the realist, annoyed at the intrusion on my fantasy. Vampires are immortal.

Gemma stood up, holding both my hands over the table, and yawned, showing her pink mouth like a cat while she arched her body in a stretch.

"I'm so tired," she said, "like I've been hypnotized."

Were my pale blue eyes that strong? I felt a bit frightened of my power, if in fact it was mine.

"Come take a nap with me," she said with a smile that let me know she was playing with me, as though I were her prey.

She took my hand to lead me to her bedroom, the bed turned down to reveal mahogany sheets that matched the wood of the bedposts. I saw that she'd taken my advice about the red and purple paisley for the curtains, adding a thin undercurtain of rose silk voile behind them that gave the room a pink glow.

She pulled her T-shirt over her head, stepped out of her shorts, and stood for a moment in her red bikini to let me admire the rough silk against her glowing skin.

"I found this when I was traveling. I'd been looking for it for months and there it was, waiting for me in Paris." She untied the top and slipped off the bottom, then stretched out on the bed, where her body disappeared into the smooth sheets as though she were colorless. When she lifted her hands, palms up, reaching to me as she spread her thighs, I saw the white string between her legs like a fishing line holding what I wanted at the other end, a string that quivered as she swam across her smooth sheets.

"These are great sheets to use when I have my period," she said, warning me.

I nodded, unable to say how much I desired the smell and taste of her blood. She reached under the bed, taking out a roll of plastic wrap and one of those boxes of plastic gloves that pull out like Kleenex. "I have these if you want," she said.

Lovers' bodies must be covered in plastic now, though the memory of a time when that wasn't necessary aroused me: blood on my fingers, in my cuticles, caught under my nails, the blood I didn't appreciate when I would have been free to lap it up. I held my hands out to her, seeing they were still dead white despite the pink light, then sat on the bed, kicking the plastic wrap and gloves back under. When she stroked my arm, I could feel my own blood begin to wake, to move, to pick up strength from her fingertips.

Slowly Gemma raised her hands to my breast and began to unbutton my long white dress. After she slipped it down over my shoulders, I continued to unbutton it to the floor, stepped out of it, then peeled off the bathing suit I still wore underneath. I had to show her what I was because the aging body can be a shock to someone who doesn't know what to expect. I looked in her eyes for signs of disgust, the widening pupils, the diffraction of the iris I'd glimpsed lately in others who looked away, but her eyes took in the whole of me, the drooping breasts with soft dry skin between them and nipples so pale they were hardly visible, the sagging stomach, the flabby ass, all the bits of me that had been lifted and covered by my suit. Her eyes seemed to approve of this picture.

She sat up and took my hands, pulling me onto the bed again, pulling me on top of her, wrapping those warm dark arms around me. Life flowed from her to me, a gift I took. She sucked my nipples until they turned red, rubbed my hands until they flushed rosily in the pink light.

"You're cold," she said. "How could your hands be so cold on such a hot day?"

Gemma imprisoned me between her warm legs, pressing against me with her clit, which felt like a lit match on my thigh. I leaned into that flame, feeling my flesh glow, picturing my skin turning dark and rich as life burned into it. She pulled away, separating her legs and pointing down with her fingers to the white string that floated out from her cunt.

"Okay," I whispered, "yes," nuzzling my nose down there, but with a hand on my crotch she pushed me down, separating my lips to reveal my pale clit, then sat up to reach under the bed, pulling out the roll of plastic wrap, ripping off a small piece to put carefully over my clit before sucking it until my whole cunt quivered and turned a dark, moist pink as though by sucking she had given me her blood.

"My turn," I murmured, reaching my pink hand to her dark cunt. Spreading her lips apart was like opening a flower, with the outer petals a red so dark it seemed brown while the inner petals increased in lightness until I reached the pink interior, which gradually darkened as my fingertips swooped over the stamen in the middle. As I tugged her string with my teeth, I recalled an examination I'd had years ago when I had my period and the doctor, a woman, pulled out my tampon, richly dark with the blood I still had in those days, and held it up for a second before tossing it in the garbage, a second of unembarrassed admiration which united the two of us.

I wanted to drink this woman's blood, to become whole and darker than I'd ever been, but the realist intruded on my fantasy again: blood can carry AIDS and death, those riders on life's liquidity. Can dykes give each other AIDS through their menstrual blood? Some say yes, some say they don't know—so many rumors feed every legend. I tugged on that string until I felt it give like a cork, then eased the thing out of her, a tiny birth of red-soaked cotton. I held it up like my doctor had before swaddling it in the plastic wrap from my clit and putting it carefully into the wastebasket beside the bed, then pulling off another, larger piece of the wrap to spread between her legs. I lowered my face until I could reach her cunt with my tongue, which I moved back and forth from clit to opening, probing the plastic where the dark blood oozed out and spread like vermilion paint over a clear canvas. As I imagined lapping her blood, its scent seemed to change to that of a good rare beef.

When I was a child I went with my mother to one of those new supermarkets where the meat counter was spread with roasts wrapped in clear plastic instead of paper, price tags stuck to the top so you didn't have to ask the butcher for anything, but could just quickly make your selection. While my mother examined the frozen goods opposite the meat counter—beans and strawberries in February!—I furtively stuck my tongue against a chunk of beef to taste the red juices just beneath the surface of the plastic. I moved on to a leg of lamb, a chicken, secretly licking and savoring the different flavors the sanitary wrappings had allowed to leak, all the while watching my mother's back so I'd be able to stop the moment she turned around.

Was I deprived of meat during war rationing in the '40s? I remember occasional liver and chicken, but not much else. Is that what fed my hunger for blood then and now? The super-markets of the '50s were a revelation, and so was the woman now beneath my tongue. After those marches in the '70s, holding signs saying "We are not meat!," how could I lick a woman I compared to beef? But all of us are meat to each other: I'm a stringy old piece of chicken, past its prime but still great for soup, and the woman beneath the plastic wrap, a rich, raw, tender heifer, making my tongue young as I lap at the wrapping.

Gemma gave an annoyed groan, whispering, "Other side," so I slurped my tongue over her clit, stage right, until her breathing quickened. Beef doesn't give orders. My tongue moved quickly from clit to cunt, pulling back so I could watch the red juices pool beneath the plastic, which had a bloody, meaty taste to it. Was it just her scent's influence on my taste buds, or was the plastic permeable?

Desire was beginning to overcome doubt. Why not drink her blood? I wanted that moment of pleasure, I wanted to die into it, to die old and depraved, to die now. My tongue's motions grew more violent, as though it had developed a life of its own along with a desire to break through all barriers. She threw herself from side to side while my head followed, my hands holding tight to the edges of the plastic.

Who knows what's safe and what's not? What are the long-term effects of sucking on plastic heated by a body hot as a microwave oven, releasing God knows what poisonous chemicals into your mouth? Once, just this once, taste her blood, Gemma's good, she's safe, and if she's not, it doesn't matter, you're old enough to retire soon from life as well as from work, you've got to have it one last time. How many more chances will there be to die in such ecstasy?

And so I lifted that wrap, turning it over and licking every drop of her sweet bloody essence from it, then lapping her cunt clean, and then her clit until she came with a final rush of blood that soaked my chin and ran down my breasts, painting my nipples as I drank it along with all the men she knew nothing about and the women she thought she knew so well. I was both a vampire who couldn't die and an old woman who would die soon, a daredevil in a collapsing balloon. As I drank her orgasm I had my own, quivering like a baby as I sucked her.

I was sated; I wanted only to lie beside Gemma on her mahogany sheets and stroke her thigh lubricated with her rich blood. I raised my hand, ruddy around the fingernails, and rubbed my arms with her blood until they looked soft and brown in the light that filtered through the rose curtains.

"What would your Aunt Belle say about this?" I whispered in her ear.

She sighed, then laughed a deep, relaxed laugh I'd never heard from her before. "Oh, Belle. She's terribly jealous, of course, if she's looking down from anywhere. She could be possessive as hell, but I'll bet she's glad for me at the same time, glad I'm alive and glad I learned so much from her."

"You never told me," I murmured, less surprised than I felt I should be.

Again the deep sigh, the rich laugh. "I wasn't sure how to begin. I thought you didn't matter enough to tell, until I went away. Belle wasn't a relative, of course, but I often called her Aunt Belle, which was pretty funny, considering what our relationship became. She was my mentor, my freshman English teacher at the university and then my lover after she retired; she continued to be my teacher in so many ways. We never lived together because she had this house and I preferred to live with roommates my own age. Of course it was hard and there were conflicts." She sat up, wrapping a dark sheet around her shoulders. Though the room was still cool, I could see the sun pulsing through the thin curtains.

"And that's the mystery," I said.

Gemma smiled, but her eyes were liquid, which made me afraid she'd start to cry. I'm not good at sympathy.

"We both had no one else," she said. "I have no family except a stepmother I don't get along with, and she had no family left. We were everything to each other. I just regret my rebellion. I couldn't live here under her wing, I wasn't ready yet, and then she was dead, she left me this house, and so here I am, living with her ghost."

"And her coffeepot, her cooker, all the ghosts of my childhood," I said to make her laugh, which to my relief she did.

"Well, I'm updating. I've put in circuit breakers instead of fuses, and I've got a microwave and my computer's connected to the Internet."

When I got up to use the bathroom, I saw in the mirror that my skin was no longer parchment, but a healthy pink, and I could swear my hair was darker, my eyes a deeper blue. Was this an illusion? I looked back to see Gemma sitting on the bed as she tied on the top of her red bikini, seeming darker and more beautiful than ever, as though the transfusion she gave me had been returned to her with interest. I felt human again, with Belle's good old hardwood floor solid under my bare feet, while Gemma, smiling at me, licking her lips, blew me a kiss as she got off the bed.

She Who Waits

Catherine Lundoff

It's another Thursday night down at the Crypt and there you are. Eyes rimmed black and face powdered white until you look like Gaiman's Death. Nothing but blood-red velvet and black lace will do for you tonight because you are the Countess of Bathory. The Bride of Dracula. The look is you and you are it because that's all there is.

All the little posers from the burbs who watch you walk in want to be you or have you. Some don't care which. Neither do you. Bad case of existential ennui all around. Just the sight of the crowd makes you yawn.

You skirt the dance floor on spiky black heels. The walls are humming to Nine Inch Nails and you can barely see your friends on the other side of the bar through the clouds of smoke. That's when you see her. The blonde at the dark end of the bar in the biker-chick-from-hell outfit looks up and meets your incredulous eyes. Long blonde hair yanked back from a bony face, really odd blue eyes, lots of tattoos, some of them homemade. Definitely looking for the Iron Hog Roadhouse down the street, you think dismissively.

Then she smiles and those weird eyes take over. You're drowning in a sea of blue. Warm salty waves lap at your clit and you can feel your nipples harden. Suddenly it doesn't matter that you're drooling over a chick who's in the wrong bar on the wrong night. You're not even worthy to lick the dragon tattoo that wraps the length of her muscular right forearm. The impossible just came calling.

The smell of black leather overrides smoke and perfume and you realize you're standing between her legs in front of the barstool. She keeps smiling. Her teeth are very large, long, yellowish. One of them (not a canine) is even tipped with gold. The view's enough to tell you that this is what you've been waiting for.

But then, you've already guessed that. You reach out a tentative hand to touch the exposed skin of her stomach and it's cold, colder than anything that breathes. Just like you knew it would be. She's not even cute. Not that you care. You realize that it isn't going to be like Anne Rice. The thought is vaguely disappointing.

A callused hand reaches out and pinches your right nipple through the velvet dress. It's a casual gesture, like she's your new girlfriend and she doesn't care who's watching. The stubby fingers roll your nipple around into a hard point, tearing a groan from your throat. The black lace panties that you put on for tonight are getting soaked. A line of moisture runs down your leg. She keeps smiling. Her eyes never leave yours. The smell of your sex rises up between you. She slips a hand between your legs and sticks a finger inside.

Classy, you think with the last little corner of your mind that you still call yours. You grab her black leather chaps and hold on for balance. The blood rushes to your face in embarrassed desire and your hips rock forward of their own accord, riding her finger. She pulls it out and licks it off. Almost against your will, you moan. She could take you now and she knows it. It wouldn't matter. There's no one else here but her.

Instead she rises to her booted feet and pulls you out onto the dance floor. Now Dead Can Dance is filling the room. The burb kids all mill around trying to figure out what they should be doing. The band's not real Goth, but the blonde favors the DJ in her distant booth with a small ironic smile. Pretty eclectic biker, you think fuzzily in the seconds that her eyes don't own you.

You ride the music in a trance. When she breaks eye contact, you can see your friends trying really hard not to see you. It almost makes you laugh to know that you're fuck-dancing with something who's almost everything they wish they were. You wish you were. She reaches up and runs her fingers through your dyed black hair, tugging on it to pull your head back. It makes you feel vulnerable and you savor the novelty. Especially when she starts kissing your neck, long teeth just grazing your skin.

You're about the same height so it's easy for her to slide a black leather-covered leg between your lace stockings. Your soaking-wet panties ride up between your pussy lips as you rub yourself against her thigh. She turns you slowly, teeth still sauntering over your exposed collarbone and shoulder.

Your eyes are shut as she circles you to press against your back and nip her way along your neck. One cold hand rises from your waist to come to rest on your breast, short fingers stroking an already pebble-hard nipple. Her thigh is back between your legs and you grind your ass into her as you float away on the slow music.

Then the music's changed and the crowd around you is starting to notice things. Like the queen of the local scene practically fucking on the dance floor with someone that no one can quite remember seconds after they see her. She's got you by the hand. You're headed for the door. You see eyes slide away from the two of you as you go past. You wonder if they'll remember you. You wonder if you'll be back to find out.

This is it then.

That cold fact scares you for a moment. You glance around briefly at what you had. It wasn't much, but it was yours. You go with her anyway. It'll be worth it. You hope. The frat-boy bouncer gives you a nasty grin on your way out the door. She looks at him. He stops smiling and looks away, quickly.

You think about how he looks at you and your friends and you step up to him. Close, very close, you whisper against his beer-scented skin, "I'll be back." He shudders and doesn't meet your eyes. You smile tightly and follow her out-side. Definitely worth it. She's got her bike parked in the alley around the corner. It sits there, chrome gleaming under the lone lightbulb in its metal cage. For a moment, you think you see a saddle and a flash of red eyes, but then they're gone. It's just you and her and a big Harley. You start breathing faster. She's right behind you now, pushing you up against the bike, bending your face down over the seat. You've never done it like this before and you're shivering as you spread your legs and she slides up your tight velvet skirt, exposing your ass. There is the sound of tearing as she shreds your panties off and the light breeze cools your bare skin.

All of a sudden, you're rubbing your face on the leather of the seat, breathing it in. She runs a hand over your ass, then shoves one finger up your hole. You gasp into the black leather, writhing against it. She pushes her other hand inside you, and you arch your back, thrusting against her hands.

The sound of the zipper on your dress fills the alley, echo-ing with your moans, as she pulls it down with her teeth. The dress slides off your shoulders as you lean your hands into the bike. The cool air hits your breasts, shrinking your already-hard nipples. You lean back down to rub them on the seat, teasing them until you can barely stand the touch of the cool leather.

By now, she's got her whole fist in your pussy and three fingers up your ass. You thrust and thrust against the icy cold of her hands. Your juices are pouring down your legs under the lacy garters and pooling in your shoes. There are voices nearby, leaving the club, and you wonder if they can see you. You hope they can. The first orgasm hits hard and you howl into the seat, muffling the sound.

She pulls her fingers out of your ass and slips off a glove you didn't know she had on. You shudder as a sharp nail draws its way down your back. The skin parts behind it and the warm blood runs quickly over your cool flesh. The pain makes you whimper. You feel her laugh quietly as she licks the wound, savoring your fear, your desire. She thrusts into you again with her other hand, and you come, every nerve screaming for more. This time you don't care who hears and you shriek. You want more. It has begun.

As her hand tugs out of you, she pulls you around to face her. You look up through a blur of smeared makeup and desire into those blue, blue eyes. They're almost glowing now. She knows what you want. She probably wanted the same thing once. Maybe. She shoves you back onto the seat and bends over you, one nail still barely tickling your clit. You squirm against her and she pulls on your hair to turn your face to the side. Her tongue caresses your neck and the pressure on your clit sends you over, bucking against her hand. Her teeth find your vein and she begins to drink.

It isn't the way you thought it would be. You had more elegant circumstances in mind, something very eighteenth century. This is more like Sturgis. It hurts. You gasp as the finger on your clit twists, fingers sliding inside you. Her insistent mouth draws on the holes that she's punctured in your neck. You ride her hand. You ride her power. It leaves you floating away on the high.

Just before you pass out, she pulls away. You look dreamily at her bony face and bloodstained teeth as she smiles down at you. She's almost glowing with health now; even her long face is rounding out a little, softening. You feel dizzy. She pushes you onto the pussy pad and climbs up in front of you.

The bike roars into life and you speed out of the alley just as you are. Dress pushed down around your waist, breasts bare, wet crotch grinding against her leather chaps while you hold on as tight as you can. No one walking on the sidewalk or passing in the surrounding cars seems to notice. You wish they would. You feel sleazy. The seat is soaking and you squirm against her on the wet leather, letting your body beg for more.

The building looks familiar as she pulls up in back of it. Dazed as you are, you realize that she's coming home with you. Good thing that your last roommate flaked out and you're living there alone now. She stops the bike and you climb off. She walks you up the back stairs with her hand holding the back of your neck. The ice of her skin wars with the heat from your clit.

You have no idea where your purse is. It had your keys in it. The two of you stand before your locked apartment door for a moment. "You're invited in," you whisper. She laughs softly. It's a dry, chuckling sound, like bones rubbing together. You start to shiver, out of control. She looks hard at the door. You can't imagine it defying her, and it doesn't. The deadbolt clicks and it opens slowly. You can almost feel Mrs. Arnold across the hall spying through her peephole.

The blonde stops you in the doorway and leans down to run her tongue over your bare breasts. You groan, clutching her long blonde hair while your nipples burn, burst into flame under the pressure of her tongue and teeth. She looks up at

Mrs. Arnold's peephole and you hear a gasp, and the sound of feet thudding away. You meet her eyes and smile, sinking back into the ocean that calls you. You're not shivering anymore.

Then you're inside the apartment. It's clear that you blow most of your money on clothes. She doesn't stop to admire your minimal decor or your CD collection, though she smiles slightly at your poster from *The Hunger*. She doesn't remind you of Catherine Deneuve. For the first time, you wish that she would tell you what she was like before, how she became what she is. But it's too late. You try anyway. "How did you...cross over?"

The blue of her eyes is starting to change, growing darker as she reaches out and casually pulls your dress down. She doesn't answer, but she grimaces speculatively, running her tongue along those long canines. You shudder a little, an involuntary reaction. She runs a hand up your thigh. You dimly remember that you still have your stockings on and you stand there shivering again while she paces slowly around you. You stifle a mental picture of tigers at the zoo. Of goats staked out at the edge of the jungle. You remember that you want this. She reaches out and lifts your chin in her hand. There is no pity in her eyes.

You reach out for what is there and fall in. Heat rushes up from your clit and you ask no more questions. She pinches your nipples hard, pushing you back onto the ratty sofa. You spread your legs as she drops between your thighs, long tongue beginning to tease your clit. All fear gone now, you ride her tongue, groaning as it tickles and coaxes you.

Her fingers thrust into you one by one, thrusting and pushing, until her whole hand can fit inside. You moan, spreading your legs up and onto her shoulders to make more room. She fills you, grinding up and into your pussy walls, and you are wide open. All the while her tongue circles. You come with a shout, hands involuntarily clutching her head. She turns, sinking her teeth into the vein in your inner thigh.

Each time she drinks from you, you wander a little farther out. This time, you're soaring through the clouds on a moonlit night, just like you've always dreamed of doing. There's just a small pain tying you down and you try to ignore it as you sail near the full moon. The white light shines down on you and you close your eyes against it. You fly under it, the cool winds lifting your leathery wings. This, at least, is just as you dreamed it would be. The pain becomes sharper.

You come back to find that she's not ready to let you go yet. You are spread-eagled and facedown on your bed. A rope runs around each of your wrists and under your dilapidated mattress. She is kneeling above you, naked, with a candle in her hands. Hot wax trickles onto your back, sending a river of fire that runs from your skin to your clit and you scream.

She runs an ice cube over the small burns, and you jerk away from the sensation. Her knee drives into your pussy as she does it again. And again. You tug on the ropes, fully awake as you grind back against her knee. Your clit rubs her hard cold flesh. The heat and cold and the ice of her knee all push you back into your body. You hear your voice begging hoarsely for her to stop, for her to do it again, for her to take you completely.

And she does. She bends over your writhing body, sinks her teeth into the side of your throat and drinks. You feel the blood leaving your body and you twist, tensing, muscles convulsing, as you come so hard that the rope breaks. You look up to see her, head tilted back in ecstasy, mouth open and howling, your blood running down her jaw onto her small white breasts. Then, the clouds are back and you are soaring away, your body still coming on the bed below you. Upward you glide until the moon winks out.

When you awaken, it is sometime—hours, days, weeks— later. You are alone and it is after sundown. Things have changed. That awareness fills you with a cold happiness, like

197

a good feed. She pulled the curtains of your room shut before she went, and you mentally thank her for this kindness, as you would thank another pack member for not killing you as a cub. You reach an almost reluctant hand up to your mouth. They're there. You almost stand to look at yourself in the mirror before you remember that there is probably no point.

You feel restless, filled with a driving hunger. It's feeding time. You try to concentrate on being elegant, coldly sophisticated. But it's hard to feel much of anything around the need to hunt, so you rise sinuously and pace over to the closet. A black vintage dress comes to hand and you pull on your costume for the night. You go out, heading for a new bar, because that is something you understand.

It's a seedy place, the kind that the old you would have been terrified to stay in. Before the change that is running through your veins tonight, filling them, glowing, burning everything in its wake. You watch the pimps and the hustlers and the whores dispassionately, pushing their attention away when it becomes too focused. You're waiting for the right one to arrive while the scent of warm blood fills your nostrils. It's almost too much and you begin to dream as you sit at the bar, dreaming about bathing in blood, feeding until you are sated.

The big man who walks in then has dreams, too. You can read them by simply looking deep into his eyes. They're a meal in themselves. You reach out.

He's at your side in moments, cautious, but unable to say no. He's another kind of predator, but not tonight. The fight whets your appetite as he struggles to turn away, to imagine that the coming night will fulfill his fantasies. You pretend to sip your drink, sparely, elegantly, deflecting the interest of the bartender.

Just for fun, you run a casual hand over his crotch. His arousal is sweet and you smile at him, watching his eyes widen a little in fear, his tight jeans bulging at your touch. You leave together. No one will remember you. You draw his dreams of power and pain out of him with his life's blood and leave him in an alley some blocks from the bar.

Your veins burn until you want to howl your success at the moon. Survival dictates that you do not call attention to what you are and what you have done. Not until you're better at it, at least. You note the lack of sophistication in this thought, but it doesn't bother you now. You are living dead. Child of the night.

As you walk past the Crypt on your way home, you notice that they have a flyer up for a new bouncer. It makes you laugh quietly. Perhaps you'll come back and apply for the job.

Blood and Silver
Pat Califia

Once upon a time (and still), there was a young woman who was very tired of being treated like a little girl. Her name was Sylvia Rufina. Like most female persons in her predicament, the only available avenue of rebellion was for her to pretend to obey the commandments of others while protecting a secret world within which she was both empress and impresario. Having frequently been told, "Go out and play," more and more, that was what she did. Her family lived in a small farmhouse that felt smaller still because of the vast wilderness that surrounded it. She was at home in this untamed and complex landscape, if only because there was nothing false or sentimental about it.

One of the games she played was "holding still." This was a game learned under confusing and painful circumstances at home. But hidden within a stand of birches or scrub oak, she was not molested. Instead, if she learned to let her thoughts turn green and her breath slow to the pace of sap, she became privy to an endless variety of fascinating events: how beavers felled trees, how mice raised their children, the way a fox twitched its nose when it spotted a vole.

One day, when she was studying the spots on a fawn that dozed in a copse just a few dozen yards from where she held her breath, the wolf appeared. He (for there was no mistaking the meaning of his big face, thick shoulders, and long legs, even if she had not espied his genitals) was an amazing silver color, with dark black at the root of his stippled fur. His teeth were as white as the moon, and his eyes were an intelligent and fearless brown. They studied each other for long minutes, wolf and woman, until he lost interest in her silence and relaxed limbs, and went away.

The next time he came, he walked right up to her and put his nose up, making it clear that he expected a greeting of some sort. So she carefully, slowly, bonelessly lowered her body and allowed him to examine her face and breasts. His breath was very hot, perhaps because it was autumn and the day was chilly. His fur smelled of earth and the snow that was to come, and the air he expelled was slightly rank, an aroma she finally identified as blood.

Satisfied with her obeisance, he went away again, tail wagging a little, as if he were pleased with himself. This was the only undignified thing she had seen him do, but it did not make her think less of him. She appreciated the fact that the wolf did not caper, bow down, yelp, or slaver on her, in the slavish and inconsiderate way of dogs. The wolf was no whore for man's approval. He fed himself.

She did not see the wolf again for nearly a week. But when he returned, he brought the others: two males and three females, one of them his mate. This female was nearly as large as her spouse and as dark as he was metallic, the eclipse to his moon. Some instinct told Sylvia Rufina that she must greet them on all fours and then roll over upon her back. This seemed to excite everyone to no end. She was nosed a good deal, fairly hard, licked three or four times, and nipped once. The surprisingly painful little bite came from the leader of the pack, who was letting her know it was time to get up and come away with them. It was later in the day than she usually stayed out-of-doors, and as she fled, lights came on in the little house, dimming the prettier lights that bloomed in the deep black sky.

Racing with the wolves was like a dream, or perhaps it was normal life that was a dream, for the long run with the wolf pack was a flight through vivid sensations that made everything that had happened to her indoors seem drained of color and meaning. She never questioned her ability to keep up with them any more than she questioned the new shape she seemed to wear. Her legs were tireless; running was a joy. Even hunger was a song in her belly. And when the group cut off and cornered a deer, she knew her place in the attack as if she had read and memorized a part in a play.

After they ate, most of them slept, yawning from the effort it took to digest that much raw, red meat. Unaccustomed to so much exercise and the rich diet, she slept also.

And woke up miles from home, alone, in harsh daylight. Every muscle in her body hurt, and her clothing was ripped, her hair full of twigs, leaves, and burrs. Her shoes were gone and her stockings a ruin. Somehow she made her way home, hobbling painfully, trying to think of a story that would excuse her absence without triggering a proscription against hikes in the mountains.

There was no need for an alibi. Her family had already decided what must have happened to her. She had followed a butterfly or a bluejay or a white hart and gotten lost in the woods. When she crossed the threshold and heard inklings of this story, she saw that each of her family members had picked a role, just as the wolves had memorized their dance of death with one another. And she gave herself up, too exhausted to fight back, letting them exclaim over and handle and hurt her with their stupidity and melodrama. Though a part of her sputtered indignantly, silently: Lost! In the woods! Where I've roamed for three-and-twenty years? I'm more likely to get lost on my way to the privy!

Unfortunately, when she had gone missing they had called upon the Hunter and asked him to search for her. He was someone she avoided. His barn was covered with the nailed-up, tanning hides of animals, and thatched with the antlers of deer he had slain. Sylvia Rufina thought it grotesque. Her father had taught her to recognize certain signals of an unhealthy interest. After having finally grown old enough to no longer be doted upon by her incestuous sire, she could not tolerate a stranger whose appetites felt revoltingly familiar. When the Hunter lit his pipe, waved his hand, and put a stop to the whining voices so glad of their opportunity to rein her in, she gaped at him, hoping against her own judgment that he would have something sensible to say.

He had brought something that would solve the problem. No need to restrict the young woman's love of nature, her little hobbies. No doubt it gave her much pleasure to add new leaves and ferns to her collection. (In fact, she did not have such a collection, but she was aware that many proper young ladies did, and so she bit her tongue, thinking it would make a good excuse for future rambling.) The Hunter shook out a red garment and handed it to her.

It was a scarlet sueded-leather cloak with a hood, heavy enough to keep her warm well into winter. The lining was a slippery fabric that made her slightly sick to touch it. He had kept hold of the garment as he handed it to her, so their hands touched when she took it from him, and her eyes involuntarily met his. The predatory desire she saw there made her bow her head as if in modesty, but in fact to hide her rage. Even during a killing strike, the wolves knew nothing as shameful and destructive as the Hunter's desire. She knew, then, that he had bought this red-hooded cloak for her some time ago and often sat studying it, dreaming of how she would look laid down upon it. If she wore it in the forest, she would be visible for miles. It would be easy for a hunter, this Hunter, to target and track her then.

She was poked and prodded and prompted to say thank you, but would not. Instead she feigned sleep, or a faint. And so she was borne up to bed, feeling the Hunter's hard-done-by scowl following her supine body up the stairs like an oft-refused man on his wedding night.

It was weeks before she was deemed well enough to let out of the house. The red cloak hung in her closet in the meantime, its shout of color reducing all her other clothes to drab rags. It would snow soon, and she did not think she would survive being stranded behind the pack, in human form, to find her way home in a winter storm. But she must encounter them again, if only to prove to herself that the entire adventure had not been a fevered dream.

Her chance finally came. A neighbor whom nobody liked much, a widowed old woman with much knowledge about the right way to do everything, was in bed with a broken leg. This was Granny Gosling. As a little girl, Sylvia Rufina had gone to Granny Gosling with her secret troubles, mistaking gray hair and myopia for signs of kindness and wisdom. Her hope to be rescued or at least comforted was scalded out of existence when the old woman called her many of the same names she had heard in a deeper voice, with a mustache and tongue scouring her ear and her long flannel nightgown bunched up painfully in her armpits. The child's hot sense of betrayal was quickly replaced with stoicism. We can bear the things that cannot be altered, and now she knew better than to struggle against the inevitable.

Other neighbors, a prosperous married couple with a bumper crop of daughters overripe for the harvest of marriage, were hosting a dance with an orchestra. People were to come early to an afternoon supper, dance in the evening, and spend the night. Mother and father had their own marketing of nubile damsels to attend to, but their house stood closer to Granny Gosling's than anyone else's. They were expected to go and lend a hand. What a relief it was to everyone when Sylvia Rufina said quietly at breakfast that she thought it might do her soul a great deal of good to visit the sick and unfortunate that day. She was young. There would be other cotillions.

As the other women in the household bustled around, curling their hair and pressing the ruffles on their dresses, she made up a basket of victuals. She picked things she herself was especially fond of because she knew anything she brought would be found unpalatable by the injured granny. She helped everyone into their frocks, found missing evening bags and hair ribbons, sewed a buckle on a patent-leather shoe, and kissed her mother and her sisters as they went off, consciences relieved, to the dance. Her father, realizing no embrace would be offered, avoided the opportunity to receive one. As soon as their carriage disappeared around a bend in the road, she set off in the red cloak and kept the hateful thing on until she had gone over a rise and down the other side and was out of her family's sight.

Then she took off the cloak, bundled it up as small as she could, and put it inside a hollow tree, heartily hoping that birds and squirrels would find it, rip it to shreds, and use it to make their winter nests. At the foot of this tree she sat, snug in the nut-brown cloak she had worn underneath the Hunter's gift, and ate every single thing she had packed into the basket. By the time she finished her feast, it was nearly dark. Cheerful beyond measure to be free at last from human society, she went rambling in quest of her soul mates, the four-footed brothers and sisters of the wind.

Faster and faster she went as her need for them became more desperate, and the world streamed by in a blur of gaudy fall colors. The cold air cut her lungs like a knife, and she found herself pressing the little scar the wolf had left on her collarbone, using that pang to keep herself moving forward. The sun plunged below the hills, and she ran on four legs now, chasing hints among the delicious odors that flooded her nose and mouth. At last she found a place where they had been, a trail that led to their present whereabouts, and the reunion was a glad occasion. There was a happy but orderly circle of obeisances and blessings—smelling, licking, and tail wagging—and favorite sticks and bones were tossed into the air and tugged back and forth.

Then they hunted, and all was right with the world. She was happy to be the least among them, the anchor of their hierarchy. Despite her status as a novice, she knew a thing or two that could be of value to the pack. The crotchety neighbor would never be in pain again nor have occasion to complain about the disrespect of young folk or the indecency of current ladies' fashions.

But this time, forewarned that dawn would put an end to her four-footed guise, the young woman took precautions. While everyone else turned in the direction of the den, where they could doze, meat-drunk, she bid them farewell with heartbroken nudges of her nose, and retraced her footsteps back to the hollow tree. There, she slept a little, until dawn forced her to put on the hateful red cloak again and return home. She was lucky this time and arrived well before her hungover, overfed, and overheated relations.

She thought that perhaps, with what she now knew, she could endure the rest of her life. She would have two lives, one within this cottage and the other in the rest of the world. Knowing herself to be dangerous, she could perhaps tolerate infantilization. And so she made herself agreeable to her mother and her sisters, helped them divest themselves of their ballroom finery, and put out a cold lunch for them. She herself was not hungry. The smell of cooked meat made her nauseous.

She had not planned to go out again that night. She knew that if her excursions became too frequent, she would risk being discovered missing from her bed. But when the moon came up, it was as if a fever possessed her. She could not stay indoors. She pined for the soothing sensation of earth beneath clawed toes, the gallop after game, the sweet reassuring smell of her pack mates as they acknowledged her place among them. And so she slipped out, knowing it was unwise. The only concession she made to human notions of decorum was to take the hated red cloak with her.

And that was how he found her, in the full moon, catching her just before she took off the red leather garment. "Quite the little woodsman, aren't you?" he drawled, toying with his knife.

Sylvia Rufina would not answer him.

"Cat got your tongue? Or is it perhaps a wolf that has it, I wonder? Damn your cold looks. I have something that will melt your ice, you arrogant and unnatural bitch." He took her by the wrist and forced her, struggling, to go with him along the path that led to his house. She could have slipped his grasp if she had taken her wolf form, but something told her she must keep her human wits to deal with what he had to show her.

There was something new nailed up to his barn, a huge pelt that shone in the full moonlight like a well-polished curse. It was the skin of her master, the lord of her nighttime world, the blessed creature whose nip had transformed her into something that could not be contained by human expectations. The Hunter was sneering and gloating, telling her about the murder, how easy she had made it for him to find their den, and he was promising to return and take another wolf's life for every night that she withheld her favors.

His lewd fantasies about her wolfish activities showed, she thought, considerable ignorance of both wolves and women. The wolves were lusty only once a year. The king and queen of the pack would mate; no others. The big silver male had loved her, but there was nothing sexual in his passion. He had been drawn by her misery and decided out of his animal generosity to set her wild heart free. And her desire had been for the wilderness, for running as hard and fast and long as she could, for thirst slaked in a cold mountain stream, and hunger appeased nose-down in the hot red mess of another, weaker creature's belly. She craved autonomy, not the sweaty invasion of her offended and violated womanhood. But the Hunter slurred on with his coarse fancies of bestial orgies, concluding, "After all this time I pined for you, and thought you were above me. Too refined and delicate and sensitive to notice my mean self. Now I find you're just another bitch in heat. How dare you refuse me?"

"Refuse you?" she cried, finding her voice at last. "Why, all you had to do was ask me. It never occurred to me that such a clever and handsome man would take an interest in someone as inexperienced and plain as me. I am only a simple girl, a farmer's daughter, but you are a man of the world." Where this nonsense came from, she did not know, but he lifted his hands from his belt to wrap his arms around her, and that was when she yanked his knife from his belt and buried it to the hilt in the middle of his back.

He died astonished, dribbling blood. She thought it was a small enough penance for the many lives he had taken in his manly pride and hatred of the feral. She took back the knife, planning to keep it, and let him fall.

By his heels, she dragged him back into his own house. Then she took the hide of her beloved down from the barn wall, shivering as she did so. It fell into her arms like a lover and she wept to catch traces of his scent, which lingered still upon his lifeless fur like a memory of pine trees and sage-brush, rabbit-fear and the froth from the muzzle of a red-tailed deer, the perfume of snow shaken off a raven's back. It was easy to saddle the Hunter's horse, take food and money from his house, and then set fire to what remained. The horse did not like her mounting up with a wolf's skin clasped to her bosom, but with knees and heels she made it mind, and turned its nose to the city.

Since a human male had taken what was dearest to her, she determined, the rest of the Hunter's kind now owed her repa-rations. She would no longer suffer under a mother's dictates about propriety and virtue. She would no longer keep silence and let a man, too sure of his strength, back her into a corner. The wolves had taught her much about wildness, about hunters and prey, power and pursuit. One human or a thou-sand, she hated them all equally, so she would go where they clustered together in fear of the forest, and take them for all they were worth.

In the city, the Hunter's coins obtained lodging in a once-fashionable quarter of town. Down the street, she had the red cloak made into a whip with an obscene handle, cuffs, and a close-fitting hood. For herself, she had tall red boots and a corset fashioned. The next day, she placed an advertisement for riding lessons in the daily newspaper. Soon, a man rang her bell to see if she had anything to teach him. He wore a gray suit instead of the Hunter's doeskin and bear fur, but he had the same aura of barely controlled fury. He was wealthy, but his privilege had not set him free. It had instead deepened his resentment of anything he did not own and made him a harsh master over the things that he did possess.

Since he despised the animal within himself, she forced him to manifest it: stripped of anything but his own hide, on all fours, forbidden to utter anything other than a wordless howl. He could not be trusted to govern himself, beast that he was, so she fettered him. And because he believed the animal was inferior to the man, made to be used violently, she beat him the way a drunkard who has lost at cards will beat his own dog. He forgot her injunction against speech when it became clear how the "riding lesson" was to proceed, but she had no mercy. Like most men, he thought of women as cows or brood mares, so if he wanted to experience servitude and degradation, he would have to experience sexual violation as well as bondage and the lash. Bent over a chair, wrists lashed to ankles, he bellowed like a gored bull when the wooden handle of the whip took his male maidenhead.

In the end, he proved her judgment of his character was correct—he knelt, swore his allegiance to her, and tried to lick her, like a servile mutt who wants a table scrap. She took his money and kicked him out with a warning to avoid attempts to sully her in the future. He went away happy, his anger temporarily at bay, his soul a little lighter for the silver that he discarded in a bowl on the foyer table.

Soon Sylvia Rufina's sitting room was occupied by a series of men who arrived full of lust and shame and left poorer but wiser about their own natures. But their pain was no balm for the wounds the Red Mistress, as she came to be called, carried in her psyche. Her self-styled slaves might prate about worship and call her a goddess, but the only thing they worshiped was their own pleasure. She knew, even as she crushed their balls, that they remained the real masters of the world.

Her consolations were private: the occasional meal of raw meat, and nightly slumber beneath a blanket of silver fur. For one whole year, she tolerated the overcrowding, bad smells, and disgusting scorched food of the city. Her fame spread, and gossip about her imperious beauty and cruelty brought her paying customers from as far away as other countries. The notion that one could buy a little freedom, pay for only a limited amount of wildness, bored and amused the Red Mistress.

But she kept her thoughts to herself and kept her money in an ironbound chest. She lived like a monk, but the tools of her trade were not cheap, and she chafed to see how long it took for her hoard of wealth simply to cover the bottom of the box, then inch toward its lid.

When spring came, at first it simply made the city stink even worse than usual, as thawing snow deposited a season's worth of offal upon the streets. There was a tree near Sylvia Rufina's house, and she was painfully reminded of how beautiful and busy the forest would seem now, with sap rising and pushing new green leaves into the warming air. Her own blood seemed to have heated as well, and it grew more difficult to curb her temper with the pretense of submission that fed her treasure chest. An inhuman strength would come upon her without warning. More than one of her slaves left with the unwanted mark of her teeth upon their aging bodies and thought perhaps they should consider visiting a riding mistress who did not take her craft quite so seriously.

The full moon of April caught her unawares, standing naked by her bedroom window, and before she willed it she was herself again, four-footed and calm. After so many months of despicable hard work and monkish living, she was unable to deny herself the pleasure of keeping this form for just a little while. The wolf was fearless and went out the front door as if she owned it. Prowling packs of stray dogs were just one of the many hazards on this city's nighttime streets. Few pedestrians would be bold enough to confront a canid of her size and apparent ferocity. When she heard the sound of a conflict, she went toward it, unfettered by a woman's timidity, ruled by the wolf's confident assumption that wherever there is battle, there may be victuals.

Down a street more racked by poverty than the one on which the Red Mistress plied her trade, outside a tenement, a man in a moth-eaten overcoat and a shabby top hat held a woman by the upper arms and shook her like a rattle. She was being handled so roughly that her hair had begun to come down from where it was pinned on top of her head, so her face and chest were surrounded by a blonde cloud. She wore a low-cut black dress that left her arms indecently bare, and it was slit up the back to display her calves and even a glimpse of her thighs. "Damn you!" the man screamed. "Where's my money?"

The wolf did not like his grating, hysterical voice, and her appetite was piqued by the fat tips of the man's fingers, which protruded from his ruined gloves, white as veal sausages. He smelled like gin and mothballs, like something that ought never to have lived. When he let go of one of the woman's arms so he could take out a pocket handkerchief and mop his brow, the wolf came out of the shadows and greeted him with a barely audible warning and a peek at the teeth for which her kind was named. He was astonished and frightened. The same pocket that had held his handkerchief also contained a straight razor, but before he could fumble it out, the wolf landed in the center of his chest and planted him on his back in the mud. A yellow silk cravat, darned and stained, outlined his throat and was no obstacle.

The wolf disdained to devour him. He was more tender than the querulous granny, but dissolute living had contaminated his flesh. She did not want to digest his sickness. Licking her muzzle clean, she was surprised to see the disheveled woman waiting calmly downwind, her bosom and face marked by the pimp's assault. "Thank you," the woman said softly. She knew her savior was no domesticated pet that had slipped its leash. Her life had been very hard, but she would not have lived at all had she not been able to see what was actually in front of her and work with the truth.

Human speech made the wolf uneasy. She did not want to be reminded of her other form, her other life. She brushed past the woman, eager to sample the evening air and determine if this city held a park where she could ramble.

"Wild thing," said the woman, "let me come with you," and ardent footsteps pattered in the wake of the wolf's silent tread. The wolf could have left her behind in a second but perversely chose not to do so. They came to the outskirts of a wealthy man's estate. His mansion was in the center of a tract of land that was huge by the city's standards and stocked with game birds and deer. A tall wrought-iron fence surrounded this land, and the golden one made herself useful, discovering a place where the rivets holding several spears of iron in place had rusted through. She bent three of them upward so the two of them could squeeze beneath the metal barrier. The scent of crushed vegetation and freshly disturbed earth made the wolf delirious with joy.

Through the park they chased one another, faster and faster, until the girl's shoddy shoes were worn paper-thin and had to be discarded. The game of tag got rougher and rougher until the wolf forgot it was not tumbling about with one of its own and nipped the girl on her forearm. The triangular wound bled enough to be visible even by moonlight, scarlet and silver. Then there were two of a kind, one with fur tinged auburn, another with underfur of gold, and what would be more delicious than a hunt for a brace of hares? One hid while the other flushed out their quarry.

Knowing the potentially deadly sleep that would attack after feeding, Sylvia Rufina urged her new changeling to keep moving, back to the fence and under it. The two of them approached her house from the rear, entering through the garden. The golden one was loath to go back, did not want to take up human ways again. But Sylvia Rufina herded her relentlessly, forced her up the stairs and into the chamber where they both became mud-spattered women howling with laughter.

"You are a strange dream," the child of the streets murmured as the Red Mistress drew her to the bed.

"No dream except a dream of freedom," Sylvia Rufina replied, and pinned her prey to the sheets just as she had taken down the hapless male bawd. The wolf-strength was still vibrant within her, and she ravished the girl with her mouth and hand, her kisses flavored with the heart's blood of the feast they had shared. Goldie was no stranger to the comfort of another woman's caresses, but this was no melancholy gentle solace. This was the pain of hope and need. She struggled against this new knowledge, but the Red Mistress was relentless and showed her so much happiness and pleasure that she knew her life was ruined and changed forever.

The bruised girl could not remember how many times she had relied on the stupor that disarms a man who has emptied his loins. No matter how bitterly they complained about the price she demanded for her attentions, there was always ten times that amount or more in their purses. But instead of falling into a snoring deaf-and-blind state, she felt as awake as she had during the change, when a wolf's keen senses had supplanted her poor, blunted human perceptions. The hunger to be tongued, bitten, kissed, and fucked by Sylvia Rufina had not been appeased; it drove her toward the small perfect breasts and well-muscled thighs of her assailant and initiator.

Goldie did not rest until she had claimed a place for herself in the core of her lover's being. It was the first time in her life that Sylvia Rufina had known anything but humiliation and disgust from another human being's touch. Her capacity to take pleasure was shocking, and yet nothing in the world seemed more natural than seizing this cherub by her gold locks and demanding another kiss, on one mouth and then upon and within the other. They fell asleep on top of the covers, with nothing but a shared mantle of sweat to keep them warm. But that was sufficient.

Dawn brought a less forgiving mood. The Red Mistress was angry that someone had breached her solitude. She had not planned to share her secret with another living soul, and now she had not only revealed her alter ego but made herself a shape-shifting sister.

Goldie would not take money. She would not be sent away. And so the Red Mistress put her suitor to the severest of tests. Rather than imprisoning her with irons or cordage, Sylvia Rufina bade the blonde postulant to pick up her skirts, assume a vulnerable position bent well over, and keep it until she was ordered to rise. With birch, tawse, and cane, she meted out the harshest treatment possible, unwilling to believe the golden one's fealty until it was written in welts upon her body. The severest blows were accepted without a murmur, with no response other than silent weeping. When her rage was vented, Sylvia Rufina made the girl kiss the scarlet proof of her ambition that lingered upon the cane. And the two of them wept together until they were empty of grief and could feel only the quiet reassurance of the other's presence.

That night the refugee from the streets who had been put to sleep upon the floor crept into the bed and under the wolf hide that covered the Red Mistress, and made love to her so slowly and carefully that she did not fully awaken until her moment of ultimate pleasure. It was clear that they would never sleep apart again as long as either one of them should live.

They became mates, a pack of two, hunter and prey with one another, paired predators with the customers who were prepared to pay extra. With the comfort and challenge of one another's company, the work was much less onerous. The Red Mistress's income doubled, and by the time another year had gone by, she had enough money to proceed with her plan.

On a day in the autumn, a month or so before the fall of snow was certain, she locked up her house for the last time, leaving everything behind except the trunk of coins and gems, the maid, and warm clothing for their journey. They went off in a coach, a large silver fur thrown across their knees, and headed toward the mountains. No one in the city ever saw them again. On the way out of the city, they stopped to take a few things with them: a raven that had been chained to a post in front of an inn; a bear that was dancing, muzzled, for a gypsy fiddler; a caged pair of otters that were about to be sold to a furrier.

They had purchased wild and mountainous country, land no sane person would ever have a use for, too steep and rocky to farm, and so it was very cheap. There was plenty of money left to mark the boundaries of their territory, warning hunters away. There was a cabin, suitable for primitive living, and a stable that had already been stocked with a season's worth of feed for the horses. Once safe upon their own precincts, they let the raven loose in the shade of an oak tree, freed the old bear from his cumbersome and painful muzzle in a patch of blackberries, and turned the otters out into the nearest minnow-purling stream.

And that night, amid the trees, with a benevolent round-faced moon to keep their secrets, Sylvia Rufina took the form she had longed for during two impossible years of bondage to human society. The golden-haired girl she loved set her wild (and wise) self free as well. Then they were off to meet the ambassadors of their own kind.

They lived ever after more happily than you or me.

I've told you this story for a reason. If your woman has gone missing, and you go walking in dark places to try to find her, you may find Sylvia and Goldie instead. If they ask you a question, be sure to tell them the truth. And do not make the mistake of assuming that the wolf is more dangerous than the woman.

About the Authors

TONI AMATO is a redneck gentleman living in Boston and trying her damnedest to make the girls happy. Her work has appeared in *Best Lesbian Erotica 1998, 1999,* and *2000* and in *Best of the Best Lesbian Erotica.* When she's not writing smut, she's working on too many projects and hoping to finish one of them soon.

RACHEL KRAMER BUSSEL is a freelance writer living in New York City. She is the review editor for *Venus or Vixen?,* is an editorial assistant (and recent model) for *On Our Backs,* and writes the "Lusty Lady" column online at *Check This Out.* Her writing has been published in the anthologies *Starfucker* and *Faster Pussycats,* as well as in the *San Francisco Chronicle, CitySearch NY, ROCKRGRL, Clean Sheets,* and on LesbiaNation.com.

M. CHRISTIAN'S stories have appeared in publications such as *Best American Erotica, Best Gay Erotica, Best of the Best Gay Erotica, Friction, Best International Bisexual Erotica,* and over one hundred other books and magazines. He is the editor of seven anthologies, including *Rough Stuff* (with Simon Sheppard), *Guilty Pleasures, Best S/M Erotica,* and *The Burning Pen: Sex Writers on Sex Writing* (Alyson Books). His columns appear in *Blue Food Magazine, Venus or Vixen?, Scarlet Letters,* and on the Web site of the Erotica Readers Association. A collection of his gay male erotica, *Dirty Words,* is forthcoming from Alyson Books in 2001.

MR DANIEL is an African American writer, spoken-word artist, film and video curator, and educator. Her erotic writing has appeared in *Hot and Bothered 2, Lip Service, Best of the Best Lesbian Erotica,* and *ISSUES: The Magazine for Lesbians of Color.* She was thrilled to read "sex hall" on a live Webcast of Good Vibrations's "One-Handed Reading" event for National Masturbation Month.

GITANA GAROFALO grew up in the Great Lakes region and is interested in how the erotic lives of those living in rural areas are shaped by cars and the land. She writes, "The Midwest, beautiful, isolated, and home to a more diverse population than most realize, presents both pleasure and challenge to its queer people—those who stay and those who leave. Thanks to Ann and Jennifer, my favorite Midwesterners; la Peligrosa; and my readers, Ruth and Mary."

SACCHI GREEN leads multiple lives in western Massachusetts and in the mountains of New Hampshire. She's published a modest number of science-fiction and fantasy stories, some for children, but the erotic side of the force seduces her all too often. Some of the results can be read in the 1999 and 2000 editions of *Best Lesbian Erotica* as well as the forthcoming anthologies *Zaftig: Well-Rounded Erotica, Set in Stone,* and *Best Women's Erotica 2001.*

THEA HUTCHESON came of age in the '70s with permission to explore sex, but like most women, no understanding of how to traverse that unknown country. She has spent the years since refining her understanding of that slippery, tricky paradise and she wants to share. Not because she is a exhibitionist, she writes, "but because women need to know, and, culturally, we have few avenues to share. So here's a little something for your toolbox."

CATHERINE LUNDOFF is a computer geek, belongs to an anarchist bookstore collective, and lives in Minneapolis with her fantastic girlfriend. Her stories have appeared or are forthcoming in *Taste of Midnight, Set in Stone, Zaftig: Well-Rounded Erotica, Clean Sheets,* and *Best Lesbian Erotica 1999,* as well as other erotica and fantasy anthologies.

SHELLEY MARCUS grew up in a family where she couldn't talk about sex, so she wrote about it. While she occasionally writes less sexual fiction, Shelley's real obsession is erotica. Her stories run the gamut from bondage to vanilla, and have appeared in erotic anthologies such as *Herotica 6* and *Strange Bedfellows.* Shelley makes her home on the East Coast, and like her "Inquiring" narrator, likes her lovers young and enthusiastic.

SKIAN MCGUIRE, formerly a Philadelphian, is a Quaker sadomasochist who now lives with her dog pack and her partner of eighteen years in the wilds of western Massachusetts. Her work has appeared in *Best Lesbian Erotica 1999* and *Black Petals,* and she has recently completed a novel called *Nights at the Bijou.*

ELAINE MILLER is a publisher, writer, and editor (among other things) who thrives in Vancouver, Canada, with her yummy lover and their freaky cats. President and cofounder of Paronomasiacs Synonymous, she wages a constant battle with her sense of humor, which threatens to take control of her life. As cocreator of Psycho-Ex.com, she dabbles in web design and other techy stuff.

PEGGY MUNSON is the editor of *Stricken: Voices from a Hidden Epidemic of Chronic Fatigue Syndrome* (Haworth Press). She has published in four other editions of the *Best Lesbian Erotica* series, and in numerous other books and publications such as *On Our Backs, San Francisco Bay Guardian, Margin: Exploring Magical Realism, Our Own Voices, Hers3,* and *Literature and Medicine.* She has been awarded fellowships at the MacDowell Colony, the Ragdale Foundation, and Cottages at Hedgebrook.

AIMÉE NICHOLS is not to be taken internally or sold to children under the age of eighteen. When not being a dangerous and/or illegal substance, she is a freelance Australian writer, a student, and the editor of *Biblio Eroticus,* Australia's premier pansexual erotica magazine. She has never made love on a sultry night with the scent of jasmine in the air, and fervently hopes this remains the case.

KARIN POMERANTZ's work can be seen in *Best Lesbian Erotica 2000, Best of the Best Lesbian Erotica,* and *Skin Deep: Real-Life Lesbian Sex Stories.* Although arrogant, she is still willing to attribute part of her success to her muses, who shall remain nameless but who know who they are.

ELSPETH POTTER was born in the 1960s in a hospital run by nuns. She now lives in Philadelphia. She pursues several genres, including erotica, but some of them are hard to catch. She firmly believes that truth is stranger than fiction. The idea for "Water Music" came from a post-Holocaust utopian novel that just happened to have a hot spring with naked people in it.

SHAR REDNOUR published the award-nominated 'zine *Starphkr,* picked up for publication as a collection by Alyson in 2001. In 1995, Shar began the current trend of erotic "true story telling" by creating the best-selling *Virgin Territory* anthology series. "How to Fuck in High Heels" inspired Shar and her partner Jackie to create the hit movie *Hard Love & How to Fuck in High Heels,* which premiered in the 2000 San Francisco Gay & Lesbian International Film Festival and continues to play in film festivals worldwide.

JEAN ROBERTA is an instructor of first-year English at a university on the Canadian prairies. She has never broken the rules that apply to her job. She perceives herself as a marshmallow, but has been told that she is a grammar dragon. Her lesbian erotica has been published in *Batteries Not Included, Hot and Bothered 2, Desires, Best Lesbian Erotica 2000,* and in various journals.

LAUREN SANDERS is the author of *Kamikaze Lust,* a novel. She is coeditor of the anthology *Too Darn Hot: Writing About Sex Since Kinsey.* Her fiction has appeared in *Best Lesbian Erotica 2000, Best of the Best Lesbian Erotica,* and *On Our Backs.* She has written for *Time Out New York, American Book Review, Poets & Writers Magazine,* and numerous other publications. She is currently at work on another novel, *With or Without You.*

ALISON L. SMITH has been a director in residence at the Northampton Center for the Arts and a featured director in Lincoln Center's American Living Room Series. This spring,

Minneapolis' Eye of the Storm Theater produced *Dismember Mine,* her musical comedy about female serial killers. Her work has appeared in *Best of the Best Lesbian Erotica, Best Lesbian Erotica 1999, Hot and Bothered 2,* and *Curve.* She lives in Northampton, Massachusetts.

SUSAN ST. AUBIN lives and writes in the San Francisco Bay Area. She has been published most recently in *Best American Erotica 2000* and *Best Women's Erotica 2000.*

A. J. STONE was born and raised in New York City. A feature film producer, she currently resides in Los Angeles. This is her first published erotic short piece.

About the Editors

PAT CALIFIA is now **PATRICK CALIFIA-RICE**, an FTM who lives in San Francisco with partner Matt Rice and their son. Patrick is in private practice as a therapist, and feels good about the fact that every day he learns a little bit more about how to spoil his cat. Many of the books he authored prior to transition are of interest to lesbians, or to anyone who cares about radical sex and the politics of desire.

TRISTAN TAORMINO is series editor of *Best Lesbian Erotica*, for which she has collaborated with Heather Lewis, Jewelle Gomez, Jenifer Levin, Chrystos, and Joan Nestle. The 1997 collection was nominated for a Lambda Literary Award, and the 1999 edition was a Firecracker Alternative Book Award nominee. She is the author of *The Ultimate Guide to Anal Sex for Women,* which won the 1998 Firecracker Award. She is director, producer, and star of the video *Tristan Taormino's Ultimate Guide to Anal Sex for Women,* distributed by Evil Angel Video. She is editor of *On Our Backs,* a columnist for the *Village Voice,* and sex advice columnist for *Taboo* magazine. She was publisher and editrix of the sex magazine *Pucker Up,* and is webmistress for www.puckerup.com. She has been featured in *Playboy, Penthouse, Entertainment Weekly, Details, New York Magazine, Out Magazine,* and *Spin,* and on HBO's *Real Sex.* Her new book on sex will be published by Regan Books in 2001. She teaches sex workshops and lectures on sex nationwide.